VALENTIN & THE WIDOW
VOLUME ONE

THE MANDRAKE MACHINE
AND
THE FLOWERS OF MRS MOORE

THE VALENTIN & THE WIDOW SERIES

VALENTIN & THE WIDOW
VOLUME ONE

THE MANDRAKE MACHINE
AND
THE FLOWERS OF MRS MOORE

ANDREW WHEELER

CHAPTERHOUSE
TORONTO

Printed in Canada

First Printing, 2017

ISBN 978-1-988247-22-9

Chapterhouse Publishing Inc.
Toronto, ON

www.chapterhouse.ca

FOR MUM

CONTENTS

AN INTRODUCTION

It starts as a voice in your head. That is the call to adventure.

Or that's the romantic ideal, at least; a whisper in your ear that could be destiny, or the divine, or a manifestation of your own ennui expressed as something outside yourself, luring you onto the road to explore beyond the borders of the known.

In this case, the book you're reading now really did begin as a voice – and it was my voice! The adventures of Sacha Valentin, a troubled Russian soldier, and the widow Eleanora Rosewood, a headstrong English aristocrat, were originally read aloud as a weekly podcast. The format allowed me to get these stories out into the world in a style reminiscent of old timey radio dramas. Now you can read these stories for yourself, and the voice in your head is your own.

This book collects the first two installments of the Valentin & The Widow series, and these stories will take you – and our heroes – from Shanghai to Havana in the mid-1920s, to face a terrifying doomsday device and a deadly conspiracy. Future stories explore high society Paris, Prohibition-era Chicago, and the terrible secrets of weird Soviet science, as well as several corners of the world struggling under the yoke of colonial rule.

These stories are set in a world recovering from one great war and hurtling towards another, and the people of this era were straining for the right to establish their own identities and determine their own futures. These are themes and ideas that recur throughout the series.

I've always loved adventure fiction, from Sinbad to Tintin, via Indiana Jones, Richard Hannay, and James Bond. Adventure stories take their heroes to far-flung destinations and into unfamiliar cultures, and paint the world in rich colours of derring-do and wicked deeds. Yet there is an element of colonialism that runs through all adventure fiction. The cultures being explored tend to be exoticised and othered.

With these stories, I want to acknowledge that our world is both strange and familiar wherever you go, and that people deserve a chance to define themselves wherever they come from. You will still find many of the tropes of adventure fiction in this work, but hopefully delivered with enough sensitivity and smarts to make them worth returning to, and with one eye on the idea that the world is not a playground or a battlefield. Every place you go is someone's home.

I am both a product of empire and a subject of oppression. My two heroes are reflections of that experience, and of a journey that I'm still undertaking. Even the stories in this book have undergone changes since the audio version, both major and minor, as my journey continues.

I'm inviting you now to join me on this journey. This is a call to adventure. This is the voice in your head.

— Andrew Wheeler.

Toronto, ON. July 2017.

THE MANDRAKE MACHINE

Eleanora Rosewood could see the far edge of the world from the porthole window of her cabin. Wizened men in smock shirts balanced on driftwood barges; rangy Indian traders trooped the docks with baskets of oranges on their heads; a fishing junk bobbed in the harbour, its decks awash in guts and blood; and ribbed iron warehouses formed a fortress wall between the sea and the city. It was alien and extraordinary, and it made Eleanora's heart race. She was a fool to have come here.

Eleanora set down her teacup and took one last look at the cabin. The porter waited in the doorway with her bags and hatboxes.

This had been her sanctuary for the last few days. She had rarely ventured beyond the comfort of her wood-panelled room: an elegant retreat from a world that she no longer trusted. It had afforded her the precious peace and loneliness that she needed.

Now there was no more time for reflection. The treacherous world awaited.

Eleanora pulled on her black gloves, fixed her cloche hat with a pin, and adjusted her veil. Her mourning weeds were her armour.

'Are you ready, Lady Rosewood?' asked the porter.

'Am I?' said Eleanora. 'Yes. I suppose I must be.'

The porter led Eleanora up to the main deck, and she stepped out into the cooling winds of a bright April morning. As the ship sailed into the harbour, she caught her first sight of the true city beyond the docks, and a rush of relief swept over her.

The city was beautiful. It was not so strange and forbidding after all. It offered the same elegance of the more handsome European cities, flush with the thrill of the modern world: romantic arches, grand balconies and old stone buildings nestled in among the crisp edifices of the new architecture.

Yet it was the touch of difference that made it magnificent: the crimped curling red roof tiles; the golden statues of angry dragons and grimacing dogs; the fluttering banners bearing script that more resembled dancing figures, to her eye, than written words.

Neatly paved streets bustled with men in sober, smart dark suits. Women gathered at Parisian-style cafés in fine pastel dresses. The air thrummed with criss-crossing telegraph lines, the whirr of trams and the chirp of their bells. A brass band on the harbour wall stirred up with boisterous joy, and the sweet scent of unfamiliar spices travelled on the trade winds to welcome new arrivals.

'Shanghai, Shanghai, arriving in Shanghai,' shouted the steward. 'All passengers are invited to disembark.'

Eleanora had set off on this journey with only the loosest sketch of the city in her mind's eye, and the broadest notion of the task that awaited her here. Until this moment, the mission had seemed fanciful. Now it was a fact and it waited at the foot of the gangway, and Eleanora faced a daunting truth.

She was a woman alone in a strange new city. There were dangers in Shanghai, and the grief that had driven her here would not protect her.

The sun-bleached Traveller's Assistance desk was empty and littered with ticket stubs.

'The desk is no longer in service, my lady,' said the porter. 'Have you anyone coming to meet you?'

Eleanora shook her head, and the admission brought a flush of embarrassment to her cheeks. 'I haven't planned as thoroughly as I meant to,' she said. 'If you would be so kind, could you set the bags down here and call the Grand

Hotel to send a car? I would be most grateful.' She handed him a few coins for his trouble. He touched his forehead and stepped away.

Eleanora waited by the unattended desk and watched as the other passengers met their loved ones and took to their automobiles. The civilised city stood just out of reach across the harbourfront, and the hustle and roughness of the docks seemed to crowd too close.

'You're a thief! You're a bandit! I'll cut you, do you hear me? I will rip you from belly to throat.'

Eleanora flinched at the language. A peg-toothed old man stood on the prow of his fishing boat about forty feet away, brandishing a huge and fearsome fish hook. The subject of his invective was a hulking fellow who did not seem to care what he was called. He was brutish and broad-shouldered, with a broken nose and a thick black beard. He pulled on a long dark pea coat that was far too warm for the weather, and walked away from his abuser with his hands in his pockets.

The brute glanced over at Eleanora. His face was shadowed by the brim of his flat cap, so she could not see his eyes. Eleanora shuddered, lowered her gaze, and gripped the handle of her portmanteau.

'Vagabond,' the old man continued. 'From belly to throat! You hear me? I'll rip you from belly to throat!'

The sailor shook his head and resumed his pace.

Eleanora turned from the scene. With alarm, she faced a new stranger: a man with the look of a shaven rat, wrapped in gold and crimson livery.

'Madame, bonjour,' said the man-rat. 'My name is Jean-Jacques, and I am with the Grand Hotel.' He looked her over with a smile that was entirely inappropriate.

'That was very quick, monsieur.'

'Oui, madame. I was sent to receive the St Bride. The steward tells me that you are staying at the Grand?'

'That is my hope. I am the dowager Lady Rosewood. I trust you have transportation?'

'Bien sûr, Lady Rosewood. The rest of your party is where, my lady?'

It was the question that Eleanora feared the most. A young woman travelling alone could easily be taken for a fool.

'The rest of my party will join me there,' she said. 'May we go, please? They may be waiting already.'

'Á votre service, my lady.' He clicked his fingers and called out, 'Jana! Ruyi! Assist the lady!'

Two men rose from a bench and shuffled over. Jana was a wiry Indian with a cracked glass eye; Ruyi was a stocky Chinese man with plaited hair and a tattoo of a flaming bird on his left arm. Jana took control of Eleanora's wheeled portmanteau. Ruyi picked up her carpet bag and her hatboxes.

Eleanora followed them across the tram tracks towards

11

a row of shops and restaurants. She was grateful to be on her way to the safety of the world-renowned Grand, and the promise of a warm bath and a comfortable bed. With a backward glance, she bid silent farewell to the St Bride.

The brutish sailor in the heavy coat watched from the harbour wall.

Yes, she would be grateful for a safe place to hide away.

'This way,' said the porter. He gestured to an alleyway. It was dark and narrow, and gave off an awful sour smell. It was not the sort of place that a lady should venture into.

'It is the quickest way, your ladyship,' said the Frenchman. 'The car is on the other side of this building.' He gestured for her to proceed. 'I promise you, it is well. You are safe.'

Eleanora watched her luggage disappear into the alley. She had little choice but to follow. Having come all this way, to a strange city on the far side of the world, she felt an obligation to be fearless.

The alleyway was not a straight line. It turned left, and passed between the back doors of restaurants on either side. Eleanora was out of view of the street, and her doubts re-asserted themselves. Fear was a counsel to caution, and this was not a time to disregard good reason. She should not have followed these men.

No sooner was she certain of her indiscretion than was she punished for it.

The Chinese man, Ruyi, threw the lady's portmanteau

into a pile of rotting scraps. Jana dropped the carpetbag. The pair turned on her with sickening leers.

'What are you men doing?' asked Eleanora. 'Why have you so mistreated my luggage?' She turned to Jean-Jacques. He held a wicked little blade in his right hand.

'You should not have come here, your ladyship,' he said. 'This city is not safe for delicate creatures.'

Eleanora gritted her teeth and took two steps backwards. 'Put that knife away immediately, sir.' She tried to suppress the tremble in her voice. 'If anything happens to me, it will not go unnoticed.'

'A respectable young woman, alone in the heathen lands, fallen into the hands of bandits?' said Jean-Jacques. 'I am sure the newspapers will find some amusement in it. You will be a cautionary tale. Your countrymen will shake their heads when they read about you over breakfast.'

Eleanora looked to the other two. Jana held a large tarnished machete. Ruyi wrapped an iron chain around his fist.

'Scream if you want to, lady,' hissed Jana. 'We will be finished here before anyone finds you.'

Eleanora took a deep breath, bunched her skirt, and kicked the Frenchman in the shin. Jean-Jacques winced and struck her with the back of his hand. He grabbed her by the shoulder and threw her into a pile of wet restaurant filth.

'You cannot want to do this,' said Eleanora. 'Think of your souls!' She looked from one man to the next to the next, hoping that any of them might have a better nature that she could appeal to.

'We've done worse,' said Jean-Jacques. 'We will do worse again.'

'I will pay you,' said Eleanora. She picked up her purse from the dirt.

The Frenchman snorted. 'We will take it anyway,' he said.

'I have more. I can get more from the hotel. My late husband was a wealthy man.'

Jean-Jacques seemed to consider this for a moment. The possibility of a richer payday gave him pause.

'I am sure you are a woman of your word,' he said, 'but I have given my word to another, and they would be dangerous to cross.'

The Indian pressed the flat of his machete to Eleanora's cheek.

'You should have screamed,' he said.

She spat at him.

'Enough play, Jana,' said the Frenchman. 'Slice her across the throat, and be quick about—'

His words were lost as his face slammed into the wall. A hand wrapped around his neck and another punched him on the nose. Jean-Jacques' head bounced off the bricks and he dropped to the ground.

Jana and Ruyi raised their weapons to greet the newcomer.

Eleanora recognised him at once. It was the same sullen sailor she had seen on the docks, but now he had a smile on

14

his face – a grim smile beneath two humourless eyes.

The sailor shrugged off his overcoat and hung it on a masonry nail. He stretched out his broad shoulders and flexed his enormous arms. Eleanora shrank against the wall. She remembered the hatpin in her cloche, pulled it free and hid it in her palm. It was only three inches of steel, a pathetic match for a machete, but it was something.

Jana came at the sailor first, his machete slicing shapes in the air. He lunged. The sailor dodged and knocked the Indian into the wall. He drove his fist into Jana's stomach, grabbed the back of his head and slammed it into his knee. Jana dropped with a whimper.

Ruyi whipped his chain at the sailor's head. Eleanora cried out a warning. She did not know the sailor's intentions, but she hoped they were better than the other men's.

The sailor avoided each swing of the chain, but it kept him on his back foot, and he would soon be forced against the wall. On the next swing, he caught the chain and yanked it, and blood gushed from his palm. Ruyi refused to let go, and was dragged head-first into the sailor's elbow.

Eleanora found the wit to get to her feet. She made her way on unsteady legs to the end of the alley in the hope that it would take her to the main street. Instead, it took her deeper into the bare brick warren among the buildings.

Someone cried out, and Eleanora looked back to see who it was. Ruyi and the sailor still each held one end of the chain wrapped around their fists, but the sailor was reeling like a drunk, and blood poured from his nose. He let the chain slip from his slick red hand.

Ruyi drew back the chain to strike. The sailor charged forward and knocked Ruyi onto his back. He landed on top of him and punched him repeatedly, until the chain slipped out of his grip.

The sailor looked up at Eleanora. He was bruised and battered, with the blood of at least two men splashed across his grimy white shirt. He offered his bloody hand, and Eleanora recoiled.

'Please,' said the sailor. 'You are safe.'

Eleanora held out her hand but swiftly snatched it back. 'Behind you,' she said.

He turned too late. Jana struck him in the face with a broken brick, and he went down.

Eleanora screamed and covered her mouth.

Jana stood triumphant over his fallen foe. He seemed to smile, but his face was such a wreck that it was impossible to be sure. He dropped the brick, picked up his machete, and closed on Eleanora.

The sailor kicked him behind the knee and he buckled forward. He whipped around and slashed the air with his blade, but the sailor caught his wrist and twisted his arm behind his back. Jana cried out and dropped the knife.

Yet Jana was nimble. He twisted his arm in such a way as

to spin out of the sailor's lock and kick him in the thigh.

Not to be undone, the sailor wrapped both arms around his slippery foe and crushed him against the wall. The Indian slammed his head against the sailor's already gushing nose, and as the sailor cried out in pain, Jana slid out of his grasp and raced past Eleanora and into the maze of alleys. The sailor wiped a streak of blood along his bare arm and gave chase.

Eleanora leaned against the wall and tried to catch her breath. Ruyi was still on the ground, and he did not look like he might get up. The Frenchman had disappeared, and she hoped he had run for his life.

Eleanora found her cloche hat in the dirt, and bunched it into her sleeve. She slipped the hatpin into the collar of her coat and picked up her purse, but she left her luggage where it was. With shaky steps, she felt her way along the alley towards the docks. She turned the corner and saw the bright glow of the morning sun on the sidewalk, and her stately sanctuary, the RMS St Bride, just a few hundred yards away. She opened her mouth to call for help, but her voice had fled with her courage.

Jean-Jacques stepped into the alley. His nose was broken, his lips were swollen, his face steamed with red rage, and his handsome jacket was smeared with filth and blood.

His knife was pristine.

He moved in close and ran the blade along the collar of Eleanora's coat, slicing through the velvet.

Eleanora put a protective hand to her throat. She held her head high and kept her eyes fixed on his.

'You should run,' she managed to croak.

The Frenchman sneered. 'I do not think so. I think it is solely you and I.'

Eleanora looked over his shoulder and smiled. 'No,' she said. 'It is not.'

The Frenchman paled. He turned to look over his shoulder. There was no-one there.

He turned back and Eleanora drove her hatpin into his eye.

The scream was as terrible as any sound she had ever heard, but she steeled herself against sympathy and ran back into the alley.

'I will destroy you,' screamed the Frenchman. 'You are dead. You are dead, do you hear me? I will bring you such pain as you have never imagined, you little witch, and then I will—'

There was a crack, and a thump. Eleanora fell against the wall and looked back to see if the Frenchman had followed.

Instead she saw the sailor. His face was pale, his mouth was pulled into a frown, and his hands were shaking.

'They will not harm you now,' he said. He reached past her, and she shivered with dread at what he might do.

He only grabbed for his coat from the nail in the wall.

'You are safe now, miss.'

Eleanora peered past the sailor and caught sight of Jean-Jacques' foot lying very still and very awkward in the dirt.

18

The sailor shifted to block her view.

Eleanora wiped tears from her eyes.

'I am not safe,' she said. 'I will never be safe again.'

∾

Eleanora Rosewood was cast adrift on dangerous waters the day she became a widow.

Her husband Edgar, the 7th Baron Rosewood, had been a hero. He had made his name as a champion race car driver while still in the flush of youth, with a vehicle of his own design, the Angel E-1. The newspapers had hailed his glory and raised him up as a national hero: not only a brave champion, but a young genius; the exemplar of English achievement, and a bright beam of sunlight in the dark days before the war.

Whitehall deemed the young lord too valuable to risk in the trenches, not because of his aristocratic heritage, but because of his gifts as an engineer. With the advent of war, he was assigned a role drafting blueprints for contraptions that they hoped might end the conflict. To his great frustration, his designs were deemed too extravagant, too impractical, too expensive to build, and each one was filed away in a drawer.

The lack of vision in Whitehall was intolerable to Edgar. Desperate to make a real contribution, he asked to be reassigned to the front. Five times his request was denied.

With the sixth, he promised to share his frustration with the press, and that threat was enough.

It was in the mud and smoke and bodies that Edgar Rosewood truly earned the title 'hero'. In the trenches, he gained a reputation as a man who placed himself in peril without fear or hesitation. More than once he risked death to pull a fallen ally back from No Man's Land. On one occasion, he led a break through German lines; on another, he fought back an enemy advance beneath a cloud of chlorine gas; on a third, he threw back an enemy grenade before it could wipe out his fellow men.

It was this last act that earned him the Victoria Cross, the highest distinction that any living soldier could hope to achieve.

And still he sketched his strange engines in the smoky half-light of the battlefield, and still he sent his designs back to the boys at Vickers.

His efforts were not for nothing. His contributions led to the occasional useful modification to a British gun or tank or plane. Yet his more outlandish proposals were still dismissed and filed away.

After the war, Edgar set to work on his own engineering projects. He established a new land speed record in the Angel Lux-F racing car at Daytona Beach in the United States. The following year, he piloted his Angel Ceto hydrofoil to a new water speed record at Bras d'Or Lake in

Nova Scotia. By the age of thirty, his achievements had made him a national treasure.

And through all his years of heroics, adventure and veneration, one woman stood by his side.

Eleanora Penfold was the sort of beauty that any man would be proud to have, but she possessed such wit that only the best man might stand a chance. Eleanora was 19, and Edgar 23, when they wed at her father's church in Hindsmere, just months shy of the outbreak of war.

Eleanora responded to the call of duty in her own way. While Edgar was at Whitehall, Eleanora joined the Voluntary Aid Detachment as a nursing services coordinator. When Edgar went to the front, Eleanora served at the field hospital in Rouen. Husband and wife spent their days just miles apart without ever seeing one another, surrounded by the dead and the dying. Though they wanted for each other every day, they prayed that events did not conspire to bring them together.

Eleanora learned many things at Rouen. She learned to be resilient in the presence of horror. She learned to be defiant in the face of the enemy. She learned that one person could make a difference, even if it were only to one soul at a time. She took these lessons home with her after the war, and rededicated herself to the human good.

These were the golden days. Europe was at peace, and optimism reigned. Edgar was adored wherever he went, and Eleanora found new purpose, and they were as giddy with love as two people could be.

It ended on April 3rd, 1924, at Villesauvage in France.

Edgar hoped to add the air speed record to his claims on land and water. He designed and built his own floatplane, the Angel Tiamat, and on a crisp spring morning he kissed his wife and took to the sky with the hope of becoming the fastest man the world had ever known.

He had barely left the ground when he seemed to lose control. The plane made a sudden dip, its engines buzzed a complaint, and a gasp escaped the lips of every person in the watching crowd.

Edgar recovered, the plane ascended, and Eleanora remembered very clearly that someone behind her laughed, such was their relief.

They were still laughing when the plane dipped again. This time she could read Edgar's panic in the plane's movements. It jerked and twisted for a mile or so, just a hair's breadth above the ground. She knew he meant to land the plane, but it resisted his every effort.

One wing brushed the ground, and that was the end. The plane flipped nose-over-tail. It cartwheeled across the furrowed soil of an old battlefield and shed a wheel here, a wing there, a tail fin, an engine. It shattered into a hundred pieces until all that was left was the broken fuselage, like a cigar stubbed out in the dirt.

She ran.

Her arms tangled in her coat.

Her feet sunk in the mud.

She fell and pushed herself up. She threw off her coat, she dropped her gloves, she lost a shoe.

She ran as fast as she was able, and when the energy left her, she staggered on, and when the emotion overtook her, she crawled. She did not hear people calling behind her. She did not notice the fire truck until it was well ahead of her. The stands were a mile from the crash site, and as Eleanora advanced, she thought it seemed like a hundred miles or more.

Two men picked her up out of the mud and tried to pull her back, but she would not go, and she fought them until they agreed to help her press on. They walked her to the edge of the crash, and she walked the last few feet on her own.

Eleanora took her husband's broken body in her arms and screamed at all the heavens so that they might tremble at her grief.

On the day that Edgar died, Eleanora did not yet know how much grief was still to come. In that day on the field at Villesauvage, she did not know what dangers she would

23

be exposed to.

She knew it now. As she staggered along the street towards the Shanghai Grand, with blood on her boots and dirt on her gloves, she knew it very well. Everyone she passed looked at her with open-mouthed horror, and recoiled again at the sight of the bloodied brute that followed behind with her luggage. The extent of their troubles was apparent enough for all to see.

The sailor was a Russian named Sacha Valentin. He had a hard, square face under a short black beard, and grey-blue eyes that watched the world sadly from the shadow of his boxer's brow. Though he looked hard-lived, the lady could tell from his voice that he was young; perhaps no older than twenty-five. Though his voice was low and his tone was serious, he lacked the note of gravity that she heard in the voices of older men.

The Russian walked a short distance behind the lady, perhaps afraid that someone would think him a thief if he stood too far away with her luggage.

He whispered to the lady as they walked.

'You are certain they did no serious harm?'

Eleanora held her poise and answered as brightly as she could manage. 'They scared me, Mr Valentin, but they hardly touched me. A cup of tea, and I will be right as rain. You are the one I worry about. They might easily have killed you.'

'Not so easily,' said Valentin. Eleanora heard a lift in his voice and looked back to see that a smile had cracked his face. He would have seemed dumbly charming if it were not for the sticky red wash of blood that coloured his teeth. The smile faded easily into a grim scowl.

'You, they would have killed,' he said. 'You should not have gone with these men.'

'I do not argue the point. I am afraid I am unused to travelling alone. When we reach the hotel, I will pay you for your time and call for a doctor to see to your wounds.'

'Thank you, no. I do not seek pay. I do not need doctor. The hotel is near; I will leave you there.'

'Absolutely not. What a foolish thing to say. You risked your life for me, and that makes you a Samaritan. Your kindness will not go unrewarded.'

'I am not a man you should be seen with, ma'am.'

'I don't see how that's your business to decide,' said Eleanora. She hoped her tone indicated that this was not a subject for further discussion.

A group of gossiping European women watched the pair with undisguised alarm from the pavement table of a café. Eleanora caught a glimpse of her muddied, unkempt state reflected on the menu glass. Her face was smeared with grime. Her hair was a tangled mess. A splash of blood coloured her neck and chin.

She stopped in full sight of the women and took a compact from her purse and powdered her face. Her hand trembled. The sponge came away black. Eleanora stared down the women until they looked away, and she walked on.

'Can you drive, Mr Valentin?'

'Da. I was denshchick to General Karolyev.'

'I'm afraid I don't know what that means.'

'I was… military driver. I drove Moscow to Paris for military conference after war.'

'Did you indeed? How marvellous. It happens that I have need of a valet. I am a widow travelling alone, with no-one to see to my safety. I would like to make use of your services here in Shanghai, even if only for a few days. You would of course be handsomely compensated.'

'Thank you, ma'am. I must refuse.'

'I must insist. It is a widow's prerogative to choose her own company. We will discuss it after you have been seen to by the hotel doctor. Here we are, Mr Valentin.'

The Shanghai Grand was as imposing and magnificent as its name suggested, and the doorman watched their approach with wide eyes. He clapped his hands, and three bellhops raced down the steps to take the bags. Eleanora held up her arms and waved them off.

'Thank you, but my man can manage perfectly well.'

The bellhops seemed not to listen, and Valentin offered no protest as they snatched the hatboxes and portmanteau from his hands. The doorman took the carpet bag.

Eleanora grabbed the umbrella that stuck from its side and cracked the doorman on the arm. She snatched the carpet bag from his hands and thrust it back into Valentin's.

'I said my man can manage.'

'Yes, ma'am,' said the doorman. He hurried back to the door and held it open.

The staff inside greeted them with unreadable faces as their sense of propriety wrestled with their sense of politesse. The prim receptionist met the ruffled pair with pursed lips. His darting eyes seemed to silently direct the other staff to their positions.

'Good morning, ma'am,' he said. 'Welcome to the Shanghai Grand Hotel.'

'Good morning. I am the dowager Lady Rosewood and I am looking for a suite.'

'Certainly, Lady Rosewood. One moment, please.'

As the receptionist ran his finger down the page of an open ledger, Eleanora took a moment to peel off her gloves and press her bare hands to the cold marble counter. She found familiarity and reassurance in the chill of hard stone against her fingertips, in the shimmer of harp music from the lobby bar, and in the perfume of flowers all around her. Though she had never seen this city before, this was the world she was used to. There was no whiff of the street at the Shanghai Grand.

'The Palace Suite is available, your ladyship, if that would be agreeable?'

27

'That sounds quite lovely. If you would be so kind as to send for the hotel doctor to see to my man?'

'Your man, my lady?'

Eleanora gestured over her shoulder. 'We ran into some difficulties on the way here, and I…' She realised from the receptionist's expression that Valentin was no longer behind her. She turned and saw him disappear through a back door at the other end of the lobby.

'Lady Rosewood, we would be honoured to provide you with appropriate household staff both within and without our walls,' said the receptionist. 'You should not be placed at any discomfort during your stay.'

Eleanora felt a stir of panic at the loss of her new champion. She was resolved not to let him away so easily. 'You are very kind,' she told the receptionist, 'Nevertheless, I would see that man rewarded for his troubles. Please have one of your staff detain him. Send for the doctor, and send up a maid to draw a warm bath, would you please?'

'Very good, my lady.'

The receptionist passed the key to a bellhop while another pushed a loaded luggage cart towards the elevators.

This was the other side of the world. This was the farthest, strangest and most dangerous place that Eleanora had ever visited. She was lost here, alone and overwhelmed, desperate for refuge or some fond remembrance of home.

She wanted Edgar here. She wanted the Edgar she knew.

Eleanora saw an old man across the lobby in a leather armchair reading the morning news with his spectacles perched on the edge of his eagle's beak nose. She knew him. She knew him very well.

It was the devil himself. The farthest thing from a fond remembrance.

The devil looked over the top of his newspaper and he smiled.

⟡

The eyes of the dead beheld him. Two dull pearls above a bloated red nose on the bony face of a miserable old man. The corpse lay crashed out across crates of potato peel and vegetable cuttings in the alley behind the Grand, his thin-lipped mouth set in a grimace that suggested he had felt the full terror of his death. It might have been the first true thing he had felt in more than forty years.

Sacha knew him from the docks. They had worked together sometimes – never on the same ship, but often in the warehouses. His name was Aristotle, but everyone called him Ari, and he traded in simpler lies than his philosopher namesake.

For every port that Sacha ever visited, from Anchorage to Saigon, Ari had spun a hundred tales of reckless nights, fallen women, and foolish crimes, all amounting to nothing at all. Ari had belched and vomited his way around the world, numb and loud, and with one hand cupped to a breast, the other fixed to a flask. Even when at work with a needle, a net or a gutting knife, Ari saved one hand for the flask.

Now he was dead, alone, and empty handed. He had lived decades longer than anyone might have predicted, but he had been dying all that time.

Three kitchen hands sat further down the alley playing cards on a barrel top.

'Do you see there is a dead man here?' said Sacha.

None of the men acknowledged him. Sacha repeated the question in French. This earned only a shrug from one man and a dismissive gesture from another. A leather-bound flask stood on the barrel, and Sacha knew it was Ari's, and that they had prised it from his dead hands.

Sacha resolved to notify the doorman, hoping that the police, the army, or a few men eager to earn easy money could be persuaded to drag Ari away in a potato sack and take him to a pauper's grave.

It shocked him to realise how little the man's life meant at the end. Those who knew Aristotle, the ones who had heard his tales, would not know he was dead unless Sacha informed them. It was not unusual for men of their sort to go unheard from for months. If they never reappeared, they were forgotten, not mourned.

A hotel porter stepped into the alley and looked towards the street. He turned and noticed Sacha standing over the corpse.

'You have a dead man here,' said Sacha.

'Come inside, Russian. The lady has money for you.'

Sacha shook his head. 'I must return to the docks. I must seek a new ship.'

'Do I care what you do? The lady has asked for you. I was ordered to tell you so.' He slammed the door shut.

Sacha crouched down and closed Ari's eyes.

This was the future that waited for him, in fifty years or in five days. This was all such men were worth: anonymity and oblivion. The world would never offer him anything more.

And yet a woman had asked for his help. Why, he wondered, had he helped her once? Why would he not do it again? For as long as the woman was in Shanghai, she could be in danger. A man of worth would never allow such a thing, whatever his station.

Sacha crossed himself and offered a prayer for Ari's soul.

'What are we, Aristotle?' asked Sacha.

The dead man gave no answer.

~❧~

Eleanora pretended not to hear. As Sir Francis called her name she kept her eyes on the elevator lights and willed the cars to descend with greater haste.

'Lady Rosewood? My dear Lady Rosewood!'

His calls were persistent, and she could not ignore him forever. The nearest elevator was still three floors up and no longer moving. A confrontation was inevitable. Eleanora steeled herself and turned with a brittle smile to face his yellow rictus.

'There you are, Lady Rosewood,' said Sir Francis. 'I knew it must be you.'

'Sir Francis. How lovely.'

Eleanora offered her hand without enthusiasm. Sir Francis held it a moment too long while he looked her up and down.

'Was there an accident?' he asked. 'You look distressed.' He raised his hand to her cheek and she flinched. The look in her eyes was enough to warn him off.

'Nothing for you to be concerned about,' said Eleanora. 'I behaved incautiously, and wandered into a little trouble.'

Sir Francis tutted.

'This is a land of savages, Lady Rosewood. You should not be here. What can we do to make sure that this never happens again?'

This was the testing moment. He meant to make her small and send her home, and she would try her resolve in resisting him.

'I ask nothing of you, Sir Francis, except that you let me go about my business.'

Sir Francis lowered his spectacles. There was no kindness in his eyes, and none of the intimacy of old friends. 'There is no business for you in Shanghai, my dear.'

'My husband had business here. I have come to settle it.'

Sir Francis leaned closer and whispered through clenched teeth: 'Your husband's politics are no matter for a lady.'

Eleanora wiped flecks of spittle from her face. 'My husband was an engineer, Sir Francis. He never spoke of politics.'

'Women have had the vote for less than a decade and already our nation suffers under a weak government of socialist fools. Is it any wonder that men do not share the complexities of politics with their wives? Go home, Lady Rosewood. Leave the politics to those who know better. You have reform society meetings and philanthropic committees to attend to. You have a husband to mourn. In my day, widows were not seen out of their houses for the first year of their grief.'

'Your day has passed, Sir Francis, and the war has taught us well: mourning is a luxury when there is work to be done.'

'I will repeat myself only once. Go home, Lady Rosewood.'

A large dirty hand pressed against Sir Francis's chest and eased him away from Eleanora.

'Sir, you are imposing on the lady,' said Sacha Valentin. 'It is my place to keep her safe.'

Sir Francis was furious at the intrusion.

'Unhand me, you filth. I will have you removed from the building.'

'Have you met my valet, Sir Francis?' asked Eleanora. 'Valentin, this is my very dear friend Sir Francis Hardie. Sir Francis, this is Valentin. He will ensure that I suffer no more unfortunate incidents.'

Sir Francis glowered at the larger man with palpable contempt, but he swallowed his indignation and forced his features to a neutral formation and turned his focus entirely back to Eleanora.

'How bold you are to have a valet in place of a lady's companion,' said Sir Francis. 'Your generation takes such a fresh view of the way we've always done things.'

'We live in the modern age, Sir Francis, and I find I have modern needs,' said Eleanora. The ring of a bell sounded the elevator's arrival. 'One must not stand in the way of progress.'

'I quite understand, Lady Rosewood, but I fear if one speeds towards uncertainty, one is likely to come to some harm. I would hate to see you come to any harm.'

'Let us hope you have no cause to.'

Eleanora stepped into the elevator, and Valentin followed.

'You will excuse me. I am weary from my travels, and I will need a surfeit of energy for all the dabbling I intend to do in Shanghai. Will you be at dinner, Sir Francis?'

'I shall.'

'Then I shall dine in my room. Good day.'

The elevator doors closed, and Eleanora allowed herself a smile.

Sacha frowned at his reflection in the bathroom mirror. He had scrubbed away weeks of grease and grime in a scalding shower. He had shaved off his beard and clipped his nails. He had steamed away the familiar smell of the ocean that usually followed him, and masked the last lingering traces with sandalwood. The man left behind, the man he saw in the mirror, was not the man he knew.

The mark of that other man was now everywhere around him. A spray of grey water speckled the walls, filth covered the floor, the towels were pink and black with blood and muck. Sacha had painted his ruination across the pristine white space and left himself clean and strange.

The only mirrors Sacha ever saw himself in were tarnished saloon bar-backs, and the man in that reflection was the only wrecked and wretched creature he recognised. The man in this mirror was a fraud, and if he scratched through his pale new skin he would find layers of dirt underneath. He was not meant to be here.

Sacha covered himself in a robe and went to the bedroom, which was eight times the size of the cabin he had shared for weeks at a time with four other men at sea. He surprised a maid as she set out a change of clothes on the bed.

'Pardon me, sir. I am sorry, excuse me.' She scooped up the folded pile of Sacha's discarded clothes and picked up his boots from the foot of the bed.

'Wait,' said Sacha. 'You are taking my things?'

'Her ladyship asked us to clean and repair your jacket and replace the rest, sir. Your belongings are on the side.' She nodded to the dresser, where she had set out the contents of his pockets – a battered cigarette tin and a handful of coins.

'I do not need new boots,' said Sacha. 'Leave them, please. And do not call me "sir".'

The maid set down the boots on the carpet and bobbed and retreated.

Sacha sat on the foot of the bed and polished the boots with the sleeve of his robe. He kept polishing until the boots shone and the robe was brown.

Satisfied that the boots at least could stand as an equal to everything else in the room, he dressed himself in the soft undershirt, starched shirt, and crisp trousers that the maid had laid out for him. The feeling of laundered cotton on his skin was strange, but pleasing. It took Sacha back to the first time he had worn his army uniform almost a decade ago.

Appropriately dressed, Sacha stepped through to the sitting room and found the lady perched on the edge of a chaise, now in a different mourning dress and with her waves of unruly brown hair wound into a tight bun. She stared down at her hands folded on her lap.

'Mr Valentin. I'm afraid I am still a little shaken from this morning,' said Lady Rosewood. She looked up and allowed herself a small smile at his transformation. 'How very fine you look.'

Sacha ran a finger along his collar and cleared his throat. 'Ma'am, I will speak plain. You are not safe in Shanghai, and I will do as I can to protect you, and I will wear these clothes so to not embarrass you, but I am not the man you need.'

'You are the man the fates provide,' said Lady Rosewood. 'You are the man who stepped in when my life was in danger. Sit, will you please?'

Sacha lowered himself into a delicate Edwardian armchair.

'I realise this is not your sort of work, but it is only for a short time,' said Lady Rosewood. 'I will keep my stay in Shanghai as brief as circumstances will allow, and I would appreciate your company for the duration. I shall see that you are well compensated. After this morning's incident at the docks, I assume you are not otherwise employed?'

'Ma'am, the man who called me a thief—'

'I do not need to hear it. I have no qualms about your character. Having carried my luggage, am I to think you mean to steal it? Having saved my life, am I to think you mean me harm? My only concern is that I may cause undue intrusion into your business.'

Sacha shook his head. 'I am a free man. I go where there is work. But I do simple work for men with strong backs. I do not work for fine ladies. I do not know how.'

'You have seen the work I have for you, Mr Valentin. I need you to keep me alive. The man you saw downstairs was surely the one who sent those thugs to kill me, and I am in

Shanghai to upset his plans, so he has an urgent need to upset mine. I require protection, and you have stepped ably into that role.'

'The war made many capable men. You must find an officer.'

'My patience for gentlemen is at low ebb, and I have other priorities. I will not linger, Mr Valentin. I know now how foolish I was to come here without proper arrangement, and it is in my best interests to see to my husband's business and depart as soon as I am able. I believe you can help me to this end, but I will not judge you if you prefer to leave. You have done so much for me already.'

'Might I ask a question, Lady Rosewood?' asked Sacha.

'Of course.'

'It is important, your reason for coming here?'

'It is a matter of life and death,' she said. 'And I am afraid the lives of millions may be at stake.'

After the crash at Villesauvage, Eleanora returned to England as a dowager, a widow at 29. She buried her husband at their country seat in Hindsmere and withdrew to their London townhouse, where she resolved not to shroud herself with a fog of grief, but to make sense of a life she had never expected. She would honour her husband by ensuring that his work passed into the right hands.

Edgar's study had been his sanctum. It was a room that Eleanora rarely ventured into. With Edgar's death, his sanctum became her project. Sorting through his belongings gave her a chance for one last conversation with her husband. It was one last chance for him to reveal something new to her.

She never anticipated what sort of conversation it might be.

Edgar's study was large, with ample scope for discovery. Each bookcase was stacked high with uneven piles. Papers jutted untidily from between book covers. A huge Mercator projection of the world filled a wall, and a globe and a roll top desk occupied the space by the bow window.

A second desk dominated the room. It was a chipped and scratched mahogany pedestal that Edgar had used as a worktable. Several small, half-finished metal contraptions littered the leather desktop, all of them strange arrangements of cylinders, cogs and wheels. Some of them served double-duty as paperweights.

Three larger skeletal machines stood in the centre of the room on canvas sheets that were meant to protect the Persian rug, but the rug was already stained beyond repair. Eleanora thought it so typical of Edgar to think to put the sheets down only after he spoiled the rug. That thought was enough to bring tears to Eleanora's eyes, so she sat at the desk to recover herself.

One drawer of the desk sat half an inch forward of the rest.

It was the sort of detail that would never have bothered Edgar, but it bothered Eleanora at once. She tried to push the drawer in, but found it would not move any further. She pulled the drawer out and reached inside the desk to see what was causing the obstruction, and she found a leather folder bound in string.

Eleanora unwound the binding, folded back the leather flaps and pulled out a blueprint. She set the desk clutter aside and laid the blueprint flat.

It was a plan for a device she had never seen before: either a boat or a submersible. It was a horrible design, a monstrous leviathan. Its hide bristled with spikes and terrible guns. It was unlike anything Eleanora had seen before of her husband's handiwork – yet it was unmistakeably his. The sight put a sickness in the pit of Eleanora's stomach. She hated to recall that he had ever made weapons.

The handwritten words on the top right of the blueprint gave the monstrosity a name, Skylla, and a date of design: May 1923.

This confounded Eleanora's hope that it was a rogue artefact from Edgar's days at Whitehall. He had conceived of this beast less than a year ago. He had conceived of it during peacetime.

As she folded the blueprint up she noticed some handwritten words on the back. 'Proposal 3; Madras station – to keep savages in their place'.

Savages.

The word twisted Eleanora into a knot. It was common enough to hear such language among the most refined sections of London society, but it was not the sort of language Eleanora expected from her husband's pen. It was not a voice she recognised as his voice. Yet here it was, 'savages', written in his handwriting and wed to an image of a machine of terror and death. To keep savages in their place.

Eleanora told herself that she had misunderstood. She had leapt to an unlikely conclusion. The blueprint was a peculiar fancy, and the words were thoughtless scribbles; it did not mean anything at all. There would be other papers, other documents, which would show her husband's true nature.

She dug through the drawers on the hunt for the evidence she needed. She found letters that she had sent him, and newspaper clippings of his adventures that she had saved. These papers stirred memories of the man she loved.

She also found a book in the bottom drawer. It was called, 'On Mongrel Races', by Professor Fernando Miro.

It was a book that dripped with hate dressed as science.

Eleanora turned the pages in silent horror at the vile claims that Miro put forward. He wrote at length about the inferior intellects of Negroes, the moral laxity of Arabs, the strange biology that made Orientals susceptible and weak.

Miro's words were upsetting enough, but what truly shook Eleanora to her soul's foundation where the other

41

words written in the margins. They were notes of agreement, endorsement, even of extrapolation. There was one note that appeared over and again: 'Can we use this?'

It was in Edgar's hand.

Eleanora threw the book across the room. It bounced off the side of the globe and hit the floor, and the globe creaked open at the equator. A secret compartment.

The globe held two mysteries. One was a silver signet ring with a black onyx stone. The stone was engraved with the image of an angel, with its wings spread wide. It gripped a lightning bolt above its head, and it stood on one leg on the edge of the world.

The other was a black leather wallet with the same engraving. The left interior page carried a photograph of Edgar in a high-collared black shirt with a gold lightning pin on his chest. Beneath the photo were the words 'Throne: Archimedes'.

The right interior page was headlined, 'Full Clearance, Full Authority'.

Beneath that was a list titled 'Primary Projects'. The first was Tiamat, which was the name of Edgar's floatplane. That was followed by Mandrake, Calliope and Caput Mundi, none of which suggested anything of special significance to Eleanora. Last on the list was Skylla, the monster machine for keeping 'savages' in their place.

Eleanora put the wallet and the ring back inside the globe and slammed it shut. These objects exposed a betrayal so fundamental that she could not stand to look at them.

For the ten years of their marriage she had never imagined that Edgar held such odious views about his fellow man, let alone that he could have acted on them. Now she had evidence of his hate, and worse, evidence that he had placed his genius in service to hate. When she had agitated for fairness, equality and peace, her husband had acted against her.

In that moment, Eleanora felt horribly glad that her husband was dead, not because he had betrayed her, but because she hoped his projects might die with him.

Edgar's sanctuary was enemy territory, the workshop of a wicked stranger. Eleanora reviewed her surroundings to see what else the room might hide. Where in this room was the secret of the Calliope? In which hidden corner was the Caput Mundi?

Eleanora's eyes settled on one of her husband's half-finished contraptions: a small rectangular scaffold containing a brass cylinder and some metal tongues. It resembled the guts of a player piano.

Edgar had been working on a music box, which he said would be an anniversary gift. He had played it for her just once, and the music was like nothing she had heard before: a bright warm beautiful tone, strings and voices stirring in divine harmony. It had wrapped itself around her and sent shivers through her skin.

The music had lasted less than a minute before the box overheated. Smoke rose from the gears, and a liquid like quicksilver seeped from the cylinder. Edgar said that the vibrating pin was unstable, and took the machine back to his study to continue his work. That was the last she saw of it.

The guts of the music box were laid out in front of her, exactly as he had left them. There was the vibrating pin, glistening and pearlescent like oil on water. It was beautiful like no metal Eleanora had ever seen. She picked it up and held it to the light. Was this music box the only innocent object in the room?

The doorbell sounded and Eleanora jumped in fright.

Eleanora could not bear to think of another person here, intruding on her loneliness. Worse, she was fearful of sharing her discoveries about her husband. No-one else could know about this until she had decided for herself what to do with it.

Eleanora looked around the room to see if anything was out of place. She put Miro's book back in its drawer, and the Skylla blueprints back in the pedestal. All of Edgar's other secrets were safely hidden.

The doorbell rang again. Eleanora left the study and locked the door behind her. She realised that she still had the vibrating pin from the music box and she slipped it into her pocket.

Sir Francis Hardie stood at the front door with a grimace on his face and his hat in his hands.

'Lady Rosewood.' He dragged her name out with a slow drawl. 'My dear, dear friend. I am so devastated by the news.'

Sir Francis was not a dear, dear friend. He had been a friend of her husband's, and a man whose presence in her life Eleanora only tolerated because of social obligation. She found him condescending and politically regressive.

Sir Francis was a respected civil servant who had risen to the post of permanent cabinet secretary for foreign affairs. He was also a fellow of Edgar's private gentleman's club, The Mercia.

Edgar Rosewood had been a popular man, beloved by many. Eleanora knew that she would have to spend the coming weeks listening to his friends' heartfelt expressions of regret, and after what she had just learned, she was less sure than ever that she could endure it.

Nonetheless, she invited Sir Francis through to the drawing room, took his coat and offered him a drink.

'I apologise, but I have dismissed the maid for the day,' said Eleanora.

'Then allow me, please,' said Sir Francis. 'I will make us both some tea.'

Eleanora protested. Sir Francis insisted. Eleanora watched the clock on the mantle and waited. The intrusion was agony.

Sir Francis returned minutes later with a tray, two teacups, and a pot of fragrant tea. He poured, and they sat in silence, he unsure what to say, she wishing to say nothing at all.

45

The silence was more unbearable than the company, and Eleanora felt obliged to be polite.

'Thank you for visiting, Sir Francis.'

'You're very welcome,' said Sir Francis. 'I understand your grief, Ellie.'

Eleanora bristled at the familiarity.

'The war punished Anne and I more than most,' said Sir Francis. 'Rufus at Ypres. Louis at Baghdad. Gilbert at the Marne. It seems so cruel that Edgar should be spared death in the trenches only to die so young in peacetime. I lost three boys to that war, and now I feel I have lost a fourth.'

Eleanora offered no answer to that. Was she meant to offer her condolences to him? They sunk back into silence, and Eleanora sipped her tea and Sir Francis stared solemnly at his cup.

'Anne suffered terribly,' said Sir Francis. 'I thought I would lose her as well, such was her grief. I asked the doctor for something to help her rest, and he gave us a miracle powder that eased the worst of her pain. She takes it still. I hope you don't mind, but I put a little in your tea. I knew it would be a blessing.'

Eleanora set the tea down.

'Sir Francis, what do you mean? What have you done?'

'I really am sorry to presume, but it distresses me so to see you go through this alone. Anne says you should stay with us in the country for a few days. You should be with friends at a time like this.'

'I will not be cosseted,' said Eleanora. 'I prefer... I would like...' she struggled with her words and forgot altogether what she wanted to say. She felt unsteady. She swayed a little. She tried to focus on the walls, and they seemed to pulse in time with her heartbeat. She thought that such a sight ought to terrify her, but somehow it was peaceful.

Eleanora looked at Sir Francis, but she could not make out his face, and she wondered if he had perhaps transformed into an eagle. She looked for the clock and could not find it at all. She fell onto her side, and into darkness.

It was dusk when Eleanora woke on the fainting couch in her drawing room. She had indistinct memories of a woman holding her hand, mopping at her brow and singing to her in a foreign tongue. She smelled faint traces of incense, an exotic and unfamiliar smell. The tea set was cleared away, and Sir Francis was gone.

A horrible thought struck her. She staggered to the study and fumbled to recover her key from her jacket pocket. The lamps took a moment to flicker on, but even in the dim light, her first glimpse confirmed her fears.

The room had been ransacked. The bookcases were bare. The desk drawers were empty. Every paper was missing, every contraption was gone. Only the furniture in the room and the grease-stained canvas sheets remained. Eleanora found her love letters thrown in a corner, some of them open, some of them crushed.

The globe was just as she had left it, but it was locked tight. Eleanora picked up a letter knife from the desk and levered the globe open, but she knew it would be empty, and so it was.

Every sign of her husband's secret life had disappeared, and she was left with no evidence of the man she had never known. If Sir Francis had come just an hour earlier, she might never have discovered Edgar's secrets at all. Perhaps that would have been preferable?

Eleanora sat at the desk and stared at her husband's map of the world, and saw it now as a battlefield. Where she saw people and nations bucking against the bonds of Empire and inequality, her husband had seen savage upstarts pressing against the righteous might of established power. Where she had dreamed of a liberating tide that might spread across land and sea, he had celebrated the horrors of a fortress of oppression. Where she had fought for self-determination by marching, writing letters, and making scones for committee meetings, he had joined a secret league to keep the world divided, and the downtrodden underfoot. The weapons he had built for his war were far more effective than hers.

And his weapons survived him. His league survived him. Sir Francis's visit had not been charity; he was clearly part of this secret cabal, and now he had Edgar's notes and designs, and perhaps the means to continue his devilish work.

Eleanora crossed to the map and looked for Madras, site of the Skylla project. There was nothing to mark it. She looked for anything that might reveal the location of one of her husband's projects, but there were no clues. They might be anywhere. They might be everywhere.

She spotted a single silver pin in the map, stuck to the Eastern edge of China's round Buddha belly just over the city of Shanghai. Eleanora pulled it. To her surprise, it was more than a pin; it was a four-inch metal dowel. As soon as she pulled it free, the map scrolled back into the wall to reveal something quite different underneath.

It was another blueprint, pinned flat to the wall within the frame of the map: a design for an elaborate drilling apparatus. The legend in the bottom right corner gave its name as the Mandrake Earthquake Machine. Beneath were the words: 'Epicentre: Shanghai, China. Estimated population: 2 million'.

Tucked into the corner of the blueprint was a small piece of folded card. Written on it in Edgar's handwriting was a date, circled twice: April 20th. Eleanora pulled out the card and saw that it was a matchbook for a place called The Mandrake Palace. She read the words on the blueprint again.

'Epicentre: Shanghai, China. Estimated population: 2 million'.

Eleanora tore the blueprint from the wall and went upstairs to pack her bags.

∽∽∽

'Today is April 17th, Mr Valentin,' said Eleanora. 'I have travelled by plane, by train, and by liner to reach Shanghai, and I now have only days to stop an earthquake that could destroy a city of two million people.'

The Russian sat as still as a statue, his fingers steepled, his brow furrowed. Eleanora wondered if he was trying to come to terms with the scale of the danger, or if he was searching for the words to gently tell her that she was mad.

'Your husband, he has built an earthquake machine?'

'See for yourself,' she said. She picked up a copy of the Times of London from the coffee table shelf and produced the folded blueprint from inside. Valentin unfolded it and held it up.

'I can repair cars, Lady Rosewood. I cannot read this.'

'It is a drilling device,' said Eleanora. 'It is designed to deliver an explosive packet deep into the earth's crust. On the right position on a fault line, it could trigger devastation on a horrific scale. That is my belief, at least, and I have had plenty of time to study the design.'

Valentin folded the blueprint and set it down. 'Why would they do this? What can they gain?'

Eleanora took a deep breath. 'I cannot… I cannot know the minds of evil men. All I can say for certain is that the threat is real – the attempt on my life and Sir Francis's presence confirm it. I must convince the authorities of the danger, and pray that there is time to prevent it. My fear is that the authorities in Shanghai will not listen to the warnings of a grief-stricken English Cassandra.'

'You have informed your own authorities? You have informed the British government?'

Eleanora shook her head. 'Who can I trust? Sir Francis is a senior civil servant. He *is* the authorities. I know a man at the consulate here in Shanghai who may be able to lend me credibility, if I can count on him as a friend, but I must hope that I get to him before Sir Francis gets to me. That is why I need your help, Mr Valentin. That is why I need protection.'

She looked at him with earnest expectation. His stoic features were difficult to read. He picked up the blueprints again, but set them down almost at once without reading them.

'We will go to your friend at once,' said Valentin. 'You will give him the blueprint and leave Shanghai.'

'It may not be so simple,' said Eleanora. 'My friend would be risking his career for me. I need more evidence than I have. The Mandrake Machine is at least fifty feet tall. It cannot be easy to hide such a thing. Fortunately, I have an idea where to look.'

She produced a matchbook from her purse and threw it on the table.

'The Mandrake Palace,' she said. 'The Mandrake Machine. The trail begins here.'

Valentin was aghast. 'You cannot go to this place,' he said. 'It is dangerous.'

'Then I hope I won't go alone,' said Eleanora. 'Two million lives hang in the balance, Mr Valentin. Is that worth a little danger?'

⸜⸝

The Mandrake Palace stood atop a rocky outcrop at the edge of the wide brown Huangpu River. Red paper lanterns swung from its eaves, and red lacquered panels hung from the walls of the tower, each showing golden maidens picking fat fruits from thorn trees while ogres watched and gloated. The sonorous hum of gamelan music filled the air, and a sweet, spicy purple smoke wafted on the wind.

A soft-top black Vauxhall Prince Henry from the Grand Hotel parked down the street from the palace. Valentin sat in the front and watched the passing foot traffic. Eleanora sat in the back and studied the building. She was disappointed to note that there was nowhere here that the machine itself might hide.

'It looks like a temple,' said Eleanora.

'It is not a temple,' said Valentin. 'It is… nightclub. No, that is too gentle a name. These buildings, they are for opium and… other comforts.'

'Whoring,' said Eleanora.

'As you say. The tower, that is for the pit, where men lose money on fights. Fights between dogs, fights between roosters, fights between men.'

'Oh, is there boxing?' asked Eleanora.

'You would not call it boxing,' said Valentin. 'Madam Mandragora, she is the owner, her study is at top of tower. If there is anything here of your husband's machine, you will find it there.'

'Then that is where I must go,' said Eleanora.

Valentin shook his head.

'It is not wise.'

'But it is necessary. If we wait until they are closed, we might—'

'They never close.'

'Then when they are quiet—'

'They are never quiet.'

'All right. It will require a stealthy approach. I have spent enough time at terrible parties to know a thing or two about wishing myself invisible.'

Valentin leaned across the back of his seat. 'There are men everywhere, Lady Rosewood. Even if the man at the door lets you by – and excuse me, they do not admit any woman who may be some man's wife – there are others who will stop you.'

Eleanora took another look at the building. She could see no way in other than the front door. She could not scale the walls. It was too bright a night, the streets were too crowded, the overhanging roofs made it impossible, and she had not climbed any walls since childhood.

'How am I to do it, then?' she asked.

'A distraction,' said Valentin. 'You need something that will bring men running from their posts.' He stepped out of the car, peeled off his leather driving gloves and unbuttoned his jacket.

'What are you doing?'

'The man at the door will not move far, but he will turn to look inside.' Valentin folded the jacket and laid it across the driver's seat. 'When he turns, you must enter. You will find a hidden door to your right; I have seen the guards pass through it. I do not know what is beyond there, but I will do what I can to make sure that no-one notices you.'

Valentin tore the dressing from the gash on his shoulder and unwrapped the bandage from his wrist.

'Valentin, what are you doing? Those bandages are there to prevent infection!'

'They are too clean. They do not look right.' He took off his crisp white shirt so that he wore only his undershirt, and he picked up a handful of muck from the gutter and smeared it across his chest and wiped it on his arms.

'Wait in shadow and watch 'til the doorman turns. You will have only seconds. If you return safe to this car, sound your horn and I will come to you.'

'What do you intend to do?' asked Eleanora. 'What can you possibly do to draw so much attention?'

Valentin grinned from ear-to-ear.

'I will show them a fight they will not forget,' he said.

'I cannot allow it.'

'So, I am a very poor valet. I do not do as I am told,' said Valentin. 'Please remember to sound the horn.'

⁂

The man on the door was a broad-shouldered thug in the black silk uniform of the house. He made no gesture of acknowledgement at Sacha's approach. Sacha was just another itinerant sailor looking for a way to lose himself in cards, grog, girls and the opium haze. He nodded Sacha through.

A beautiful girl with red blush cheeks, redder lips, and a white lotus flower in her hair took Sacha's hand as he stepped through the door. She wore a blue dress embroidered with golden birds. All of this was designed to flatter the expectations of visitors, a foreigner's idea of Shanghai.

'Such a handsome sailor! Welcome to the Mandrake Palace. What is your pleasure today?'

Sacha ignored her question.

The entrance hall was a dark black box, an empty space that stopped the world dead and cleared the senses for the fantasies and indulgences beyond the velvet curtain. Sacha heard the swelling roar of a drunken crowd and a smile formed on his lips. The girl answered his smile with hers. She looped her arm around his, drew back the curtain and led him inside.

The main room was a bare battered wooden hexagon with bars to the left and right, and sawdust scattered on the floor. Men leaned on shaky tables of salvaged wood and waved tankards of watery ale as they cheered and yelled.

In the middle of the room was the pit, ringed by a wooden banister. The pit was a sunken hexagon about three feet deep, and it was currently host to two Western men, both stripped to the waist and soaked in sweat and blood. They circled each other like hungry dogs.

Above the pit was a ringed balcony where women in silk gowns stood at chalk boards and offered odds. They waved long sticks like fishing poles over the heads of the drunks. On the end of each stick was a wicker basket used to collect stake money and return winnings. Sober men in black silk stood around the edges of the room to ensure that no-one abused this simple system.

Above the women's heads was a hexagonal hole in the ceiling about four feet across, lit by a single lantern. Here a silhouetted figure looked down on the girls and the fights and the bawdy crowd. This was the lady of the house. She lowered a basket of her own, and the girls filled it with takings from the night's bad bets. Once full, the basket disappeared into the hole.

A loud cheer brought Sacha's attention back to the pit. The smaller of the two men, a hairy ape with a heavy brow and olive skin, lay on his back at the feet of his opponent, a bald, patchily pink fellow with a thick, red beard.

Redbeard seemed to believe he had won, and raised his arms in triumph. The ape-man shook his rattling head, sprung to his feet and drove both fists at once into his opponent's stomach. He followed with an uppercut that lifted his opponent off his feet.

Redbeard landed with a loud thump, to another roar from the crowd. The ape-man raised his foot and stamped on his rival's stomach, and this brought forth a cry of such palpable agony that Sacha heard gasps from the balcony. Redbeard tried to raise his head, but he lacked the will, and his lights faded. Ape-man waited to see if he would twitch, and the crowd waited with him, but the man was down.

A grey-haired old fellow in yellow silk stepped through the crowd to the edge of the pit.

'The contest is won,' he said. He unhinged the gate in the bannister, and two house thugs leapt down to drag the prone loser from the pit. 'Sirano the Greek now stands as our champion.' The baskets whipped through the air to reward those gamblers who had bet on the smaller man.

'Who will challenge him?' asked the old man. 'Will any man step in to the ring and take his chance? Three hundred dollars American to any man who claims three victories in the pit!'

The room still bubbled with noise in the wake of the Greek's victory, as money changed hands both with the house and among private bettors. No-one stepped up to take the challenge.

'Such excitement,' said the girl at Sacha's side. 'Please, sir, what is your pleasure today?' She pressed against him and squeezed his arm.

'I came here to fight,' he told her. He drew his cigarette tin from his coat, kissed it, and slipped it into his trouser pocket. He passed his coat to the girl.

The room went quiet as Sacha stepped up to the edge of the pit. All eyes looked to him with expectation. The old man smiled at Sacha across the pit.

'Do we have a challenger?' he asked.

Sacha nodded. The crowd roared. Sirano scowled at his new opponent and spat into the sawdust, and the baskets set about their whirling dance again.

Eleanora looked to the palace at the sound of the roar. Stationed in the cover of a boarded doorway, her face wrapped in a black motoring scarf, she was invisible to a street thronged with evening revellers. She was nervous out here alone, but her car was a short run away, and the Mandrake Palace was close enough that she hoped someone would come to her aid if she screamed. It seemed like a slim hope.

The man at the palace door did not move from his place. The roar had been enough commotion to alarm Eleanora, but it had not stirred his interest. This was not her moment. She would have to wait a little longer.

∽∾∾∾

Sirano reeled from a jackhammer punch to the jaw. Sacha smacked him again and knocked the Greek off balance so that his skull bounced off the wall of the pit.

The Greek stayed down, and Sacha bobbed from one foot to the other, a long snarl curled along his lips. Stripped to the waist, his muscles knotted and wet with tarry sweat, his chest heaved with each breath, and the tendons of his arms tensed like topmast rigging. Blood covered the knuckles of his driving gloves. It was not his blood. Sacha's eyes sparked with a smoky fire.

The crowd called for him to finish the job. There were no rules here. He could take the Greek out with a kick to the

59

head while he was down, and if his tempers were higher, he might do it. Yet he was neither so hungry nor so desperate as to need to be cruel. The animal was still in its cage.

Sirano had exhausted most of his energy in his first fight, and Sacha knew the pattern well. He had been to the Mandrake Palace enough times to see that few of these drunks had two good fights in them. The fresher fists almost always felled the champion. Sacha had never seen any man last through three fights, and the house always kept its money.

Sirano pushed himself to his knees and up on to his feet. Sacha did not indulge his recovery. He needed to end this fight to preserve his strength for the next. He delivered another brutal kiss to Sirano's cheek, and the Greek pirouetted into unconsciousness.

The crowd cheered.

'Another champion stands before us,' said the old man in his sing-song chirp. 'And he is a big one. Has any man the heart and soul to challenge our mighty Russian? Step forward, please! Make your bid at victory. Three wins for three hundred dollars! Throw your hat in the ring!'

Sacha looked up at the flurry of hands as they reached for their winnings from the cages, and he wondered if he would get a moment's respite before the next fight.

A white cap spun through the air and landed in the blood-and beer-sodden sawdust of the ring. The owner pushed his way through the bettors and stood at the bannister. He was an American, a sailor, in creased and dirty dress whites and a blue neckerchief collar. He was handsome and smooth-skinned, with cropped blond hair and an overconfident smirk, and he was almost Sacha's equal in dimensions.

'I'll fight him,' he said.

A chant rose up from the American's shipmates. 'Clay, Clay, Clay, Clay.'

Clay raised his hands in the air to accept their acclaim. He smiled at Sacha, and vaulted into the pit.

⁓

Another loud cheer shook through the walls of the club, and Eleanora looked for her moment, but again the door-man remained at his post.

Eleanora wondered now if the Russian's plan was any kind of plan at all. He had survived one fight today against three murderous thugs. Would he truly have the stamina to endure another? He might even now lie unconscious on the floor of the bar. He might be dead. He might have quit her cause entirely. What was she to him? His head might lie on the lap of a bought woman while he puffed on an opium hookah. How long could she wait here on the dark streets with such uncertainty?

Eleanora tried to think what she knew of the man for certain, given all that she had told him about herself. She knew his name. She knew his nationality. She knew he had served in the army, and she presumed he had fought in the Great War and the Bolshevik Revolution. She knew that at some point he had left his country and turned to the freedom of the seas. He was a man who went where the work was.

And she knew that he was a gallant. He had seen a woman in peril and come to her aid. He had offered to excuse himself for her comfort at every opportunity. He had listened to her tale of woe and given his full assistance. He had even placed his life in jeopardy for hers.

In this, he seemed cavalier in both the best and worst senses. He was courtly and respectful, but he showed worrying disregard for his own safety, and perhaps even an enthusiasm for peril.

There was much more that she did not know about him. She did not know why he had left his homeland and come to the other side of the world. She did not know what ties or obligations he might have, or why he seemed to have nothing more than the clothes on his back. She did not know why he was willing to throw himself in danger's way, and this mystery was cause for alarm. Had he any concern for his own life? Had he any life to speak of?

The man was brick to look at, but shadow to consider. Eleanora had only to hope that she had judged him well. If he idled on his back in the company of exotic harlots, she had no strategy to fall back on.

❧

Sacha lay on his back and looked up at the women in their pretty silk dresses. He imagined they sung and twittered like tiny birds, but he could not hear any sound above the ringing in his ears and the echoing shouts of a stranger's name.

He remembered his whereabouts just in time to see Clay's big Oxford shoe crash down towards his head, and he still had enough wit to grab the shoe in both hands and push Clay off balance.

Clay sprang back to his feet as quickly as Sacha could rise. They regarded each other like beasts and met in the centre of the ring, each man's shoulder driven into the other's chest, each man's arms tight around the other's waist, their feet scratching for purchase on the uneven sawdust floor.

Clay's angry grunts filled Sacha's ears, and Sacha felt Clay's teeth bite into his shoulder. Sacha swung his head against Clay's with a solid crack, and the blow was enough to give Sacha the advantage of momentum to slam Clay into the wall.

Clay pushed Sacha off and slid along the edge of the pit to put some distance between them. Each man caught his breath and found his feet. Onlookers pushed and pulled at each other as they sought to improve their view. One man nearly tipped into the pit, and his glass beer stein fell from his hand and landed with a dull thud in the arena.

Clay darted for the glass and scooped it up, keeping one eye on Sacha in case he attempted to do the same. Sacha did not. He shook his head to show disappointment at the American's decision to use a weapon instead of his fists.

Clay did not care. He charged at Sacha and swung the glass at his head and let a bellow fly from his mouth. Sacha ducked and pummelled a one-two to the American's gut. Clay buckled forward, and Sacha surged upwards. He lifted the American off his feet and tossed him over his shoulder.

Clay flipped through the air and landed on his back with a thud that must have shaken every bone in his body. Now it was Clay's turn to look up at the lovely ladies on the balcony, but fate did not allow him an uninterrupted view. The beer stein caught the light like a diamond as it spun through the air, and Sacha looked away as it completed its terrible arc.

The crack that echoed through the room was enough to silence the crowd. It was not the glass that had broken. It rocked on the ground by the American's head as blood gushed from his nose. He coughed and choked as blood filled his mouth. He was too stunned to move himself, and Sacha feared that he might drown, so he rolled the man onto his side. Clay threw up a foaming mouthful of spit and blood and a couple of teeth. He pounded the ground with his fist to show his concession, and the crowd lit up with a cheer.

Clay's friends leapt into the ring and dragged him away. They glared hatefully at Sacha as he lolled against the pit wall and caught his breath.

The ladies stirred back into action to settle debts and wipe down chalkboards, and the old man stepped forward, this time with a gong in his hand. He banged the gong to silence the room, and when he had everyone's attention he stepped aside.

A woman took his place.

Sacha had seen her on previous visits, but only from a distance. She was a striking woman with imperial composure. Her face was taut and handsome, and she wore white powder make-up and purple paint that shaded her eyes and shaped her lips. All part of the performance. Like the girls, she wore a silk dress, but hers was charcoal black and embroidered with jet. A purple shawl covered her shoulders, bunched like a collar, and a bronze scarf looped twice around her neck. Her hair was a black crown hung with braided loops, held in place at the back with two black daggers.

Her name was Madam Mandragora, and this was her house.

'You have won two fights.'

She spoke with a steady tone, and the silence intensified as people strained to hear her. She did not look at Sacha as she addressed him. Her words were for the room.

'Win one more fight and you will be a true champion. Win one more, and you will walk away from this place with three hundred dollars!'

She gazed out across the faces of the drunks and vaga-bonds as if they were courtiers and nobles. 'My friends, can any man here stand in his way?'

A murmur circled the room, but Sacha already knew what came next. He had seen it before. A sound of screeching came from the back of the room as a chair dragged across the floorboards. The crowd parted without a word, and the new challenger made his way towards the pit.

From where Sacha was standing the man looked at least seven feet tall. His arms and thighs were as thick and heavy with muscle as an ox's neck. His head was shaved and his bare chest was covered with tattooed black lines in the form of an eagle, and the whole of him might have been carved from one enormous tree. Above his fat flattened nose were two placid grey eyes that took in the world with an unworldly patience.

This man was why no-one ever won the house's money. He came from a small island in the South Pacific, and what-ever name he had been known by there, here he was referred to in whispers as 'Tulip'.

Tulip kicked the gate off its hinges and it shattered against the opposite wall. The cheer from the crowd was loud enough that it might be heard by boats on the river.

When you fight Tulip, everyone hears about it.

No-one could mistake this cheer. It rose of a sudden, and it did not subside. Bells rang, gongs sounded, and the rumble of a hundred stamping feet shook the ground. The noise was so raucous, so frenzied, that it filled Eleanora with dread to imagine what could incite it.

Whatever the cause, Eleanora understood that this cacophony was her cue. She peered around the stone doorframe and up at the palace. The doorman rocked on his feet for a moment, glanced left and right, and turned and went inside.

Eleanora sprang from cover and sprinted across the street. She slowed her pace for the sake of stealth as the palace loomed above her, and she climbed the wide low steps as quietly as she could, and dashed through the door.

She almost collided with the doorman, and managed to suppress her alarm. He stood with his head through the velvet curtains, and it was so dark in the entrance hall that Eleanora momentarily mistook him for another door.

Eleanora put her hand to her chest to try to quiet her thumping heart. She could not peer over or around the doorman to see what he was looking at, but she had no time for curiosity. She had to move.

The black lacquered wall to the right was ridged with lines. It had to be the door that Valentin had told her about. Eleanora pressed against it and tried to feel for a handle or a trigger, but her weight was enough to release the catch, and the panel swung open. Eleanora stepped into darkness and pulled the door closed behind her.

There was no grand spiral staircase here, only a very narrow black corridor that curved around the wall of the building. Eleanora felt her way until her foot kicked against a step. There were stairs. Eleanora climbed up and discovered that the ceiling did not rise at the same angle. She was forced into a stoop. Eleanora felt above her and discovered the edges of a trapdoor.

With caution, Eleanora pushed against the door and peered out. She saw the legs of a wooden chair and guessed that this was where a guard might sit – but there was no sign of the guard's feet. Eleanora opened the trapdoor a little wider and saw to her great relief that the chair was empty. As quietly as she could, she stepped out of the hole and lowered the trapdoor behind her.

She was now behind a painted paper wall on the second tier of the tower. The wall ran in a ring along the back of the circular balcony, but there was a gap in the wall just in front of her, and a shadow stood on the other side of the screen. This was surely the guard who was meant to sit sentry at the trapdoor. He, too, had allowed himself to be distracted by the spectacle in the pit.

Eleanora followed the corridor of screens the other way, and came to a second opening. She knew she would have to pass it if she intended to find a way up to the third level.

Eleanora crouched close to the floor and poked her head

around the corner. The balcony was wide, with some empty seats scattered about it. A large bamboo pot held canes with wicker cages hooked on their ends. Four battered old bureaus stationed at intervals around the balcony served as the girls' banks. Two large blackboards revealed the odds for the fights. At this moment, the odds for a man named 'Tulip' looked a great deal more favourable than those for 'the Russian'.

The women leaned over the edge of the balcony and watched the action in the pit intently, with occasional shrieks and gasps. None of them looked Eleanora's way. Two guards on the balcony were just as enraptured. Eleanora almost believed that she could walk right out there and not be noticed. She had half a mind to do exactly that, just so that she could have a glimpse of the fight that had snared everyone's attention – but Valentin's distraction would do her no good if she was distracted by it, as well.

Eleanora sprinted past the opening and continued around the corridor. She found an alcove, and the only window she had seen thus far in the building. The small round porthole offered a downriver view of the murky waters of the Huangpu. It was a lookout window that gave some idea of what the river had swept into town today.

Eleanora realised with a flash of triumph that there was a lacquered panel set into the wall of the alcove, exactly like the one that had brought her from the ground floor. This was the door that would take her up to the top of the tower.

She pressed against the panel and it popped open.

The room at the top of the tower was about twenty feet across and illuminated by a single burning lantern, which hung in the centre of the beamed round roof above a hex-agonal hole, ringed by a wooden railing.

This space served as both a study and a withdrawing room. On one side was a mahogany desk and a pair of stiff-backed chairs, two bureaus, three archive cabinets, and two large bookcases. On the other was a chaise and a gramophone, a drinks table, a large bow-bellied wardrobe, a dressing table, and a wooden screen of carved interlacing vines.

Yet it was the hole in the centre of the room that ab-sorbed Eleanora's attention. The cries of the crowd roared from below, and Eleanora wanted to rush over to see what was happening. A terror of the truth rooted her to the spot, and she remembered again that this distraction was not meant for her. She had business to attend to. She was here to uncover the mysteries of the Mandrake Machine.

Eleanora peered through the tall bamboo shutters on the far side of the room to see if they led to a second staircase or a hiding hole for the mistress of the house. They only led to a balcony with an upriver view of the city. Next, Eleanora checked on the large green safe tucked into the shadow of the desk. She knew she had no hope of opening it, so she looked for easier targets: some papers stacked on a bu-reau; letters on the chaise; a hatbox on top of the wardrobe, which was exactly the sort of place that Eleanora might hide her own treasures.

For that reason, Eleanora began with the hat box. No sooner had she pulled it down than she heard another terrible cry from the crowd.

This time she could not stop herself. She sped to the railing and looked down into the pit.

Sacha pushed back onto his feet, but before he could get upright the other man battered into him and knocked him down again. Tulip followed one blow with another and another. Each blow shook Sacha so much that it gave him no chance to recover, let alone to fight back. The best the Russian could manage was to take the blows to his forearms and protect his face.

Wet with blood and sweat, Sacha could barely stand. His opponent delivered his punches with calm, unshakeable ease. Tulip had not begun to make an effort.

Sacha rolled across the floor and tried to connect a kick to the giant's knee, but he managed only to graze his shin. The giant did not notice. He grabbed Sacha by his shoulders, picked him up, and threw him into the bannister.

71

Eleanora covered her hand with her mouth. She could not see the expression on Valentin's face, but she could well imagine how pained and miserable he must be. She wanted the fight to be over. She wanted the man written up on the boards as 'Tulip' to be declared the winner while Valentin still had a breath in his body.

Yet that would be a disaster for them both. A swift end to the fight would mean an end to the distraction that allowed her to be there. She would be captured, and his sacrifice would be for naught. Eleanora had to move fast and be gone from this place. She had to put the fight out of her mind.

The hat box held jewellery cases. She opened one and found a necklace of silver flowers; the second contained pearl drop earrings; the third contained two slim pearlescent cylinders.

They were the exact replica of the vibrating pin from Edgar's music box.

The pin that Eleanora had found in the study even now sat in the drawer of her writing desk in her rooms at the Shanghai Grand. She had thought of the music box as the one innocent object in her husband's study, meant as a gift of love, and she had held on to the pin as a last memento of the man she had married. It was the slightest token.

Now even that memory was sullied. These pins were proof that he had built another music box, and their presence here suggested that he had given that music box to this woman, this Madam Mandragora. Everything in here might be a gift for his criminal accomplice.

The two silver pins represented a fresh betrayal that Eleanora had never even considered.

Eleanora threw the pins back in the hat box and shoved it back on top of the wardrobe, so she would not have to look at any of it a moment longer. She pushed the thought of betrayal out of her mind and resumed her search for evidence of the Mandrake Machine's existence.

The letters on the chaise had the appearance of official documents, but they were written in Chinese. Eleanora folded these up and tucked them into her sleeve.

The papers on the bureau included detailed diagrams for parts of the Mandrake Machine; three drafts of a letter signed by a man named Zinoviev; a page torn from an encyclopaedia about something called the Star of Shah Jahan; a sketched portrait of a young Chinese man alongside a simple drawing of a mountain sheathed in cloud; and a passenger list from an ocean liner.

It was the passenger list from the RMS St Bride, the ship that had brought Eleanora to Shanghai. Eleanora's own name was circled, and question marks had been scribbled next to the names of some of the other passengers.

Sir Francis's people clearly could not conceive that Eleanora had travelled to Shanghai alone; they had looked for anyone who might be a companion.

Eleanora took all of these papers in the hope that they

might help her prove a conspiracy. She folded them and slid them into her sleeve with the letters.

The desk drawers were locked, and Eleanora saw no sign of a key. She wondered if she could force the drawers open somehow. She looked around for a lever and found a polished ivory paper knife. It did not look strong enough for the job. On the gramophone table, a silver amulet caught her eye. It bore the same image of a cloud-covered mountain that she had seen on the papers. It was beautiful, but it would not help her break open the drawers.

Next to the amulet was a little jade statue of an ugly Oriental dog about the size of a man's fist. It sat up on its haunches on its wooden stand, with its eyes bulging and its tongue lolling to one side. Eleanora picked it up and felt its weight. It was heavy enough to use as a hammer.

Eleanora noticed a sheaf of old envelopes wedged under the gramophone. She set down the statue and pulled them out, and a chill ran down her spine.

Edgar's writing.

She might have expected it, but each new example of his betrayal tore her heart afresh.

Eleanora opened the first letter. It had been sent from the Moore School, a ladies' finishing school in Havana. Edgar had visited Cuba twice. Eleanora had never been, but she had sponsored several girls at the Moore School at her husband's encouragement.

"My dear M," the letter began; "What an age. I am shocked to the core by the things we teach our girls these days. Knowing you as I do, I am sure you would take it in your stride."

Eleanora was afraid to read further in case her husband's words found new ways to hurt her.

She did not get the chance. The hard muzzle of a gun pressed against the folds of her driving scarf, and Eleanora shrieked. The letters slipped from her fingers and fluttered to the floor.

❧

Sacha could not hear any screams or calls or cries. The world was muffled from all the blows he had taken to the head. He could not see much either, because of the blood in his eyes. He could hardly breathe. It was a struggle to move. Sacha had been in many fights in his time, but he could not remember ever receiving a beating like this. He could not remember much of anything at this point.

Sacha kept his distance from Tulip as best he could. He staggered against the wall of the pit and tried to weave and dodge, but it took most of his remaining strength to stand. He knew he must have landed a blow or two on his opponent, but it did not show.

Still, Sacha was not finished yet. The bruises, the blood, and the throbbing numbness that told him to lie down; none of that would stop him. This was not real pain, after all – this was the exhilarating rush that wiped away all pain.

Here in the ring, a man might understand himself. A man might come to terms with his nature. Here in the fight, his flesh and his fire and his urges all made sense. His passion poured through his fists. The beast was free.

Sacha charged on a surge of determination and connected a blow to Tulip's nose.

Tulip was unimpressed. He smacked Sacha across the face and knocked him back down.

Sacha lay in the dirt and laughed. He knew this was not wise; he could tell from the flicker of Tulip's expression that this aggravated him, and Sacha laughed harder knowing that in this way he had finally landed a blow.

Sacha tried to push up onto his knees, but the last of his energy had fled. Tulip grabbed Sacha under his arms, almost as if he meant to help him back up, but instead he held him off the ground like a broken puppet, shook him, and glowered into his bloodied eyes.

Sacha kicked Tulip in the stomach. Tulip roared and hurled Sacha clean out of the pit.

The raucous sounds of the crowds around the fight pit rose to the rafters of the Mandrake Palace, but offered no distraction to Eleanora as she stood very still with the cold steel of a gun against the base of her skull. The woman with the gun put her lips to Eleanora's ears and whispered:

'He spoke of you in his letters.'

Eleanora shivered.

'His letters made you sound such a gentle creature,' she continued. 'I think he would be shocked to see you now.'

Eleanora tried to swallow her fear. She found a voice to reply.

'He never spoke of you,' she said.

The woman laughed. She took Eleanora by the shoulder and turned her around.

She was equal parts beauty and terror; fierce and dramatic in her elegant robes, surely at least as deadly as the daggers in her hair, and as exquisite as the dragons engraved on the barrel of her gun. Her face was painted white and her lips purple in the style of a woman from the Chinese stage, but Eleanora could see the intensity that shaped the real face underneath.

The woman slipped her pistol into the pocket of her robe as if to show Eleanora that she did not consider her a threat.

'How defiant you look in your mourning black,' said the woman. 'I imagined you sick and feeble; a snowflake or a little lamb. Yet here you are, far from home in the wicked world, wide-eyed, lost and alone.'

'You are Madam Mandragora,' said Eleanora.

'That is the name I am called by the men down there.

That is the name I am known by to all of Shanghai. But did you want to know what your husband called me? Do you want to know the names he used when we were alone together?'

Eleanora braced herself against tears. 'I shall hold to Mandragora,' she said. 'The other names I might call you would not favour my situation.'

Mandragora smiled. She gestured to the chaise, and Eleanora sat.

'Shall I tell you who I truly am?' said Mandragora. 'I am nothing. Less than a whisper. Invisible. You were to see only your husband, and nothing of the shadows at his back. You should not be here. You should never have seen my face.'

'The world is not always kind to our expectations,' said Eleanora. 'I always hoped I might be happier than this.'

'Poor dolorous widow. How absurd that he did all of this for you.'

Mandragora's words sent a fresh shock through Eleanora's body. The suggestion that any of this was done for her was grotesque. Machines of death, atrocities, devastation: she could never have asked for any part of it.

'There is a reason he kept this from me, madam,' said Eleanora. 'He knew you would be repulsive to me.'

'Certainly, he did. He brought you roses, not the dirt that they grow in. You remember Greenwich, of course?'

Greenwich. Eleanora had one precious memory of Greenwich. Even now, after all she had discovered, that memory was still a jewel.

'What do you know of it?' she asked.

'He told me the story,' said Mandragora. 'How he asked you to stand on one side of the meridian while he stood on the other. Do you remember what he promised you that day?'

Eleanora nodded. A warm bright day in early spring and the breezes were rich with lilac and lavender. The meridian marked time for everywhere in the world; it was the start and end of the day, the crossing line for the sun's full journey around the world. With the city of London laid out in glory before them, Edgar Rosewood sunk down on one knee to pledge his truth.

'Ellie, I make this promise to you. If you will do me the honour of becoming my wife, I will give you the world. Will you marry me?'

Eleanora gripped his hand as he kissed hers, and she wept with happiness.

'You cannot keep such a promise,' she said, 'but I would be your wife and ask for nothing. Of course, I will marry you.'

'I will always keep my promises to you,' he said. He stepped across midnight, took her in his arms, and kissed her.

Eleanora wept again now as she remembered it.

'I did not want the world,' she said. 'I only wanted him.'

Mandragora dismissed the park, the flowers and the city with a flick of her hand and brought Eleanora back to the black walls and the bare wood and the opium smoke on the air. She went to the drinks table, pulled the glass stopper from a decanter, and filled a small engraved glass with amber liquid.

'Your poor husband,' said Mandragora. 'Wives can be such a burden on a man. No wonder they always need someone else to escape to.'

Eleanora felt a cold rage crackle under her skin. She knew she ought to fear this woman, but she was too furious at her impudence.

'You know nothing about my husband.'

Mandragora looked Eleanora in the eye. 'I'm sure you wish that were true,' she said. She drained her glass and set it down on the gramophone stand.

Eleanora leapt to her feet and lunged at her enemy with the ivory paper knife. Mandragora smacked Eleanora's arm away, and the knife flew from her hand. She grabbed Eleanora by the throat, sank her long fingernails into her skin and pushed her against the gramophone stand. The woman's eyes seemed darker now, and washed with hate, and Eleanora was truly afraid.

'Edgar was the greatest man in a generation,' said Mandragora. 'He built his ambitions around you, you ungrateful witch. Is this how you love him? Is this how you honour your husband?'

Eleanora drew a rasping breath. 'I will not explain myself to a creature like you,' she said. She reached behind her for the little dog statue. Mandragora saw it in her hand and threw Eleanora to the ground. The statue rolled across the floorboards.

'Creature, am I?' said Mandragora. The corners of her mouth edged towards a smile and she suppressed it. 'Are you so different to him and his friends, do you think? Your whole world looks to the east and sees devils, mongrels and savages.'

'That is not what I meant,' said Eleanora.

'Is it not?' Mandragora picked up the jade statue and rolled it in her hands. 'I know what I am to you and yours. This place, this costume; it is all what you want me to be. Yet if I must be your dog, I will be the dog at the richest table. I will pick the best scraps and serve the strongest masters. I will play their games, and I will steal more strength from them than they would ever want to give me.

'And look at you, little lamb. They would have given you everything, and still you demurred. "Thank you, no, I mustn't. I shouldn't. I simply can't".'

Mandragora turned to watch the fight, and set the statue down on the rail. Eleanora untied her black scarf and put her hand to her raw red throat to see if the woman had broken skin.

A crash from the pit was followed by a thunderous cheer. The drunks chanted, 'Tulip, Tulip, Tulip'.

'The masters say you are soft and weak,' said Mandragora. 'I was told to send men to scare you at the docks, so that you would turn on your heel. As Edgar's wife, you were to be afforded a little respect. You were not to be killed.'

'Then let me go,' said Eleanora. 'Send me home.' With Mandragora's back to her she edged toward the discarded paper knife.

'You misunderstand. I was told to send men to scare you, but I sent men to kill you. What does that tell you about your hopes, Lady Rosewood? The world will not suffer for your passing.'

Eleanora reached for the paper knife. The floorboards creaked. Mandragora whipped out her gun and aimed it at Eleanora's head, and Eleanora did not dare make another move.

'If you murder me, the law will know it.'

'A hundred pieces of driftwood float through these doors every day. You are just another soul. You are less than most: a wife in want of a husband. You are of no consequence to anyone.'

Desperate for any words that might keep her alive, Eleanora remembered the passenger list she had found on the desk, now folded inside her sleeve.

'I did not come to Shanghai alone,' she said. 'I have accomplices, and they know I am here. If you fire that weapon, no force on earth will prevent my associates from taking their revenge.'

Mandragora looked Eleanora over with scepticism. She lifted her gun.

'Tell me the names of your accomplices,' she said.

'What does it profit me to betray them? Take me to Sir Francis. I will give him the names in exchange for my life.'

'Give me the names and you have my word that I will take you to Sir Francis.'

Eleanora hissed her incredulity. 'What is your word worth to me?'

'That depends, Lady Rosewood, on whether you think me a woman or a creature,' said Mandragora. 'Give up your companions, and I will let Sir Francis deal with you. That suits me very well. Refuse, and I will kill you here and now and take my chances with your friends. Do you understand?'

Eleanora nodded. It was a terrible choice, but it was the only choice open to her. If she said nothing, she would die. If she gave up a conspirator, she might walk out of here alive.

Yet she only had one conspirator, and he was downstairs, broken and bleeding, sacrificing his wellbeing for the benefit of hers.

'He is here,' said Eleanora. 'He is down below.'

❧

Chants stirred Sacha from his fog, though he could barely make out the word; just the rhythm of it ringing in his skull. Tulip, Tulip, Tulip.

Sacha felt for the solid reassurance of the floor beneath him. He expected the sawdust of the pit, but his fingers touched on bare beer-soaked splintered boards. He raised his head and saw that he was on a table top, and the table top was on the floor. Glasses lay spilled around him, and the seat of a broken stool rocked by his head.

Sacha pushed onto his elbows, but someone held him down. A man knelt at Sacha's side with his hand on Sacha's chest. He was about Sacha's age, but better weathered; he looked like he had been cast from bronze. He had blue eyes, short blond hair, a beard of golden stubble, and a wide, well-made mouth that rested comfortably in a smile.

'Stay down,' said the stranger. 'The fight is over. You lost.'

Sacha brushed him off, but made no further effort to move. He looked the stranger over and tried to make sense of him. He wore a black jacket with bare epaulettes, a coarse white cotton shirt, and dark grey trousers with a blue stripe along each leg. He also wore a gun belt and Russian boots. It was a costume stitched together from military surplus, with no two pieces from the same uniform. This was a man who belonged to nowhere and pledged to nothing. He did not look like a serious person.

'The fight is not over,' said Sacha. 'I did not concede.'

'You were knocked out,' said the stranger. 'Knocked out of the pit, and knocked out of your head.' He had a Germanic accent, but soft and filled with wry amusement.

'The fight is over, my friend. You cannot win the money. You have no reason to get back up.'

Sacha did not know if that was true. He had not heard the car horn that would signal Lady Rosewood's safe escape from the palace, but there was every chance he had missed it in the noise of the crowd, or while unconscious. He could not be sure that the lady had made her escape, which meant that he could not lie down.

'There is honour to fight for,' said Sacha. It was an excuse the stranger might believe. It was one that Sacha could believe, as well.

The stranger rolled his eyes. He took a handkerchief from his pocket and picked up a half empty bottle of clear spirit from the floor. He doused his handkerchief and dabbed it to a cut on Sacha's brow. Sacha seethed and raised a hand in protest. The stranger batted his hand away and continued his ministry.

'Let me give you some advice on dignity, my friend,' said the stranger. He offered a cocked smile from the corner of his mouth. 'There is nothing more dignified than strength. I believe it. I admire strength above all other virtues. Strength of will, or mind, or body, it is all as one, and strength alone will bring us through our dark days. Not hope or wit or charity; only strength.' He doused the handkerchief a second time and wiped at Sacha's cheek. Sacha regarded him with scepticism.

'You have proven yourself,' said the stranger. 'I am an exacting judge of men, but in you I find much to admire. No-one defeats that monster in the pit. That is the reason he exists. You survived longer than any man, and in this you are heroic. You are the second most formidable man in Shanghai, and you have your dignity. But return to the pit, and you will seem sullen and wretched, and there is no dignity there.'

'I will not be beaten,' said Sacha.

The stranger leaned forward and put his hand on Sacha's arm. Sacha felt his vodka-warmed breath against his cheek.

'Leave fighting for another day,' he said. 'I would buy you a drink in recognition of your strength. I cannot do this if that monster kills you. Please recognise the advantages of your current situation.'

The stranger spoke with such soft, insinuating charm that he might shake the confidence of a convent sister. He was an appealing companion for a man with no friends.

'My name is Arek Saxon,' said the stranger.

'Sacha Valentin.' Sacha shook his hand. Arek gripped tight and helped hoist Sacha to his feet.

'I am afraid you have flattened my table,' said Saxon. 'I'm sure we can find another. Or we can go some other place to drink, if you have seen enough of these walls?'

Sacha nodded, but recalled at once the reality of his situation. He could not go anywhere with this man. He could not abandon Lady Rosewood.

'I am sorry. I would like to drink with you, but I cannot,' he said. 'I have business to attend to. I have a fight to win.'

He took a step forward and swayed. Arek caught him and held him by his shoulders.

'You are a fool if you intend to resume this fight,' said Saxon. 'Do not throw yourself away. Find some better use.'

'This is no business of yours,' said Sacha. 'I fight. It is what I am good at.' He pushed Saxon away and steered back to the pit, unsteady with every step.

'Then cheat,' Saxon called after him. 'In the name of God, man! Life is short for honest men. Cheat, or you will die!'

Sacha tried to make a dismissive gesture to Arek, but the effort almost threw him off balance. He reached the edge of the pit and grabbed the bannister.

Tulip leaned against the far wall with a beer stein in each hand and a girl in each arm.

'We are not finished, you and I,' said Sacha.

Silence fell across the men that surrounded the pit, and it spread to the edges of the room, snatching up half-sentences and quelling the clink and clod of glass and bottle.

Tulip pushed the girls aside and handed each of them a beer. His once serene eyes now burned with fury. It was insult enough to Tulip's pride that Sacha could stand at all. That he could talk was too much to bear, and that he used his words to issue a fresh challenge was an outrage beyond imagining. Tulip pounded on the bannister and shattered it to splinters.

The old man in yellow rushed through the crowd and waved his hands like the wings of a panicked chicken.

'The fight is over! The fight is over!' He pointed a bony finger at Sacha. 'All bets are settled. You are defeated.'

Sacha looked around for the lady of the house. He noticed with alarm that she was nowhere to be found. How long ago had she slipped away? He had not seen her since the start of his fight with Tulip. Sacha looked up at Mandragora's balcony, and through bleary eyes he thought he saw the shape of a woman standing there.

'We will start again,' said Sacha. He returned his gaze to his opponent. Tulip nodded his assent.

The old man threw down his arms. 'New fight,' he declared. 'New fight! New bet.' He looked at Sacha and added: 'No prize money!'

Sacha heaved himself over the bannister and dropped into the pit with the grace of a stunned ox. Tulip brushed through the splinters and jumped down to face him. The two men glowered at each other as the betting cages whizzed above their heads. Tulip threw his arms out wide and brought them together to clap around Sacha's head. Sacha ducked and drove his fist into Tulip's stomach.

Eleanora looked at the scene below with fear heavy in

her heart. The audience stirred into frenzy as the two giants traded blows, and though Tulip clearly dealt more damage, Valentin's return to the pit had at least dented the other man's pride. Eleanora took a step back. She wrung her hands together until her knuckles were white.

Mandragora pushed her forward. 'Take a good look,' she insisted. 'Find your friend and show him to me.'

Eleanora fixed her eyes on Valentin. He was bleeding. He was dying for her.

'I do not see him,' said Eleanora.

Mandragora leaned in close to Eleanora's ear.

'Look closer,' she whispered. 'Which of these hand-some gentlemen is the travelling companion to a fine English lady? That black-gummed Irishman with only one eye? Is he your friend? The Japanese thug with the foolish moustache? The undernourished mulatto throw-ing up in a corner so that he can begin his drinking afresh? Which of these is the man you mean to throw to me, Eleanora?'

Eleanora tore her eyes away from the fight and looked over the hopeless crowd of drunkards and vagabonds. Any man she picked would be an innocent dragged into her horrors, and her word could mean his death.

Eleanora told herself it was for the greater good. Every one of these men might die if the Mandrake Machine destroyed Shanghai. Millions could die if Eleanora did not escape this house with her life. Could she sacrifice one soul for the good of a city?

Her eyes settled on a clean, handsome young soldier in unfamiliar military garb as he pushed his way through the crowd towards the pit. He looked like an officer at liberty, and he was the only man she had seen who might pass for respectable. He also looked capable and within his wits, and thus better equipped than the rest to deal with whatever misfortune came his way.

'He is…'

'Yes, lady lamb? You see him.'

Eleanora shook her head.

She could not do it. She could not nominate a stranger for death. Though it might cost her everything, though it might cost Shanghai dearly, she could not have that man's life on her conscience. There had to be some other way out of this.

'He is gone,' she said. 'Take me to Sir Francis and I will give you his name, I swear it.'

'This is a feeble ruse,' said Mandragora. 'Do you think me so dull that I cannot piece together simple truths? You were very clever to hire a man already known to me. It is the Russian, yes? The one dying slowly for my patrons' entertainment?'

Eleanora shivered. 'I do not know that man.'

'But you do. Of course, you do. I know him, as well; he has visited us many times. He does not take of the girls or the opium, and we have never coaxed him into the ring before, but he is a familiar drinker and brawler. The villains I sent to kill you were bested by a Russian that fits his description exactly. The same man came with you to the hotel. You must pay very well if he is ready to die for you.'

'He is a stranger. He is nothing to me.'

'Then why panic so? With you or not, he is about to die. We should share this majestic moment, dear lady. Perhaps it will bring us closer together?'

Eleanora braced herself against the wave of horror that flooded through her. She would not let this man die, not in the ring and not at Mandragora's hands. Not for her sake.

She snatched the little dog from the railing and shouted, 'Valentin, run!'

Mandragora grabbed her wrist and turned her around. She pressed her against the rail so that she was almost half over the pit, and the wood creaked and complained underneath her. Eleanora's black scarf slipped from her shoulders, and she knew that, if Mandragora wished it, she could easily push Eleanora over the rail and watch her follow it down.

'You fool,' said Mandragora. 'Edgar would have made you a queen, and look at you now. Desperate and murderous. Did you think you would strike out my brains with this green rock?'

'No,' said Eleanora. 'I hope to save a better life than mine.' She opened her hand and let the jade statue fall.

Sacha did his best to stay clear of Tulip's reach. He ducked and swayed and bobbed, but Saxon's words about strength rang in his ear, and he knew his strength was exhausted. Tulip's next blow might take his head clean off his shoulders. Sacha prayed that Lady Rosewood had made her escape, and his death would not be for nothing.

He heard his name, or thought he did. It was muffled by the other noises in the hall, and by the ringing in his ears. Perhaps it was the voice of God, calling him home?

Sacha looked up to heaven as Tulip's shadow fell across his face. A black scarf drifted down. It turned and curled on the drafts of the old building. He had seen that scarf before. He knew that scarf.

Tulip tensed his muscles for the finishing blow. Sacha knew it was coming, and he had no will to avoid it. He had given as much as he could. It was a dream now. A scarf in the sky. The echo of his name. A small dark sun plummeting to the earth. What did it all mean?

The fist sped towards Sacha's face, and Sacha remembered. He ducked. He dived under Tulip's legs and caught the small dark sun before it hit the ground.

It was a jade statue of a little pug dog. It stuck its tongue out at Sacha.

'Life is short for honest men,' said the dog – or else the words came from somewhere in Sacha's memory. 'Cheat,' it said, 'or you will die.'

Sacha rolled onto his back. Tulip raised his foot to crush his cowardly prey, and the black scarf touched down on Tulip's head and covered his face.

Sacha grabbed Tulip's foot and threw his blinded opponent off-balance. Tulip recovered and pulled off the scarf. Sacha was up, as well. He smacked the statue against Tulip's temple with a terrible and almighty crack.

His fingers sore and trembling, Sacha slumped against the wall and watched as Tulip swayed a little. Tulip spun a little. Tulip finally tumbled down.

Everything was noise. Sacha looked up through the stew of electricity that buzzed from the crowd and peered into the lantern light. He understood at once that the lady was still up there. She had not yet made her escape.

The little jade dog was still in Sacha's hand, and it still had that strange look on its face. The dog was not done. Sacha was not done. He looked at the lantern and picked up the scarf, and folded it into a sling.

❧

Mandragora dragged Eleanora from the railing, threw her to her knees, and levelled the pistol in her face. A huge roar swelled up from below, and Eleanora whispered a prayer of hope that she had done the right thing, that her last act had been valiant and good. She looked up at Mandragora, de-

93

termined to face death without shame. Her murderer stared down at her, a shadow of hate crowned by lantern light.

The lantern exploded.

A crash of glass, a plume of flame; the room plunged suddenly into darkness. Eleanora dropped to her side just a moment before the gunshot. She felt the rush of air and was deafened by the sound, but the bullet missed and splintered the floorboards.

Mandragora was dimly lit by the light from below, but she was lost and confused. Eleanora had only a moment. She remembered the paper knife, found it and sprang forward, taking hold of Mandragora's gun arm with one hand and pressing the ivory blade to her neck with the other. It was a poor weapon, but it would suffice.

'Drop the gun or I will slice you open,' said Eleanora.

Mandragora did not question her resolve. She let the gun slip from her fingers. Eleanora stepped away and picked it up. She threw away the letter opener and backed towards the bamboo shutters that she knew would take her out onto the roof.

Mandragora shouted a few words of Cantonese to the guards whose footsteps Eleanora could hear pounding up the stairs. Eleanora fired twice into the door as a warning, and pushed through the bamboo shutters onto a balcony. She slipped the gun into her coat pocket and climbed over the balcony onto the roof.

Eleanora looked down across the sloping tiles of the palace at the vast Huangpu River, which waited ready to swallow her up if she missed her footing. She stepped as swiftly as caution allowed along the beam of the roof. She heard cries from the guards, but she did not stop to look back. She lowered herself over the edge of the roof, dropped onto the next set of tiles, and scrambled for the street.

All hell broke loose inside the Mandrake Palace. Sacha struggled out of the pit and pushed through the crowd, shaking off the tiny shards of shattered glass from the lantern. He had no way of knowing if he had done enough to help Lady Rosewood, but he had done as much as he could, and the current chaos was the last chance either of them would have to flee the scene.

Some men clamoured for their money, others insisted that the fight was fixed, and the women on the balcony had no idea what to do. Tulip had been defeated, and the payout was more than the house could cover.

The guards were also in a panic. Some of them rushed for the top of the building, which left the girls unprotected. The old man yelled at two guards by name and pointed at Sacha, and they heeded his call. One raised his pistol; the other drew a blade.

Fortunately for Sacha, the room was a swamp of rowdy drunks. The guard with the gun could not hope for a clear shot, and the guard with the blade could not close the distance through the tide of bodies.

Sacha dropped his shoulder and forced his way through. He vaulted through the hatch of the cloakroom, grabbed his overcoat, and dashed for the entrance. He paused for a moment to look for Arek Saxon in the crowd.

Saxon stood in a far corner with a glass of vodka in his hand. He looked unruffled and untouched by the commotion that surrounded him. He raised his glass in recognition of Sacha's accomplishments. Sacha smiled at him, punched the doorman in the gut, and raced outside.

The car was not where he had left it, but he heard men thumping down across the rooftop behind him, so he had no choice but to run.

A blinding light hit Sacha in his eyes and froze him in his tracks. Tires screeched, a car horn sounded, and the Prince Henry sped towards him with its soft top down. Sacha threw himself over the side of the car and landed painfully on the back seat.

'I hope you don't mind if I drive,' said Lady Rosewood. 'I just found that I was rather in the mood for it.'

Sacha grunted his reply. As they rocketed through the Shanghai night, he was grateful for the chance to close his eyes.

In the small hours of the night, Sacha stood at the hotel window and watched the shapes that passed on the Shanghai streets.

On their return from the Mandrake Palace, the lady ordered the doctor to return, to sew up Sacha's cuts and wrap him in fresh bandages. The doctor gave Sacha something to dull the pain to a throb, and ordered him to rest. Sacha's body cried out for it, but neither need nor drugs were any match for his anxiety. The events of the day had set a charge to his thoughts, and after a few hours of fitful turning, Sacha gave up on sleep.

The lady was now at rest in her chamber. The rooms were quiet, and Sacha could indulge in solitude.

Sacha turned the cigarette tin over in his hands. It had taken a couple of blows in the fight, which had knocked it out of shape and left a welt on his thigh. Sacha prised the tin open with some effort.

First, he took out the silver cross and wrapped the chain around his fingers. Then he picked out the old sepia photograph.

The photograph showed two boys dressed in the belted tunic jackets of the Russian army. Their arms were slung around each other in a gesture of familiar camaraderie, and each had a broad grin on his face. Behind them was the massive spoked wheel of a Lebedenko tank, a towering armoured tricycle with a canon turret.

'Childish things,' said Sacha.

He held the picture up to the window so that the light from the street illuminated the boys' faces.

'I should not long for the simple passions of war.'

An urgent knock sounded at the door. The hour for civilised visitors was well past. Sacha folded the photograph back into the tin, set the silver cross on top, and tried to force the lid back on, but it resisted. He set the tin on the coffee table and took the foreign documents stolen from Mandragora and slipped them under the rug. He put the chain on the door, and opened it an inch.

The girl in the corridor was about eighteen. She leaned against the opposite wall, breathing hard. She had an Indian complexion. Her short brown hair was tangled around her face. Her black shift dress almost slid off her shoulders, and she held a pair of black satin heels in one hand.

'Help me,' she said. She did not look at Sacha, but along the corridor, watchful. 'You have to help me. Please.'

Sacha closed the door, took off the chain, and opened it again. The girl almost ran, almost fell into his arms. Sacha looked along the corridor and saw nothing. He pulled the girl inside and led her to the recliner, and returned to lock and bolt the door.

The girl draped herself across the recliner, one arm pressed to her temple, the other trailing on the ground. Her skirt rode along her thighs as she raised her knees onto the seat. She was a very pretty girl with wide green eyes. Her lips trembled and her bosom heaved.

'What is wrong, miss?' asked Sacha. 'Who is chasing you?'

'I am sorry,' said the girl. She wiped at her cheek with the back of a fingernail. 'I am so sorry; I should not bring my troubles to your door, but these men, they meant to hurt me. I thought they were good boys. I thought they were nice.'

Sacha poured her a glass of water from the carafe on the writing desk. She took a sip, and drew her legs back to give him room on the recliner. He chose to sit on the chair.

'Tell me what happened,' said Sacha.

'It is just part of the job; to welcome people, to be friendly,' she said. 'I smile at them, they smile at me. I thought they were nice.'

'What is your job, miss?'

'I am a hat check girl at the Charteris Casino.'

'And who are these men?'

'Boys. Three boys.' The girl took another sip of water and told her story. 'We had been talking all night at the Charteris – they would come back to get something from their coat, over and over again, and they would talk to me and say nice things, and ask for my advice on places to go in the city; places to drink and places to dance. They were very nice, very sweet.

Then I was finished for the night, and one of them offered to drive me home, and he was so polite, so I did not think... I thought it was all right. I thought I could come to the hotel for one drink, and it was fine. But all three of them were there, and they...'

She sobbed again and swallowed the rest of the water.

Sacha was not equipped to deal with a situation like this. If the men were here, he could beat them, but he did not know what to do about the woman they had harmed. He tried to offer a reassuring frown, but he feared that he only managed a look of pained confusion.

'I ran for the door,' said the girl. 'They came after me. I got to the staircase – I think the one the maids use – and I ran. I could hear them above me, so I came to this floor and saw a light under your door and I knocked. I am sorry. I am so sorry.'

Sacha stood and went back to the door. 'They did not follow you to this floor?' he asked. He cracked the door open and looked up and down the corridor. 'I do not see them. Perhaps I should look for them? I will teach them a lesson, if that is what you wish.'

The girl wailed. 'Do not leave me! Close the door, please! I am safe here with you, I know it.'

Sacha closed the door. The girl patted the recliner.

'Sit with me.' She chewed on her bottom lip. 'I owe you my life.'

Sacha stared at her with an unexpected sensation of nervousness. He was not experienced in the ways of women, but he found her sudden bold manner strange and inconsistent.

The girl swept her hair out of her face and slid her bare feet along the rug. 'They call me Honey,' she said. 'What is your name?'

Sacha felt a blush bloom along his cheeks. 'I will send for a bellhop,' he said. 'He will see that you are taken to safety.'

Honey stood and walked across the floor with a cat-like slink. 'I am safe here,' she said. 'With you. And it is dark outside. Let me stay.' She rested one hand against his chest, just over his beating heart, and brushed the other across his cheek.

'Miss, I am sorry, but you should leave.'

She stuck out her bottom lip and looked up at him through her eyelashes. 'I cannot go.'

'You cannot stay.'

She looked around the room, and her eyes settled on the bedroom door. 'I understand. You are not alone. Your wife is here?'

'I do not have a wife. But I am not alone.'

'Is she your lover?'

'She is my employer.'

'Then you can let me stay.' She reached behind her back and unfastened the buttons of her dress. With a roll of her shoulders the dress slid to the floor.

They stood just inches apart, he in his cotton vest and shorts, she in her pink silk chemise.

'Please get dressed,' said Sacha. He was afraid that Lady Rosewood might awake at any moment and come through. He was even more afraid that she might not.

'You are a serious man. Are you playing the role of the sheik?' She lowered one of the straps from her slip. 'Should I fear you? Will you make me shiver?'

Sacha straightened her strap. 'You will embarrass yourself,' said Sacha. 'I do not want this.'

'You do not know what you want. Relax and let me show you. Let's have a cigarette,' said Honey. She picked up the cigarette tin from the table. Sacha grabbed her wrist harder than he meant to, and the case dropped from her hand and cracked open.

'What are you doing?' asked Honey. She looked up at him with a terrified expression, but recovered her composure in a moment and twisted her arm free of his grip. 'Would you rather fight me than make love with me?'

Sacha picked up her black shift and put it in her arms. 'Get dressed,' he told her. 'I will take you down to the lobby and call for a motor car to take you home.'

She offered a petulant frown. 'Where did you lose your manhood?' she asked. 'What sort of half-creature are you? Fine then, I will get dressed. If you are so gallant, you will at least give me some privacy.'

Sacha closed his eyes and turned his back.

The girl sighed. 'This is not the way it is supposed to happen,' she said. 'They will be very unhappy when they hear about this.'

These were not the words of an innocent. Sacha opened his eyes a crack and saw the girl reflected in the mirror. She had a knife in her hand.

Sacha turned and took a step back as the blade swept towards him. She missed with her first attack and made a desperate second lunge. He blocked her strike and slammed his palm into her chest. She flew back over the recliner.

Honey sprang to her feet, leapt onto the recliner, and kicked Sacha in the head.

'You could at least have died happy,' she said. She stepped down and drove her knee between Sacha's legs. He dropped with a hopeless groan.

Honey twirled the dagger in her fingers. She gripped Sacha by his hair and swung the knife at his throat.

A gunshot rang out over Honey's head and she hesitated mid-strike.

'Drop the knife or I will shoot you where you stand.'

Lady Rosewood stood at her bedroom door dressed in a camisole and robe. She had Mandragora's pistol in her hand.

'So, there you are,' said Honey. 'The little nothing that caused so much trouble.'

'I will not ask you a second time.'

Honey dropped the knife.

'You are both fools,' said Honey. 'How long do you think you can survive here, if a little girl can come so close to killing you? Your lives are—'

'Now get out,' said Lady Rosewood.

Honey reached for her dress, which lay crumpled on the floor. Lady Rosewood stepped on it. Honey looked up into the barrel of the gun. The expression on the lady's face did not invite debate. Honey left the dress. She ran from the room and slammed the door behind her.

Sacha dragged himself onto the recliner while Lady Rosewood locked and bolted the door.

'An assassin,' said Lady Rosewood.

'Not our first,' said Sacha. He was ashen, and his voice was a strained whisper. 'She behaved as a woman in trouble. I meant only to help her.'

'Then they have come to know you, Valentin,' said Lady Rosewood. 'They know you have a weakness for chivalry.'

'They do not know me as well as they wish,' said Sacha.

Lady Rosewood scooped up the dress. 'I assume, from her state of... dishabille... that she meant to seduce and murder you, and then take me in my sleep? Does that seem accurate?' She threw the dress in the waste paper bin. 'I am relieved to learn that you are such a gentleman that she had to resort to noisier methods.'

Sacha sank further into the recliner. 'I am a common

man, Lady Rosewood. Do not think more of me than that.'

Lady Rosewood picked up the girl's shoes. There was a mechanism under the left shoe for secreting a dagger. She threw both shoes in with the dress.

Sacha closed his eyes. He could hear Lady Rosewood as she paced the room on the lookout for other remnants of this disturbance. He heard her set something down on the coffee table.

'I confess, this girl might have had the better of us both if I had not been sleeping so poorly,' said Lady Rosewood. 'I have been kept awake by so many questions. I wonder, for instance, if I am running away by coming here.'

Sacha shook his head. 'I do not understand,' he said.

'My heart is broken in two, and it makes me sick to think of old familiar places,' said Lady Rosewood. 'I am not the person best suited to do the things that must be done, and yet here I am. Not because I am brave, but because I am too afraid to stay where the world might catch up to me. Does that make sense?'

'You are brave, Lady Rosewood.'

'You are kind,' said Lady Rosewood. 'I wondered also…' she hesitated.

'Ma'am?'

'I have an impertinent question. Might I ask it?'

'Yes, ma'am.'

'Valentin… are you also running away?'

He opened his eyes and looked up at her. She held the dagger by its tip between forefinger and thumb, not as a weapon, but as a filthy thing she needed to dispose of. The sight made Sacha smile.

'I do not run,' he said. 'I am a man without country or home. I am as I must be. There is nothing to run from and nothing to run to. I am free.' A twinge of pain forced him to close his eyes and lie down again.

'So be it,' said Lady Rosewood. 'You should sleep. In the morning, we will discuss our next course of action. Rest assured you have earned my thanks and my respect a thousand times over today.'

He heard her open and close the door to her bedroom, and he remained still and silent for a few minutes longer. When at last he sat up, he saw what Lady Rosewood had set on the table; it was his cigarette tin, with the silver cross beside it, and the photograph of two young men in their army tunics.

Breakfast arrived with a knock and a rattle to stir Sacha from his hard-won rest. He washed and shaved and found new clothes laid out for him by the bathroom door. He dressed in the coarse black wool trousers and dark navy shirt, but again forewent the offer of new shoes in preference to his worn-in boots. He presented himself to the lady, who sat at a table laid out with tea, toast, marmalade and jam, and the stolen documents from the Mandrake Palace.

'Do you drink tea?' asked Lady Rosewood.

'Of course.'

'Sit down and have some breakfast.'

Sacha stepped back from the table as if it were booby-trapped. 'It is not right, ma'am.'

'Ridiculous. I insist. You are my protector; I shan't have you wasting away.'

'I will eat when you are finished. We should not eat together.'

'We have much to discuss, Valentin; I shan't shout to you through a locked door while I enjoy my toast and your stomach rumbles. I can order some coffee, if you would rather?'

'I prefer tea.'

'Then sit, please, and help yourself to anything you would like.'

Sacha took a seat and poured himself a cup. He stirred a spoonful of strawberry jam into the tea. The lady watched with an alarmed expression that made him regret it at once, but she returned her attention to the papers and pretended not to have noticed. Everything about this room made Sacha feel awkward, from the small cup to the small chair to the small woman opposite him.

'I have decided to return home,' said Lady Rosewood. 'The RMS St Bride leaves for Singapore at three this afternoon. I have asked the hotel to secure a cabin.'

The announcement caught Sacha by surprise. 'You will leave today?'

The lady did not look up from her documents. 'I am afraid so. After our little visit last night, I realise what a mistake I have made in coming here,' she said. 'The truth of the matter is, there is little more I can do but place myself in peril. Once I have trusted these papers to my friend at the embassy and told him what is to come, my best course of action is retreat. There is Havana to think about, and Madras. If I die in Shanghai, who will live to alert the authorities to my late husband's other strategies?'

'But if you can stop the machine in Shanghai—'

'I hope that the machine can be stopped, but it cannot be stopped by me. I am an emissary of my husband's ills; I am not the agent of his redemption. A woman travelling alone cannot lay siege to whatever empire of evil he made himself a part of, and my friend Mr Bloom is much better equipped than I. He has resources in Shanghai and the faith of the authorities. I can only hope that these papers will expose and incriminate Mandragora and reveal the machine's location.'

Sacha nodded and sipped his tea. Lady Rosewood offered him toast. Her hand trembled. Sacha took a slice quickly to save her from embarrassment.

'I will of course arrange for you to travel out of Shanghai, in case our efforts are not successful,' she said. 'The clothing is yours to keep.'

'Thank you,' said Sacha. 'I would prefer to stay here.'

Lady Rosewood paled at the suggestion. 'You cannot stay. If the Mandrake Machine is effective it will kill thousands. You may be among them.'

'If your friend can find and destroy this machine, I will not die,' said Sacha. 'If your friend fails, and the city falls, and somehow I still live, they will need strong men to recover the living and bury the dead.'

'And if you die?'

'If I die, I die.'

Lady Rosewood scowled.

'Valentin, you have saved my life; I cannot leave you here to squander yours.'

Sacha shrugged his shoulders. 'My life is of little value. I cannot change the world, as you can. I am only here a little while, and it is no matter to anyone when I leave.'

'That is sheer nonsense. I will not stand for it.'

'Ma'am, there is nothing you can do. Shanghai is a danger to you, even if the city stands. You have good reason to return to London. I have no reason to be anywhere but here.'

'We will talk about this further,' said Lady Rosewood. 'We must make our way to the embassy to deliver these documents.'

Sacha was sceptical. 'We are to deliver them by hand?'

'On this occasion, we must. Government can be slow and short-sighted, and I cannot risk these papers falling into the hands of anyone affiliated with Sir Francis. I trust

Dorian Bloom, though he may not entirely trust me. I'm afraid we have some past pains between us, and past pains are not easily forgotten.'

'There is a greater challenge than convincing your friend, ma'am,' said Sacha. 'First we must reach him. Your enemies know where you are. They will be watching this place, and they will—'

A knock at the door alarmed them both. Lady Rosewood went to the writing desk and drew the pistol and the knife. She handed the knife to Sacha. 'See who it is,' she said. She resumed her seat, with the pistol hidden on her lap.

Sacha opened the door just a crack with the security chain in place. 'It is the maid,' he said.

'Describe her, please,' said Lady Rosewood.

Sacha looked at the poor girl and attempted an assessment, to the embarrassment of them both. 'She is blonde, with blue eyes. English or German, I would say. She is pale and small. She is wearing a cap and a uniform. She has freckles on her nose, and a small mouth. She is carrying a package wrapped in white paper.'

'I know her. She has my laundry. Let her in.'

Sacha tucked the blade into the back of his trousers and slipped the chain off the door. The maid carried in the laundry, and Lady Rosewood directed her to set it down in the bedroom.

'You are right of course, Valentin,' said Lady Rosewood.

'If we visit my friend directly, we will place his life in danger.' She held up the passenger list from the RMS St Bride. 'Anyone I have contact with is suspect.'

'They will be watching this hotel. They will follow you wherever you go,' said Sacha. 'We must get to your friend without being seen.'

The maid returned from the bedroom and curtsied. 'Will there be anything else, my lady?' she asked.

Lady Rosewood looked the girl over.

'There is one more thing you might help me with,' she said.

The lady left the hotel in a thin black chiffon coat, her hair tucked up into a sun hat held in place with a charcoal scarf, and her eyes hidden from the morning sun behind black tinted glasses. Her chauffeur wore his new black and navy uniform. As they pulled away from the hotel in their rented Prince Henry, a Studebaker Special Six pulled out a little way up the street behind them.

Sacha proceeded slowly through the city. He regularly checked the mirror to see if the other car was behind them, and it always was. The roads were busy on this bright April day, and it seemed that everyone was heading in the same direction, which forced the Studebaker to crawl behind them.

After twenty minutes moving through Shanghai, Sacha

arrived at Hongkew Market, a pillared three-storey open-air building, its balconies teeming with traders calling out their offers in broken English and French, customers swarming, fighting and arguing for the best prices.

Sacha parked across the street from the market and watched the Studebaker. The other car pulled in to the side of the road about thirty feet away. Sacha waited. He heard the bell of a tram and saw it come into view. The tram stopped in the road between the two cars, and the doors slid open to let passengers off and on.

With the tram as cover, Sacha hurried out of the car and opened the back door. He gave the lady his hand and she stepped out. Two passengers climbed out of the Studebaker, and Sacha recognised them as guards from the Mandrake Palace. He smiled at them and waved.

'They are watching,' said Sacha.

'Should I do it now?'

'I think so, yes. You can catch the tram from here.'

The lady stepped onto the side of the road, took off her sunglasses, unfastened her scarf, and shook her blonde hair free from her sunhat. She handed her disguise to Sacha.

'Did I do well?' asked the hotel maid.

The boys by the Studebaker watched with fallen faces, and Sacha grinned at them in triumph. They had followed the wrong woman, and there was nothing they could do to correct their mistake.

'You did very well,' said Sacha. He took the maid's hand and walked her to the tram. 'Do not worry. You will be safe now. They have no interest in you.' He pressed a folded banknote into her hand. She thanked him and disappeared into the crowd of passengers. Sacha watched as the tram drew away.

Once the tram was out of sight, Sacha turned to the boys from the Studebaker.

'If you are looking for Lady Rosewood, I am sorry, but you have missed her,' he shouted.

The driver barked at his colleagues. The men jumped back into the car and Sacha retreated to the pavement as the Studebaker executed a reckless U-turn and sped back to the hotel.

Left alone, Sacha headed to Hongkew Market. His shopping list contained only two items; bullets and medicine. Lady Rosewood was certain that they would feel happier with both.

Sacha stepped between barrels full of sad lobsters and cages of angry ducks and almost collided with a man coming the other way. They each apologised, and they each took a second to recognise the other.

'Mr Valentin,' said Arek Saxon. 'What a great surprise!'

'Mr Saxon,' said Sacha. He suppressed a smile. The reunion struck him as suspicious. 'What are you doing here?'

'What am I doing here? What are you doing on your feet?' asked Saxon. 'How can you even stand? Come, Mr Valentin, let me buy you some coffee.'

Sacha hesitated. He had spent the last years of his life avoiding friendships of any stripe. He was an exile by choice. His new arrangement with Lady Rosewood was an exception to a rule that he was not otherwise inclined to break, and Saxon made him nervous. He was too genial, too warm, and too familiar. He was the sort of man who was better avoided.

'I am sorry, I have business,' said Sacha.

Arek shook his head and put his arm around Sacha's shoulder. 'That's what you said last night, as well. Never use the same excuse twice, my friend; it is hopelessly transparent.'

'I am not making an excuse,' said Sacha.

'You can't mean to tell me you have another man to fight.'

Sacha allowed a smile to sneak on to his face. 'I have no fights today,' he said.

'Then do not fight with me. Come and have a coffee.' Arek propelled Sacha away from the market and across the street. 'I was planning to track you down anyway. There is a matter we must discuss.'

Sacha wrinkled his battered brow. 'What do you mean?' he asked.

Arek glanced around to see who might be listening in. He leaned in close. 'Have you heard of a device called the Mandrake Machine?' he asked.

The Mandrake Machine. The blueprints lay spread out on a desk in a small room at the British Consulate. They had arrived that morning addressed to Dorian Bloom and marked 'Urgent' and 'Confidential', and they had been accompanied with a most mysterious letter.

It was an intrigue.

Dorian Bloom had been warned about these by his erstwhile mentor, Sir Barnhard Baxter. It had all seemed very fanciful at the time, but now Sir Barnhard's words rang in his ears.

'They will try to seduce you,' Sir Barnhard had told him. 'They will come to you with money, or power, or women, or the promise of these things. They will try to intimidate you with a smile to hide their daggers behind. They will come to you in confidence, to flatter your office, with conspiracies and contracts. They will wear the mask of a friend, and they will bring brown envelopes and unsigned letters and ask for secret meetings in parks and at railway stations.

'Through it all you must remember your duty. For as long as there have been diplomats, there have been intrigues. You serve king and country and the great good of your fellow man. Be true to that mission in every action and you will do nothing wrong. Yes, your parents are motley, but you were born an Englishman. When these people come to you with intrigues, remember what that means.'

Despite all this, there had been no intrigues for Dorian.

He had never established the sort of profile that attracted them. His ambitions had been thwarted by scandal, which was why he now worked from a windowless closet room while the lugubrious Mr Pelham Davis Wadworth commanded the office of British consul at Shanghai.

Mr Davis Wadworth had a generous office with tall arch windows that offered splendid views of Soochow Creek, and even a balcony where he might take tea in the blossom-scented air. Yet Mr Davis Wadworth was an agoraphobe with terrible hay fever, so he kept the windows closed and the curtains drawn, the better to sleep through the day.

Dorian had a skylight. It offered occasional glimpses of fleeting clouds, and on windier days Dorian caught flashes of the union flag on the rooftop. For a time, Dorian had been able to open the skylight with a pole, but the pole had disappeared weeks ago.

No-one offered intrigues to the man in the windowless room—not because they think he can't be turned, but because they never learn of his existence. There had been no daggers, no flattery, and no brown envelopes for Dorian.

Not until today.

Dorian had not reported the envelope yet. The consul had cancelled all meetings with claims of a migraine, and Dorian knew it would offend the consul if he brought the envelope's contents to anyone else.

Dorian pushed aside the blueprint and read the letter again.

Dear Dorian,

I write to you as a friend in distress. The enclosed papers describe a machine of devastating power that is intended to shake the city of Shanghai to its foundation. The machine is due to be deployed on the 20th of April. The threat may seem incredible, yet I swear that it is real.

You are the only person I can trust with this information. There are those in the British government who are privy to this scheme, and they will quash any inquiry. It falls to you to do what you can to locate this monstrous machine and prevent a tragedy, and to do so with urgency and discretion. I know that is much to ask, but I trust your good character and ingenuity.

I will contact you again when I have more information to share with you, and I hope that you will have information to share with me. Please be careful who you speak to. No-one can be trusted.

Yours,

A friend.

It was a letter of extraordinary invention. The blueprints were brilliantly convincing, but Dorian was certain that they had been concocted to drive a wedge between himself and his government, to an end that had not yet been touched upon. This was how it began. This was how diplomats became double agents.

Daisy from the typing pool knocked on the door and pushed it open. Dorian folded the letter with guilty haste.

'This just came for you.'

She handed him a note. He unfolded it, pushed his spectacles up his nose, and read it.

Meet me now on the red bridge in the park. Your friend.

The handwriting was the same.

'Who delivered this?' asked Dorian.

'One of the fishing pole boys. Is it anything important?'

Dorian read the message again. He crushed it into a ball. 'No, it's nothing,' he said. 'Thank you, Daisy.'

Daisy nodded and left.

Dorian flattened the note on the desk and read it a third time. There was so little to it, yet it meant so much. This was his moment of temptation. Dorian could not imagine how or why he had been chosen for whatever scheme this was, but he was determined to prove that he was not the weak link in His Majesty's defences. He would meet with this mysterious 'friend', yes, but he would report back at once to the consul. He would do his duty to his country.

Dorian looked in on the consul and found that he was asleep, which was usual for this time of day. He stuck his head in on the typing pool.

'I'm just going outside for a moment, Daisy. I should be back before the consul wakes up.'

He returned to his office, tidied away the blueprint and the letter, grabbed his jacket and hat from the back of the door, and raced down to the park.

As he hurried through the park between dog walkers, elderly amblers, and giggling office girls, Dorian tried to imagine what sort of man he would find at the red bridge. He expected a figure dressed all in black; a man in a coat with a turned-up collar and a hat turned down at the brim; a grim man with his face in shadow; perhaps a dour Eastern European émigré or a sour Chinese government factotum?

His guesses were only correct in two details; the figure on the bridge was dressed in black, and her face was obscured, albeit by a veil and not a shadow.

Dorian had a good idea who he was looking at.

Eleanora Rosewood was the reason Dorian worked in a windowless closet in Shanghai. She was the reason he had accomplished so much less in his career than he had hoped to. Eleanora Rosewood was not to be trusted. Dorian turned his back and walked away.

'Dorian!' she called after him. 'Dorian, please!'

Dorian bit his lip and walked on. This was not an intrigue. This was some ridiculous fancy designed to lure him back into the confidence of a lost friend. This had nothing to do with his duty to his country, and everything to do with his duty to himself.

'Dorian, I need your help.'

Yet duty can be such a complicated concept.

Dorian stopped and turned

꧁

'I need your help,' said Arek.

He sat across from Sacha at a small table in the window of a noodle shop. Sacha kept an eye on the door, and the people passing through it. He liked Arek, but he could not let his guard down.

'What help can I be to anyone?' asked Sacha. 'I am a fisherman.'

'You know about the Mandrake Machine,' said Arek. 'According to my sources, a woman broke in to Mandragora's offices during your fight last night, and she was seen leaving the scene with a handsome Russian.'

'They must mean some other Russian,' said Sacha.

'I think they meant you,' said Arek.

Sacha folded his arms and narrowed his eyes. 'Who are you?' he asked. 'What is this Mandragora to you?'

'I work for the Secret Intelligence Service, Sacha. I work for the British government.'

'You are a spy?'

Arek pressed a finger to his lips as the waitress delivered one Turkish coffee and one tea. He held his finger there until she was out of earshot, and his bright blue eyes flashed with amusement.

'Quietly, please,' he said. 'You make it sound sordid. I am an agent of the crown.'

Sacha was sceptical. 'You do not sound like an Englishman.'

'I was born in Poland, but my mother is English, and it is England that I serve.'

'So, you are a Pole in China, working for the English, and you ask the help of a Russian?'

'Such are the circumstances,' said Arek. He stirred brown sugar into his coffee and took a sip. Satisfied, he continued. 'I was sent here to investigate some irregularities in Sir Francis Hardie's activities in Shanghai. You are familiar with Sir Francis?'

Sacha nodded.

'There was some concern in Whitehall about the movement of government funds into a regional stability project. A junior clerk noticed that the paperwork went in circles. He informed his superior, who informed the SIS, and we followed the trail to the Mandrake Palace and Madam Mandragora.'

Arek Saxon was a hard man to read. He took too light a view of the world, and his charm made Sacha defensive. Yet his story was plausible, and his words were attractive. If the British intelligence service was involved, Lady Rosewood would not have to proceed alone.

'You have been scouting the Mandrake Palace?' said Sacha.

'I have, but all I have learned is that the funds are going

to something called the Mandrake Machine. I have not learned the purpose of this machine, but I may have learned its whereabouts.'

The location of the machine! That was all that Lady Rosewood needed. Sacha tried to appear unflappable, just as Lady Rosewood had done when faced with Sir Francis at the hotel, but it was clear from Arek's insoluble grin that he had not disguised his interest.

'You know where the machine is. You have no need of me,' said Sacha.

'I know where the machine might be, and I have ample need of a man of your virtues,' said Arek. 'I do not know what the machine is, so I do not know what might await me there. I am investigating one of the government's own, so I have few resources to call on. I need a partner, Sacha. That is why I need you.'

Sacha looked down at his tea. It was too bitter to enjoy.

'Tell me the location and I will speak with my employer,' said Sacha.

'I am staying at the Hotel Shangrila. Come with me and we will call your employer from there.'

There was that same insufferable grin, so persuasive and impossible to negotiate around. Sacha steeled himself against it. He was determined not to trust this man.

'I cannot come to the Shangrila with you,' he said. 'I told you that I have other business, and it is so.'

'Then I will come with you!'

'You will not,' said Sacha. 'I will inform my employer of your wishes, and she will contact you at your hotel.'

Arek nodded. 'I understand. You do not know me. I should not presume any faith on your part.' He reached into his pocket and pulled out a map. 'Take this to your lady as a gesture of good faith.'

The map showed the hills and rivers beyond Shanghai to the north-west, with a red circle drawn around a black square, beside which were the words 'Golden Orchid'.

'What is this?' asked Sacha.

'Sir Francis departed Shanghai for Singapore this morning. According to his driver, he made three visits to this location while he was here, though none of the visits were on his official itinerary. The Golden Orchid is a Buddhist Temple. I believe it is the location of the Mandrake Machine.'

Sacha looked at the map more closely. The hills seemed a likely location. They were remote enough that they would not attract much passing traffic, and it seemed very likely that they lay along a fault line.

'I think that we should go there together,' said Arek. 'I certainly don't think that you should go there alone.'

Sacha folded the map and slid it into his pocket. 'You will excuse me,' he said.

'You are always in too much of a hurry, Sacha,' said Arek. 'If you find a moment's peace, come find me at the Shangrila.'

Sacha drained his tea in one unpleasant gulp. 'I do not savour peace,' he said, and he left.

❧

Amidst the quiet of the yellow tea roses, Dorian and Eleanora took a walk. The roses reminded Eleanora of the park at Richmond and the grounds of Knole House, and of the sleepy village of Hindsmere where she and Dorian grew up together. Yet Eleanora had never stepped fearfully through those gardens. She had never watched those bushes for spies, or searched among the flowers for assassins.

It had been a few years since Eleanora had seen Dorian, and her strongest memories of him were always of the boy, pale and thin with an abundance of freckles and an apologetic smile. It always surprised her to see the man he had become – still slender, and now pinked by the Shanghai sun, but handsome and determined, and less inclined to smile when he saw her, apologetically or otherwise.

'Do you remember the old tumbledown wall in the churchyard?' asked Eleanora. 'You used to take the odd cuts of cloth from your father's shop and we would dress up as kings and queens and use that broken wall as a throne. Father refused to have the wall rebuilt because of the roses that grew there. He said it was the way it was meant to be.'

'Do you hope to appeal to my sentimentality, Eleanora?' asked Dorian.

Eleanora stifled a sigh of exasperation.

'Are you so turned against me, Dorian? You must know how sorry I am about what happened. I never expected Edgar to tell Bibi's father about your arrangement.'

'The problem is, you never know when not to interfere,' said Dorian.

'It is not an altogether terrible characteristic,' said Eleanora.

'It's not altogether a virtue, either. You've changed, Ellie. Edgar changed you. He made you a wife, when you always promised to be so much more.'

'I know that you and Edgar did not get along, but I have lost Edgar now, and I have lost him forever. I would hate to think that I have lost you, as well.'

The bushes moved and Eleanora took a sudden step back. A little white dog pushed through the leaves, followed by a giggling girl who chased it up the path. Eleanora froze with her hand to her mouth. Her cheeks blazed with embarrassment.

'What the devil is going on?' asked Dorian. 'Why are you on the far side of the world, sending me mad letters about fantastical contraptions?'

'Did you look at the papers I sent you? Have you made inquiries?'

'A machine that can destroy a city? I can well believe that you believe it, but I suspect that someone is having you on.'

Eleanora ignored the implication and stooped to smell a perfect rose.

'Then you have made no inquiries at all?' she said.

'What inquiries am I to make? Am I to look for new building projects in a city that prides itself on its reach for the future? Am I to look for suspicious imports at one of the busiest trading posts in the world? You are asking for the impossible, without a shred of evidence to suggest it is worth my while.'

'You have the blueprint.'

'I have seen many pictures of unicorns, Ellie.'

'Then consider the risk! If I am right about this machine, it could mean the end to hundreds of thousands of lives. How can you do nothing in the face of such a threat?'

'The world is in constant danger of falling to pieces. I read security dispatches every day, and if I acted on every one of them we would all be terrified prisoners in our own homes. Why are you so convinced of this danger, Ellie? What is it about this fantastical threat that has lured you all the way to Shanghai?'

'It was Edgar,' said Eleanora.

'I'm sorry?'

'It was Edgar. He devised this machine.'

'Edgar? Why would he ever...?'

Eleanora threw up her arms. 'I don't know! My god, Dorian, I have asked this every day since I learned the truth.

His politics were secret and mad, and he led some other life that he never shared with me, and this was its manifestation.'

This at last seemed to soften Dorian's manner. He may not have liked Edgar, but he admitted that he had been a genius, and the idea of the Mandrake Machine was less implausible when paired with Edgar's miraculous knack for invention.

'But Edgar is dead, Ellie. Even if he conceived of this machine…'

'He was not acting alone. He was part of a cartel. I don't know how many were with him, but I know two of their names. Madam Mandragora was the group's agent in Shanghai, and she continues Edgar's work here.'

'Mandragora? I know her name. A very vile woman. And the other?'

'Oh, Dorian. I hate to tell you.'

'How much worse can it be if your own husband—'

'It is Sir Francis.'

Dorian stopped in his tracks and his expression stiffened.

'Sir Francis? Sir Francis Hardie?'

'I know, Dorian. I know you take your ambitions seriously—'

'It is not ambition, Ellie. It is service. I have two masters: the foreign minister and the secretary for foreign affairs. You devastated my fortunes with the former when you reported on my arrangement with his daughter. Now you want me to turn spy against the latter? It is only by his good graces that I hold any position at all!'

'I know this is delicate, but if Sir Francis is involved, you will be right to turn on him.'

'*If*, Ellie? *If*? By God, I do not have much, but I have my purpose, and you would cast it away on the whims of your grief.'

Now it was Eleanora's turn to take umbrage.

'The whims of my grief? This is not hysteria born of tears, Dorian. I abandoned imagination at the field hospital in Rouen! I tell you, I have seen the evidence of this conspiracy first hand. I have been attacked and threatened for what I know.'

Eleanora pressed her manila envelope into Dorian's arms.

'Here; make what you can of this. I took these papers from the Mandrake Palace. Begin your investigations here and see what you make of my whims.'

Dorian pulled the papers half out of the envelope and sifted through them. He settled on the torn page from an encyclopaedia.

'What does this tell me?' he asked. 'The Star of Shah Jahan? What does a long lost stolen diamond have to do with your machine?'

'I do not have all the answers, Dorian! Perhaps it was stolen by Mandragora?'

'Is she very old? It has been missing for centuries. I'm sorry, Ellie, but none of this looks persuasive. Perhaps your husband did fantasise about some fabulous city-shaking machine, but I am sure he would never build such a thing.

You have let yourself be captivated by implausible fancies. I will not throw my career away over this.'

Dorian offered Eleanora the envelope.

'Keep it,' she said. 'I know you are a good man, Dorian. You may play clerk to a pompous agent of the old guard today, but I hope some spark of compassion stirs in you tomorrow and compels you to look again at these papers. Seek me out at the Grand if you have a change of heart. I had planned to return home, but it seems this city still needs me, and if Shanghai is destroyed, I will die with it.'

Eleanora opened her parasol and walked away through the gardens. She wanted to look back, to see if her words had moved Dorian at all, but she was too afraid to do so, in case they had not.

❧

The road ahead was rough and winding. Eleanora tried to lose herself in the view of mournful willows and bursting blossoms on the river banks, but the Prince Henry bounced on every stone and lurched at every corner, and there was no calm to be found in the lady's thoughts.

'We can still make the boat, ma'am,' Valentin called back from the driver's seat. 'I will turn around, yes?'

'No, Valentin. The boat will have to leave without me,' said Eleanora. 'We must investigate your friend's map. If the

Mandrake Machine is out here, we have some hope to destroy it, and I will not need to leave Shanghai.'

'And if it is not here?'

'Ah, well. You do not trust your new friend?'

'Not enough to travel with him, but I mean to be hopeful.'

'Very good; we will both be hopeful.'

In truth, Eleanora felt more desperation than hope. Her meeting with Dorian had shattered the last of her confidence. She could not trust in others. Sacha Valentin was her first and last ally in this quest.

'What sort of a man would you say he is?' Eleanora asked. Valentin had been circumspect in his description of the self-professed spy whose map was now their only clue, though circumspection seemed to be his nature. Eleanora's question hung unanswered between them, and she thought he had not heard her.

'I say, what sort of a man would you say he is?'

Valentin kept his attention on the road ahead, which took them between the jagged walls of a ravine.

'I do not know,' said Valentin at last.

'Well, was he pleasant?' asked Eleanora. 'Did he seem educated, would you say?'

Valentin shrugged to show his ambivalence, but he thought it over for a moment and then offered: 'He is an officer, I think, so he must be educated.'

'Yet you met him first at the Mandrake Palace? Do officers often go there?'

'He was there to investigate. But, yes, they do.'

Eleanora thought back to the Mandrake Palace. She had seen little of the crowd around the fighting pit. The one man there that looked anything like an officer had been the one she had almost falsely identified as her accomplice.

'Was he wearing a dark jacket with epaulettes? Rather smart?'

'Today?' asked Valentin. 'He wore a waistcoat and shirt today.'

'Yesterday; at the fight.'

Valentin nodded. 'Yes. That was him.'

Eleanora sighed and sat back in her seat. Evidently Valentin had nothing more to say about the young man, nor much to say on any subject.

More than anything, Eleanora wanted to ask him about himself. She wanted to know how he had come to Shanghai, and why he had left Russia, and where he had served in the war. Most of all she wanted to know about the photograph he carried with him. One of the men in the photograph was clearly Valentin, but who was the other? Her instincts told her that he would not be forthcoming on any of these questions.

'My meeting with Dorian did not go as hoped,' said Eleanora. She knew she might as well offer her words to the wind, but it gave her some comfort to share her thoughts. 'Our relationship is still strained, and he thought my story fantastical. We cannot count on him to help us, which means we must do as much as we can – which, I suppose, was always the case. We must always do as much as we—'

A screech from the tires cut Eleanora off, and the car swerved violently, throwing her across the seats. Eleanora grabbed for the back of the passenger seat and tried to steady herself as the car scraped against jagged stone.

Valentin hauled on the wheel and hit the brakes to bring the vehicle under control. As soon as they stopped, he leapt out to check the road behind them. He returned holding a metal star made of welded bent nails.

'Jacks,' said Valentin. 'We are expected.' He jumped back in the car and started the engine. 'Stay down. Keep your weight to the left. The front right tyre is shredded.'

Eleanora nodded and slunk down into the well behind the front seat. The ravine was too narrow to allow them to turn, and this was not a safe place to change a tyre. They had to drive on.

The car sped through the ravine like a limping runner. It shuddered on every turn of the wheels, and the axle groaned as if it might snap.

All at once, the river valley opened on their right, and a juniper-lined bank rose on the left. Eleanora looked for a safe space to pull over, but Valentin, fixated on the mirrors, seemed more interested in the road behind them. Eleanora looked back and saw a Studebaker Special Six break cover from a rocky outcrop and speed onto the road at their back.

'Ah. We are not stopping, are we?' said Eleanora. Valentin grunted. Eleanora ducked back into the well and braced herself.

The Studebaker rammed the back of the Prince Henry

with enough force to make the wheels scream. It peeled back and slammed a second time, pushing the car towards the precipitous drop at the edge of the road. Valentin struggled to keep them on course, and only a favourable curve in the road kept them from going over.

'Give me the gun,' said Eleanora.

'We cannot outrun them, and you cannot outshoot them,' said Valentin. 'Hold on, please.'

'God damn you,' said Eleanora. She reached over the front passenger seat for the glove compartment, and only then saw just how steep and rocky the slope to the right of the road was. She glanced back and saw the Studebaker closing in, determined to send them crashing to their deaths.

'You must hold on,' said Valentin.

Eleanora sunk back into the well and covered her head. The car shook horribly as Valentin built up speed, and the broken wheel slapped against the fender with a sound like the wings of death descending. The growl of the Studebaker closed in, and the car tipped sideways.

Eleanora screamed. She peered out between her fingers and noted with amazement that the sky was not in somersault. They had tipped and stayed tipped. Eleanora peeked out of the well and saw that Valentin had driven them on to the verge, placing the Studebaker between them and the drop.

The thugs knew they had lost their advantage, and retreated so that Valentin could not swerve them off the road.

The fatal precipice eased to a steep grassy hill, and Valentin brought them back to the road.

'Stay down,' said Valentin.

'What are you going to do?' asked Eleanora.

'We cannot stay on the road. We cannot let them drive us off it. We must make our own way.' He spun the wheel and bounced the Prince Henry down the hill towards the river.

Eleanora let out another cry as they rattled down the grassy banks over rocks and shrubs. The axle shook and the car frame complained.

The river looked slow, but wide and deep, and they were headed directly towards it. Valentin tried to turn them parallel as he crunched the breaks, but weight and momentum were against them, and a tumble into the water seemed inevitable.

'Get out,' Valentin shouted.

'Are you mad?'

'We are going to tip. Get out.'

Eleanora swung open the door and stepped onto the running board. Though they were not travelling at great speed, the ground beneath her seemed to whip past at a heart-stopping rate.

Eleanora closed her eyes and threw herself from the car.

She met the ground with a thud that bruised her bones and scraped her skin. Her skidding spin ended in the tangled briars of a rose bush. Eleanora gasped to catch her breath and struggled to extract herself from the thorns.

The Prince Henry bounced to the brow of the bank at what now seemed like a sputtering crawl. It bucked onto its right wheels at the crest of the ridge, hung for a moment in the air, and rolled over with a terrible crunch, and another and another, and a final loud thrash as it hit the water.

'Oh, God. Oh, Valentin!'

Eleanora ran for the river. She heard a gunshot and dropped to the ground.

Two Mandrake men ran down the hill towards her, carrying large firearms. A third stood by the parked Studebaker with his smoking pistol raised to the sky. He had fired a warning shot.

The first man wore a bowler hat. He stopped his approach to raise and aim his weapon. Eleanora recognised it as a Thompson submachine gun. The second man overtook him, his rifle slung over his shoulder. He was a square-headed fellow with a ponytail, and he wore a smart white shirt and grey waistcoat that marked him as more than a hired thug – perhaps a trusted lieutenant to Mandragora. He held out a hand to show Eleanora that she should stay where she was.

Eleanora stood up, brushed the grass off her dress, and pulled some leaves from her hair.

'I demand that you take me to Sir Francis,' she shouted.

The lieutenant grinned.

'Sir Francis has left Shanghai, but Madam Mandragora has extended an invitation to tea,' he said. 'Come with us

and I will see to your safety.' He cocked the rifle and nodded to his bowler-hatted companion. 'Make sure that the
bodyguard is dead. The invitation is for one.'

'Stay where you are,' said Eleanora. 'Tell madam that I
decline her invitation. The police are behind us on the road.
I will travel back to Shanghai with them.'

Bowler Hat ignored her and continued off after Valentin.

'Go to the car, lady,' said the lieutenant. 'We will drive you.'

'Thank you, no.'

The lieutenant walked right up to her and grabbed her arm.
'I insist,' he said.

Eleanora twisted out of his grip. He spun the rifle around
and raised the butt to strike her. Eleanora flinched and rose
her hands to cover her face, but the crack of a gunshot
made both of them freeze.

On the brow of the riverbank the thug in the bowler
stumbled. The machine gun dropped from his hands and he
fell, blood spilling from a crack across his skull.

The lieutenant reached for Eleanora and she backed away
and grabbed for the knife she had sheathed in her boot, the
one she had recovered from the previous night's visitor to
her suite. It was gone. She had lost it in the fall from the car.

The lieutenant grabbed Eleanora by the hair and held
her between him and the riverbank. He pressed the rifle
between her shoulder blades. 'Walk,' he said.

They walked to the brow of the bank, to the body of the

fallen thug. The Prince Henry lay half submerged in the river, flipped on its side; a strange sight amid the springtime tranquillity. The sky was bright, the flowers plentiful. There was no armed angry Russian intruding on the view, and there were no trees or bushes large enough to hide him. The only place he might be was under the car itself.

'Forward,' said the lieutenant. He nudged Eleanora on. Eleanora looked down at the cracked bloody head of the dead man to avoid stepping in his spilled brains. An orange ladybird crawled across his matted hair. Eleanora covered her mouth.

The lieutenant crouched down and picked up the dead man's Thompson. He dropped the rifle, pushed Eleanora to the ground, and unleashed a storm of machine gun fire into the Prince Henry. The weapon jumped and juddered in his hands and the sound rattled the air around them.

The car made a pop and a bang. A burst of fire sprung from the engine block, followed by an explosion that consumed the Prince Henry. Eleanora clambered back. Her fingers touched on blood-wet grass. She shielded her eyes with the crook of her arm and searched the smoke and steam for any sign that Valentin had survived. It was Villesauvage again, and she was powerless to stop it.

The lieutenant swung the smoking Tommy with one arm. His moment of satisfaction was short lived, as further gunshots sounded from the road. The driver was firing warning shots into the sky. He gestured behind them.

Eleanora turned and saw Valentin soaking wet and running. He charged into the lieutenant and knocked him off his feet, and the two men tumbled down the bank.

Eleanora thought she should intervene in the brawl, but she saw that the driver had left his car and was coming towards her. His pistol could not reach her from the road, but he would soon close the distance.

The lieutenant's rifle lay on the grass.

Eleanora knew how to handle a gun. A soldier had taught her how to fire a pistol in Rouen, and she had been hunting often enough to know how to use a rifle. She had shot and killed a deer in the New Forest last year.

She had never shot a man. She had seen too much of the damage that a gunshot could do, and the freshest proof of that horror was here at her feet.

Eleanora picked up the rifle, lay on the crest of the ridge, and lined up the driver in her sights.

He was a man. She did not know his name, or even his face. She had never encountered him before. The full extent of their relationship was that he had been paid to stop her from interfering in his mistress's plans. They would not otherwise be enemies. If it were not for Edgar and his plans, Eleanora would not be here in Shanghai. She would not have a dead man beside her, and a living one stepping into her sights.

Eleanora looked to the scene behind her. She hoped that

Valentin might have despatched one man so that he could turn his attentions to the other, but Valentin and the lieutenant were still knotted in a violent embrace. The lieutenant attempted to choke Valentin, Valentin gouged at his eyes with his thumbs, and each man tried to crack the other's skull with his own.

Eleanora picked up a pebble and pushed it into her gun-side ear. She pressed the stock to her shoulder, lined up the sight against her target, found his shoulder, and fired.

The man jumped back and dropped. Eleanora adjusted the sights to find him on the grass. He did not get back up. He was likely either dead or dying. She could try all she wished to blame that on Edgar or Sir Francis or Mandragora, but it was her finger that eased the trigger. She had shot a man to save her life, and she prayed she could save more lives in the living of it.

Valentin managed to get the advantage over his opponent by rolling on top of him, but Eleanora offered a stronger advantage. She pressed the barrel of the rifle to the lieutenant's head and pulled on the bolt that loaded the next shot in the chamber.

The lieutenant let Valentin go and showed his palms either side of his head. Valentin stood up and recovered his breath.

Eleanora took a step back and ordered the lieutenant to his feet.

'Please send madam my regrets,' said Eleanora. She could

barely suppress the tremor in her voice. 'I have no time for tea. Valentin, if you would be so kind?'

Valentin grabbed the lieutenant by his shirtfront and cracked him in the nose. The lieutenant slumped to the ground, unconscious.

Eleanora cracked the back of the rifle and tossed it into the river. She picked up the Tommy gun and handed it to Valentin. He unclipped the drum and threw both gun and drum in the water.

'I have shot a man,' said Eleanora. She looked into the flames of the Prince Henry in the river. 'If he is alive, perhaps we should take the Studebaker and drive him to a hospital in Shanghai?'

'What of the Golden Orchid?' asked Valentin.

'There is nothing at the Golden Orchid. It was a lie to lure us to danger.'

Valentin set his jaw and cracked his bloodied knuckles. 'Perhaps they followed us?' he suggested.

'They were ahead of us, Valentin. We passed them when we left the ravine.'

Eleanora set off up the hill towards the road.

'They are Chinese,' said Valentin. 'They will know roads we do not know.'

Eleanora looked back at Valentin and noticed that he had the look of a disappointed schoolboy about him, albeit one who had been in more brutal scrapes than most.

He picked up the dropped assassin's knife, and that rather spoiled the image.

'I am sorry, but I fear we now understand rather more about the character of your Arek Saxon,' said Eleanora. 'He sent us here to die. He is in league with Mandragora.'

Valentin nodded. He followed Eleanora at a sullen trudge. Eleanora was glad to stay ahead of him so that he could not see her tears.

<hr />

He saw ghosts.

Sacha sat in the dark and looked out through his own reflection at phantoms by the poolside: colonists and émigrés in dinner jackets and furs taking cocktails under an indigo sky while a string quartet played swirling melodies that lacked all urgency. They seemed unreal in their numb contentment, a fantasy in hollow black.

Or perhaps *he* was the ghost. A revenant lurking in the dark, a man without a life, scorning the pleasures of those who dared to enjoy theirs.

One man at the Shangrila soiree appeared more real than all the rest. Arek Saxon pushed himself out of the pool on arms taut as steel. He took a cotton towel from the poolside dresser and wiped his skin and ruffled his hair. Despite the chill of the night he did not wrap himself. Dressed only in a pair of high-hoisted square-cut swim shorts and a skimpy woollen tank top, he stood golden and beautiful, a striking contrast to the black ghouls around him. He walked among his fellow guests with the suave assurance that he was the most eye-catching figure at the poolside.

Arek waved to a few admiring ladies in chiffon dresses. He plucked a canapé from a passing tray and headed for his apartment.

Sacha slid behind the cover of a wardrobe and waited.

The glass door slid open. The lights came on, a wet towel landed on the bed, the sodden tank top landed on top of it, and the door slid shut with a click.

'So, you came,' said Arek.

Sacha did not move. He had not made a sound, and he knew he could not be seen. He did not believe that Arek truly knew he was there.

'The lock on my front door is splintered,' said Arek. 'My holster still hangs from the valet stand, but the gun is missing. Come out, Sacha, please.'

Sacha stepped from behind the wardrobe and aimed his pistol at Arek's heart. Arek was haloed by the light of the lamp behind him, a glistening bronze silhouette. Sacha's reflection in the glass doors was a deathly pale face looming out of the darkness. An angel and an ogre.

'I hoped you would come,' said Arek. 'I did not think it would be like this. Why are you pointing my gun at me?'

'We tried to go to the Golden Orchid Temple,' said Sacha.

Arek cocked an eyebrow. 'I meant for us to go together.'

'We were expected. Assassins on the road.'

Arek stretched his hand out to Sacha as if he had forgotten the gun. Sacha reminded him by aiming it between his eyes.

'The lady says they could only have known if they were working with you,' said Sacha.

'And you believed her?'

'I did not want to.'

Sacha pulled a silver signet ring from his pocket. It bore a black onyx stone engraved with an angel symbol.

'I searched your room. I found your weapons, and I found this.' He threw the ring, and Arek caught it.

'What would you say if I told you I took this from one of Mandragora's men? What if I told you they followed me to the noodle shop and overheard our conversation?'

'I would say that you lie very easily,' said Sacha.

Arek laughed. His smile grew broad and the protest in his eyes gave way to knowing. His eyebrows lowered from a wide arch to a predatory chevron, and he slipped the ring onto his finger.

'Very well. I have no wish to deceive you, Sacha. I believe you will find the truth more persuasive. I am not an agent of the British crown. This is my signet ring, and it marks me as an agent of Dominion.'

Dominion. That put a name on it. The word bound conspirators and assassins together, with Arek now counted among their number.

'I am not your enemy, Sacha,' said Arek.

'You tried to have me killed,' said Sacha.

Arek shook his head. 'Not you. The Lady Rosewood is the obstacle. She has wrapped you up in the flags of her crusade. Step away from her, and no-one will come for you.'

'You mean to destroy my city.'

'I would save you from it,' said Arek. He glanced at the gun with nonchalant disdain and sat on the edge of the bed. 'You belong with us, my friend. You are one of the strong. You should not be some harpy's dog. Dominion will steer the world towards its best condition, and there is room among us for a man of your ability.'

'You would redeem the world with the blood of Shanghai?'

Arek shrugged his shoulders.

'I admit it sounds Old Testament, but look at the world. Mongrels want to be princes; women want to be men. The proper order is in revolt and we will all be plunged into chaos. The world cannot function if we surrender authority to the naïve and inexperienced. We might as well hand the world over to children. Blood is needed to keep these people in their place.'

'These are wicked words,' said Sacha.

'It is self-interest. You would die for this woman who is nothing to you, but you will not live for yourself? Be a

titan, man! Stand at my side and I will give you the world.'
Arek smiled and leaned back on his elbows, as if to present
himself carelessly prone and vulnerable. 'Think of the fun
we might have if you lowered your walls.'

Sacha gritted his teeth.

'Where is the Mandrake Machine?'

'I'll take you to it.' He flashed his dazzling white teeth
and ran his fingers through his still damp hair. 'Just give me
the gun, Sacha.'

'I'm not a fool. Tell me where the machine is.'

'Ah, then we must do this another way,' said Arek. He
kicked forward with his right leg and knocked the gun out
of Sacha's hand. He followed with a kick to the gut, and
before Sacha could recover, Arek was up off the bed with
his forearm pinned to Sacha's throat.

'This is not what I want,' said Arek. 'I want you with us,
Sacha. I mean it.'

Sacha cracked his head against Arek's and threw him
onto the bed. He looked for the gun and saw it lying by
the wardrobe. Arek kicked Sacha in the face and moved for
the gun himself. Sacha grabbed him by the arm so that he
could not reach it, so Arek kicked the gun under the wardrobe and threw an elbow at Sacha's face. Sacha dodged and
released Arek's arm, and Arek spun around and punched
him in the jaw.

'Don't fight me, Sacha,' said Arek.

'I am not like you,' said Sacha.

Arek grinned from ear to ear. 'You are strong. Why make yourself strong if not to be a master?'

'To live,' said Sacha. 'Only to live.'

Arek struck Sacha with a backhand and drove a fist into his chest. Sacha tried to grab his wrist, but Arek was fast and slick. He jabbed Sacha in the throat, cracked him in the side of his head and knocked him onto the bed. In a flash, Arek was straddling his chest, his knees pinning Sacha's arms.

'Everyone lives or dies by my good grace,' said Arek. 'The earth will consume this city, and water will cover their graves. Your lonely widow will die with them. If you mean to live, you must stand with me.'

Sacha banged his right hand on the bed to shake loose the hatpin secreted in his cuff. He spun it in his fingers and sunk it into Arek's thigh. Arek screamed and drew back, releasing one of Sacha's arms and giving him the leverage to throw Arek to the floor. Sacha leapt off the bed and retreated to the sliding door.

Arek stood on the other side of the room with blood running down his thigh. He held the hatpin in one hand and the gun in the other.

'Was this a trick your lady taught you?' said Arek.

'She is stronger than you think,' said Sacha. 'She is stronger than you.'

'You believe in her so much?'

'I believe she will stop you. She will stop you even if you shoot me dead.'

There was a pounding at the door, and voices without, asking in French and English what was happening. Arek did not flinch. He kept Sacha in his sights.

Sacha flicked the catch on the sliding door and pushed it open.

'If you mean to shoot me, you must do it now.'

'You will die in the dirt, Sacha,' said Arek. 'The ground will turn to sand and you will drown. It will be too late for you then. You will wish you had come with me.'

Sacha heard the rattle of keys at the door and knew that his time was up. Arek no longer looked certain and untouchable. He looked angry and hurt.

'I can save you,' said Arek.

Sacha ran out into the darkness.

❧

The dawn light cut in through the open curtains and roused Eleanora from her sleep. She blinked, rubbed at her neck, turned away from the sun, and nearly rolled off the recliner. The sudden pull of gravity was enough to jolt her awake.

Eleanora sat up and took in the room around her. She had dozed off in the sitting room of the suite, and left her bed unslept in. A cup and pot of coffee and a plate with half a sandwich sat on the table surrounded by papers. Her husband's blueprint was spread on the floor, with further papers scattered around it. She still had on yesterday's clothes.

The mantel clock told her it was not yet 6am. She had fallen asleep around midnight, not by intent, but by force of sheer exhaustion.

Upon her return from the aborted trip to the Golden Orchid Temple, Eleanora had found papers waiting for her, couriered from the British Consulate. She had taken them to her new suite, booked under a pseudonym, and set about trying to make sense of it all.

The papers included the documents she had given Dorian, which made her heart sink, but also hand-written translations of the shipping documents that she had recovered from Mandragora, which gave her some hope. Each document described a piece of the Mandrake Machine in specific detail. By matching the descriptions to the diagram, she hoped to build an understanding of how the machine worked, and how it might be sabotaged. She had made little headway, except to marvel at the ways in which the arrangements of parts echoed her husband's music box on a massive scale, suggesting a signature of sorts to his work. The silver vibrating pin she had recovered from her husband's study sat on the table and silently mocked her for her sentimentality.

Eleanora had also developed a theory about where the machine might be. The lie about the Golden Orchid Temple made her wonder how likely it was that Edgar would put a machine like this on high ground, where it would be exposed and vulnerable. That was not Edgar's style.

There were landscaped trenches on the grounds of Edgar's Hampshire estate; an archaic method of subdividing the land without interrupting the splendid views. He had often talked about expanding these trenches to use as secret hangars for flying machines that she believed he would never build. Edgar would not put his machine on high ground. He would hide it below sea level, where he could be cloistered and hidden.

Eleanora had pored over the map of the city looking for valleys and trenches that would suit her husband's needs. She had not found any answers.

Eleanora took a hot bath to clear her head, and changed into fresh clothes. She tidied the mess in the living room, put the papers in proper order on the table, and put the silver pin in her purse.

In among the papers she found her ticket for the St Bride out of Shanghai. The St Bride was more than half a day's travel away by now. Eleanora threw the ticket in the waste bin. She still had not decided when or how she would leave the city. Dorian's translations might mean that he intended to help her, or it might mean that he had passed the problem back to her. She needed to speak with him again, and she could be more persuasive face-to-face, so that would require another diversion.

Eleanora knocked on the door to Valentin's room and called his name. 'Valentin? Are you awake?'

There was no answer. There was no sound at all. Eleanora felt a chill run through her. Valentin had left her late last night to attend to personal business. He had not explained what it was, and she had not asked. Eleanora realised with growing dread that she did not know if he had returned at all. He had not disturbed her in the sitting room. She imagined he had gone to settle things with his former sea captain, who had so violently heckled him at the docks on the day of her arrival. Now she feared that the meeting had not gone well, and the captain had extracted some form of retribution for whatever difficulty existed between them. Her mind filled with horrors of shark hooks and plumb weights.

Eleanora knocked again. She pushed open the door and found the bed had not been slept in. Her protector was gone.

'Oh, dear,' she said. 'Oh, no.'

A key turned in the main door. Disturbed by the paranoid fears of her own imagination, Eleanora looked around for an object she could use as a weapon.

Valentin stepped through the door. Eleanora relaxed her grip on the clothes brush she had settled on, and realised only then what a poor weapon it would be.

'Valentin, where have you been?'

Valentin looked tired and frayed at the edges. He was red-eyed and unshaven, and his clothes were muddied and torn.

'Valentin, have you been drinking?'

Valentin shook his head. 'I am sorry, ma'am. I hoped I would not disturb you. I have only been walking the city, saying my farewells to its streets.'

'But the state of you!'

Valentin shrugged. 'I may have been fighting a little,' he said. 'I am sorry, ma'am, but I was not honest with you. Last night, I did not leave on personal business. I went to the Shangrila to confront Mr Saxon.'

'I see,' said Eleanora. The question that immediately presented itself to her thoughts was whether he had gone to seek answers or to seek revenge, but it seemed a very vulgar question to ask. Valentin sat on the chaise and reached for the coffee pot. His behaviour, his conduct, and his appearance were grossly inappropriate for a valet, and Eleanora had to remind herself that he was not a true valet at all.

'The coffee is cold,' said Eleanora. 'I shall send for some more.' She pulled on the service bell.

Valentin looked up at her with bleary eyes.

'I am sorry, ma'am. I have failed you. You should not be waiting on me.'

She sat down across from him. 'Tell me about Mr Saxon, please.'

'I did not learn anything of use,' he said. 'Only that he is one of them, and their group is called Dominion. I do not know where the machine is. I do not know how to stop him.'

Dominion. The name evoked authority and empire, but it also put Eleanora in mind of the lessons of her theologian father. The Dominion was the order of angels whose hidden work was to maintain all order in the cosmos.

'Is Mr Saxon there still?' asked Eleanora.

'I believe so.'

Eleanora got to her feet. 'Then we shall have him arrested. We shall call on Dorian at the embassy and find some reason to take Mr Saxon off the board. We can't hope to get to Mandragora, but we can get to him. Come along, Valentin. There is no time to lose.'

There was a knock at the door.

'No time for coffee, I'm afraid,' said Eleanora. 'You shall have to catch a second wind.'

Eleanora opened the door and found two Shanghai police officers in the corridor.

'Lady Rosewood, we have a warrant for the arrest of Mr Sacha Valentin on charges of assault.'

And the building shook.

The tremor came of a sudden, a vibration through the hotel floor that shook Eleanora in her boots and rattled the lampshades, and it passed in a moment, leaving her alarmed but unharmed.

The policemen at the door paused for only a moment to see if the tremor would be followed by another. They seemed satisfied that it would not be.

'Lady Rosewood, I'm very sorry, but we have to ask you to step aside.'

Eleanora looked aghast at Valentin.

'It's happening,' she said. 'The Mandrake Machine. It's happening now. They must have moved up the schedule.'

'Lady Rosewood, please step aside,' said the policeman. 'If you do not cooperate we will—'

'She will cooperate,' said Valentin. 'We will both cooperate.' He stepped forward with his hands held together in front of him. One of the policemen reached for his cuffs and squeezed past Eleanora. The other rested his hand on the butt of his gun.

Eleanora grabbed the first policeman by the shoulder. 'You can't,' she said. 'I need him. We have urgent business to attend to.'

The policeman shrugged her off. 'Ma'am, please step away.'

'He is my valet, sir. If you take him from me you will leave me abandoned in a strange city at a moment of crisis. Leave him in my custody and I swear we will report to the nearest police station to straighten this out just as soon as we are able. I assure you, he hasn't assaulted anyone. He simply isn't the sort.'

Valentin hung his head. Eleanora had to admit that it was a difficult claim to stomach, especially as it happened to not be true.

'There's no crisis, ma'am,' said the second officer. 'It was just a tremor. It's not uncommon. You are in no danger.'

'The city is on the precipice of disaster, sir! If you take my man I will have no choice but to contact the consul and have your badges.'

'My lady, I will go with them,' said Valentin. The policeman already had his cuffs locked onto Valentin's wrists. 'It is better. You must leave the city.'

The policeman put his hand to Valentin's back and propelled him through the door.

'I will not leave, Valentin,' Eleanora insisted.

'Then stop this,' he said. 'Help yourself, or help this city, but do not waste your time helping me.'

The police led Valentin to the elevator bay. Eleanora retreated into her room, grabbed her bag and slid her pistol inside.

'Damn it all,' said Eleanora to herself. 'I shall help who I damn well like.'

❧

Once a person is set on a course, it can be very difficult to shake them off it. A man might more easily change his head than change his station. That was Sacha's conclusion as the police marched him through the lobby of the Grand Hotel in handcuffs. Just two days earlier his presence in this building had been enough to scandalise a small ordered world. Now the corrective had been issued, and he was back among the refuse, and he would most likely die this day in a prison cell as filthy as the back street where Ari had gone to his rest.

There was one other course he might have pursued. He could have accepted Arek Saxon's offer. He could have watched the destruction of the very people who sneered and scowled at him now, and risen above them. A titan. These people thought him an animal; he might have outlived them all if he had exercised an animal's wit to survive by any means.

'You must speak with your masters,' said Sacha to the policemen. 'You must tell them to evacuate the city.'

'Be quiet, Russian. No-one needs to hear from you.'

As they approached the doors to the street, a red-headed man burst through from the other side and barrelled directly into Sacha. He dropped his satchel, and his papers skimmed across the tiled floor.

'Oh, goodness, I'm sorry. I was in such a hurry I just didn't look where I was going,' said the redhead. He fell to his knees and wrestled the papers into a pile. One of the policemen stepped forward to help, while the other pulled Sacha to one side. The man looked up at Sacha and pushed his spectacles along his nose. He saw the police uniforms, and noticed that Sacha's arms were fixed behind his back.

'My heavens,' said the man. 'What is all this?'

'Sir, are you an important person?' asked Sacha.

'No. I mean, perhaps, but not really. I'm just—'

'You're going to die,' said Sacha. 'You and everyone in this city. You need to tell them. The city is not safe.'

The red-headed man was wide-eyed.

'How do you know this?'

'Don't listen to him,' said the policeman. He handed the man the last of his papers. 'This Russian is a criminal. He'll say anything to get out of trouble.'

'No,' said the man. 'No, he's right. The city is not safe. We *are* going to die. Oh, dear. But how do you know this?'

'Officers. Let my valet go.'

They all turned as one and saw Lady Rosewood marching towards them from the elevator. She reached in to her handbag.

'Oh, no, Ellie,' said the red-headed man.

'Lady Rosewood, no,' said Sacha.

Someone screamed. The ground shook. The building rattled.

People were thrown off their feet. The lights flickered and swung on their chains and a glass vase fell off the concierge's desk and scattered roses across the floor.

In the moment of distraction, Sacha slammed one of the policemen into the wall and kicked the other in the stomach. He doubled over and reached for his gun. Lady Rosewood drew her pistol and slammed the policeman on the back of the head with it. He dropped his gun, and she snatched it up. The other officer tried to recover, but Sacha slammed him again, and this time kept him pinned.

'You will hang for this,' he said.

'The keys, Dorian,' said Lady Rosewood. 'This one has the keys.'

The red-headed man knelt beside the groaning police-man and fumbled through his pockets. 'What are we do-ing?' he asked. 'We can't do this.'

'I'm afraid we rather have to.'

The tremor stopped, though Sacha noticed that Lady Rosewood's hands were still shaking. Dorian handed her the handcuff keys, and she swapped them for one of the guns, which Dorian took with an expression of terror. Al-most everyone in the lobby was in too much of a state of disarray to notice the crime in progress, but one stern look-ing receptionist was making a phone call.

'Lady Rosewood, we must go,' said Sacha.

'I'm very sorry about this,' said Lady Rosewood to the policeman as she unlocked the handcuffs. Sacha took the officer's gun and Lady Rosewood cuffed him to the door handle. 'I pray you never have to understand how import-ant this was. Dorian, Valentin, come along. We have rather overstayed our welcome.'

The streets of Shanghai were in chaos as people darted from pillar to post, hoping to find a safe place to wait out the next tremor. Children were crying, a siren was blaring, and panicked voices bubbled from every direction.

'Where are you taking me?' shouted Dorian. He sat

beside Eleanora in the back seat of the Studebaker Six with his satchel clutched to his chest, casting a suspicious eye at the Russian criminal in the driver's seat.

'I'm not sure where we're going, Dorian, but we can't stay where we are,' said Eleanora. 'I'm rather hoping you were at the hotel for a reason. Do you have something for me?'

'A deadline. Tell your driver to head for the air field at Hongqiao. We have less than an hour to get you on a plane and out of Shanghai.' Dorian pulled out his pocket watch. 'Closer to half an hour, actually. Blast it.'

'Half an hour? What happens in half an hour?'

'The earthquake, Ellie. The earthquake that destroys Shanghai. The Chinese received word at 5am this morning from a group calling itself Dominion. They mean to destroy Shanghai with a man-made earthquake at precisely 7:06am. They say it will not only devastate the city, but create a wave that will sink several pacific islands.'

'What are they asking for, Dorian? What are their terms?'

'They offered none. They said… hang on.' Dorian pushed his spectacles up his nose and pulled a piece of yellow paper from his case, covered in shorthand scrawl.

'"Shanghai is a symbol of Oriental impudence. The East must abandon its ambitions and swear fealty to the West. If the Orientals do not accept their place in the white man's empire, other cities will suffer the same fate. Asia will submit or be destroyed."'

Eleanora took Dorian's pocket watch and saw the seconds tick by.

'We can still stop them. If we can just find the machine, we can stop them. What are the Chinese doing? Are they looking for the machine?'

'They don't believe it, Ellie. They're not taking any action. Neither are we. They called us as a courtesy to alert us to the threat, but they don't believe for a second that the threat is real. I'm sure I wouldn't either if it weren't for our conversation. I tried to call the consul to brief him on our intelligence. He told me to put it in a report, and he hung up. There's nothing we can do, Ellie, except get you on a plane and out of danger.'

'I won't run from this, Dorian.'

'Retreat is the only sensible option. Someone has to survive this to bring Sir Francis to justice!'

'My goodness, have you evidence on Sir Francis, as well?'

Dorian sighed and reached back into his satchel.

'I went through our files on recent business transactions between Britain and China. Sir Francis had holdings in several operations in Shanghai: hotels, casinos, shopping precincts; he even had part ownership of a ship building yard. He sold them all during his recent visit. What use is a hotel if you know it'll be rubble next week? It's not proof that will take you to court, but it was enough to convince me.'

Eleanora snatched the satchel from Dorian and tipped

the contents onto her lap. She threw him his spectacle case, his Times of London, and his copy of EM Forster's *The Longest Journey*.

'What are you looking for, Ellie?'

'You said he sold a ship yard,' she said. 'Are the records in here?'

'This one,' said Dorian. He pulled a manila folder from the pile. Eleanora flipped it open. There were two sheets, one in English and one in Mandarin. The English copy gave the name of the shipyard as Cheng-Menakee, and the sale price as little more than a peppercorn. Two signatories were listed: the seller, Francis Hardie, and the buyer.

Arek Saxon.

'There it is,' said Eleanora. 'Dry docks. The shipyard must have dry docks large enough to construct an ocean liner out of sight of the city. Large enough to build the Mandrake Machine. Valentin, drive us to the Cheng-Menakee shipyard, please.'

'Ellie, go to the airfield,' said Dorian. 'If you're sure that's where the machine is, let me contact the police. If you're wrong, at least you live to fight another day.'

'Valentin, stop the car.'

The Studebaker screeched to a halt.

'You're right, Dorian. Someone must contact the police. Find a telephone. Do what you can.'

Dorian piled his things together and pushed them back

into the satchel. 'And you will proceed to the airfield?'

'You don't have to worry about me,' said Eleanora.

Dorian got out of the car. He reached into his pocket for his watch and realised he did not have it. Eleanora pulled the door shut behind him and the car sped away. It headed in the wrong direction.

❧

The Cheng-Menakee shipyard was not quite a fortress, but its high stone walls were crowned with shards of broken glass and rolls of razor wire that would present a challenge to even the most determined saboteur.

Sacha Valentin had no intention of climbing the walls and cutting himself to shreds. He drove up to the boarded iron gates and sounded his horn.

A peeping hatch opened in the wicket door and a shadow passed across it. The hatch closed and he heard some shouts in Cantonese. Another minute passed, or maybe two. Finally, the gates drew open and Sacha drove inside.

Two men closed the gates behind him, each with a rifle slung across his back. Arek Saxon stood in the lot with his usual broad grin and one hand on the pistol in his holster. He wore his true colours now – a snug, smart, high-collared black uniform with leather gloves and boots, and a gold lightning pin above his heart.

Sacha pulled up and climbed out of the car. He kept his hands raised so that neither Arek nor his goons would have cause to shoot. Saxon watched him with a smirk as he crossed the lot.

The shipyard was a quiet, barren space. A rusted ship with a jagged broken hull sat off to one side. Wood and iron warehouses stood in clusters like the shell of an abandoned village. Beyond those was the dry dock, a wide rectangular concrete canyon with stepped walls. Within it, squatting miserably like hell's own engine, was the Mandrake Machine, a vast circular construct of jutting pistons, steel towers, and great grey gantries.

'Beautiful, isn't it?' said Arek.

Arek gestured for Sacha to stop moving. He handed his pistol to one of his goons and placed his arms on Sacha's shoulders. He patted his hands over his chest and around his waist and across his lower back, and knelt to pat down one leg then the other. He also checked his sleeves for hatpins. Satisfied, he stepped back.

'So, you're unarmed. Even so, you are still dangerous,' said Arek. He took back his pistol and gave some orders to his men in Cantonese. They nodded and headed for the warehouses.

'Tell me, Sacha; did you come all this way to return the Studebaker you took from us?'

Sacha kept his attention on the machine. He could feel Arek's hot eyes burning into him, and he found it too uncomfortable to look back. 'There are only three of you to run this machine?' Sacha asked.

'Once it's up and running, it will take care of itself,' said Arek. 'We don't want to be here when it's working, do we?'

'I felt it working,' said Sacha. 'Twice this morning.'

'Just warming up.'

'And what if it does not work?'

'That would be very embarrassing,' said Arek. 'But Edgar Rosewood was a genius, or so I'm told, so I don't think we have anything to fear. Why are you here, Sacha? How did you find me? Understand me when I say that I am glad that you did.'

Sacha matched Arek's gaze at last.

His eyes were so startlingly blue.

'I did not find you,' said Sacha. 'Lady Rosewood found you. She learned that Sir Francis owned this shipyard.'

Arek's grin barely flickered. 'And where is Lady Rosewood?' he asked.

'She is on a light aircraft leaving Hongqiao airfield,' said Sacha. 'There was no room on the plane for me, but I mean to survive this. If you will take me, Arek, I would like to come with you.'

'And be a titan, Sacha?' Arek asked.

'And be a titan,' Sacha agreed.

Arek offered his hand and Sacha lowered his arms to shake it.

'Welcome to Dominion, my friend,' said Arek. 'Come, we must prepare for our departure. I will show you a god's eye view of the world.'

✦

All was silence. Eleanora could not hear the voices of the men or the sounds from the street beyond. She listened very carefully for movement, for breath, but there was nothing. There was no-one around.

With her pistol still gripped in her hand, Eleanora threw off the black blanket that covered her, and peered out from the seating well of the Studebaker. She had heard Valentin say that there were only three men, including Saxon. Presumably that was the least number needed to oversee this man-made apocalypse, and few enough that they might make a clean escape. None of the three men were in sight.

Eleanora opened the door and raced for the cover of a Ford haulage truck. She stopped, held her breath, and listened for alarms or voices.

Nothing.

She ran to the rusted shipwreck and stopped and listened again. She checked the time on Dorian's watch. One minute past seven.

From the shipwreck, she ran to a warehouse stacked with iron girders from floor to ceiling. Her every footstep echoed too loud in her ear, but there was no-one else around to hear it. She tip-toed to the end of the warehouse and pushed open a creaking door.

The dry dock stood before her, its stepped walls like a massive amphitheatre, and there in the centre was the machine that had become so familiar to her on paper.

The reality was enough to turn her stomach. It was vast and ugly, as evil in aspect as a machine could be. It was a cage massive enough to hold a man's soul.

Eleanora scanned the edge of the dock for any sign of Valentin, Saxon, or the other men, but she could not see them, and she hoped that meant they would not see her. No-one was on the walkways that led from the dry dock to the machine, through its guts to its heart.

Eleanora made her way softly from the warehouse to the edge of the dry dock. She wove between piles of pallets and the wreckage of old iron pulleys, and reached a walkway. Only when she stood in the shadow of the machine did she pause again to take another look around. She was still alone, but for the silent giant that loomed above her.

Eleanora stepped onto the sloping metal walkway and caused a sonorous clang. She cringed and bit her lip. She listened again for any indication that she had been spotted. Luck was still on her side. She slipped off her boots and continued on her way.

Her heart perched high and heavy in her chest as she

drew closer to the machine. She felt certain it might come alive at any moment, and she feared she might be caught in its dreadful grinding parts and torn to pieces. In less than five minutes, this machine would do much worse than that.

The walkway led to an outer ring, halfway up the machine. A ladder led into the core. Eleanora took a deep breath and climbed.

She emerged onto an iron lattice platform. The pipes and struts formed a sort of chamber around her, and in its centre was a tall metal shaft that thrust up into the sky. It was linked to a metal ring held aloft by six hydraulic pistons that stretched down to the massive engine under her feet. Eleanora looked past her stocking toes and saw that the shaft continued down as well, much further than her eyes could see.

This chamber was not just the heart of the machine, but also its brain. A column in front of the shaft displayed an array of dials and meters. Beside it were three large levers.

Eleanora wondered what in the world she could do that might sabotage the machine without setting it off. She had Mandragora's gun, but if she used it she would alert everyone to her presence. She had the watch, which she could throw into the gears in the hopes that it would stop them – but the gears were so fearsome that she knew they could consume an omnibus without hesitation.

Eleanora noticed a panel on the shaft. It was an oval

of steel, held in place with a latch. She turned the latch, opened the panel, and found a shining silvery rod held in the grip of a lead collar. It was one of the pins she had seen in Mandragora's office.

Eleanora heard a creak from the catwalks behind her and looked around. There was no-one there. It had to be the machine settling under its own weight. This was no time to be skittish; she knew what she had to do.

She reached into her purse.

∽∾∽

Sacha ground his teeth, cracked his knuckles, and twitched with irritation. He had played his small part in Lady Rosewood's plan. It was up to her to sabotage the machine. He could not help her now. His only obligation was to stay in Arek's favour and perhaps distract him from the machine, but that proved unnecessary, as Arek's attention was entirely fixed on their escape. They stood in the pit of a second smaller dry dock under the shadow of the rigid white balloon of an airship.

'This, Sacha, is how we will soar above their heads as the ground cracks beneath their feet,' said Arek. His two men were inside the gondola, preparing the airship for flight. One of them waved to Arek and shouted. Arek waved back and gave a reply.

'Imagine how it will look,' said Arek. 'People scattering on the streets, buildings tumbling down as the waters roar and swell! And we will watch it all as if in the thrones of Olympus. I know you understand, Sacha. It is in your nature. There is so much beauty and majesty in destruction.'

Arek looked at Sacha with such earnest joy at this promise of devastation that Sacha wanted to reach out and choke him.

Yet part of him wanted to surrender to his words. What did he care about the world, after all? He had travelled through it like a ghost, betrayed and desolate, knowing that there was no place for a man like him. He had detached himself from all care, and only found his pulse in the face of danger. He was an outcast. If he rose and the world fell, what difference would it make to him? How hard would it be for him to take one more step, to take Arek's hand and follow him into his world of horror and hate, and live above it all, and punish a world that he had no love for anyway? And yes, to be a titan? And yes, to be a god?

Arek's hands touched the sides of his face, and Sacha looked into Arek's eyes.

'Are you with me, Sacha?'

He had done as much as he could for Lady Rosewood. He had brought her to the machine. It was up to her if the city stood or fell. If he joined Arek now, if he stepped into the airship, it would be a true ascension, above the judgement of others and beyond all care.

'Are you with me?' asked Arek again.

Sacha nodded.

Arek laughed. He threw his arm around Sacha's shoulder and slapped him on the back. 'Come on, then. Mandragora will join us shortly and we can be on our way.'

'Mandragora?' said Sacha. 'Mandragora is here?'

'Of course,' said Arek. 'It's her machine. She is the one who will activate it.'

Sacha darted away from Arek, up the steps of the airship's dry dock, and looked up at the machine. From somewhere in its darkness, he heard a woman scream.

Eleanora landed hard on the steel platform, a fresh welt forming on her cheek. Her purse spilled its contents at her feet, including the pistol she had taken from Mandragora. Its former owner now stooped to take it back.

'If only you had the sense to know your place,' said Mandragora. She stepped over Eleanora and plucked the vibrating pin from her hand. 'We moved everything forward by a day because of you. We thought your meddling might come to something. Was this all you had, lady lamb? Is this how you meet your pitiful end?'

Eleanora gritted her teeth.

'I had to try,' she said.

Mandragora scoffed. 'What a good wife you are! So desperate to redeem your husband!'

'Desperate to save a city!'

'Spare me your feeble sanctimony,' said Mandragora. She slipped the vibrating pin back into its collar, behind the open panel on the shaft. 'Do you even know what this is, this pin that you intended to steal away with?'

Eleanora did not reply.

'Of course not. That pin is the screaming root. It is the mandrake. It was Edgar's greatest creation. That small pin can channel enough energy to shake a fault line and trigger an earthquake. And he shared this creation with me, because I was the one who understood him. You were only his wife; I was his confidante. We brought this miracle monster into the world together while you were ignorant and barren.'

Eleanora ground her teeth and narrowed her eyes to keep the tears at bay.

'And did he love you, Mandragora?' she asked. 'Did he make you any promises? Did he offer you the world?'

Mandragora turned away and twisted three dials on the control panel. A thrumming noise stirred in the bowels of the machine, and the platform beneath them vibrated.

'Did he give you anything beautiful at all?' asked Eleanora. 'Did he give you even a single beautiful day? Or is this cold machine of death all you have to remember him by? The man I lost was the man who made me a music box that played the most beautiful song I have ever heard. He was not the man who would build an abomination like this.'

Mandragora laughed and shook her head. She pulled the first lever and a loud thud boomed up from the guts of the beast.

'A music box? You dull-witted sow. *This* is my music box. I will hear the screams of the city as it dies.'

She pulled the second lever and the vibrations increased a hundredfold, making Eleanora's teeth rattle in her head.

'Get up,' said Mandragora. She waved the pistol at Eleanora. 'You will watch the devastation with me, and you will see first-hand what your husband's heart has wrought.'

Eleanora got to her feet. Mandragora nodded towards the walkway.

'Go,' she said.

Mandragora pulled the third lever, and the giant piston arms exhaled, and the gears beneath their feet turned with a long low shriek.

꩜

Sacha watched in horror as the machine thundered into life, its pistons thrusting like the legs of a spider ensnaring its prey. Lady Rosewood had failed.

Back over his shoulder, Sacha saw the airship bob in the dock and strain against its ties. He had never piloted such a vehicle. Was there any hope that he could crash it into the machine? Even if he could, how would he overpower Arek and his men without a weapon?

Arek had drawn his pistol the moment they heard the scream. Sacha knew that Arek was fast, and he believed that he was deadly. Would he hesitate for a second if Sacha moved against him?

'She is here, isn't she?' said Arek. 'Your lady? The one you said had fled the city? That was her scream. Tell me, Sacha, how did your lady find her way here?'

'She is determined,' said Sacha. 'She is a hunting dog. She does not let go of her quarry. I believed her gone, but she must have changed her mind.'

'Women will do that,' said Arek. 'You did not bring her here?'

'I swear on my life, I did not,' said Sacha.

Arek did not raise his gun, but he did he return it to its holster. 'Now you pose me a challenge,' he said. 'Are you the sort of man who holds his life at any value?'

A new voice called out above the cacophony of the machine; 'Has our Russian proved immune to every charm?'

It was Mandragora, descending the walkways with Lady Rosewood before her at gunpoint.

'Perhaps you succumbed to some well-hidden charms of his own, Mr Saxon?' said Mandragora.

Arek frowned at Sacha. 'You offer a fair riddle,' said Arek. 'I think we understand each other, Sacha? I think you know I will kill you if you have betrayed me.'

'I have saved this woman enough times,' said Sacha. 'I have more than satisfied my obligations to her.'

Arek called to Mandragora. 'It hardly matters. There is nothing they can do to stop this now. We should leave. You can question him later, at your leisure.'

Mandragora laughed. 'You are a romantic, Arek,' she shouted back. 'You want to believe so much, yet you forget what a good fighter our sailor is. Tell me, Russian; will you stand by when we shoot your Lady Rosewood in the stomach and leave her here to bleed to death in the ruin of her husband's soul?'

'Give her a quick death, Mandragora,' said Arek. 'We are not monsters.'

Mandragora shoved Lady Rosewood onto the dock. She stumbled and almost fell.

'But we *are* monsters,' said Mandragora. 'The world has made us beautiful monsters. Kill her, Arek. Do it now, and make it slow.'

Arek raised his pistol, but his eyes were not on the lady, but on Sacha, imploring him to prove his new loyalty and do nothing.

Sacha took a deep breath and tried to judge the distances. Was the lady closer, or Arek? If he made a move, would Arek turn the gun on him instead? Would Lady Rosewood have anywhere to run to?

'Arek,' said Sacha.

The rest of his words were eaten by a sudden ear-shattering screech that buckled their knees and made them cover their ears. The shrill wail seemed to slice through their skin and claw at their spines.

Lady Rosewood curled up in a ball on the floor. Mandragora staggered forward and shouted something to Arek, but none of them could hear, and then Mandragora fell like a house of cards. Arek moved for the airship balloon, but he managed barely three steps before the pain of the noise crippled him, as well. He dropped his gun, and Sacha lurched towards it. He felt like he was walking through a sea of razor blades. Every slow desperate step was agony.

It was too much. Sacha buckled and fell. He sank into the red fog of his screaming mind.

❦

Eleanora tasted dust in her mouth and felt grit beneath her fingers.

She pawed at the ground and tried to push herself up. The ringing was as much in her head as in her ears now, and the scream that had coursed her spine had deadened to a horrible moan. She could think again, and she could move, but only slowly.

Eleanora got to her knees and looked around for the others. The ground was shaking, and she could barely get her eyes to focus. She saw Arek first. He crawled across the ground towards the gun. Valentin lay just beside it, but he was not moving.

A hand grabbed Eleanora's hair and yanked her to her feet. 'What did you do?'

Mandragora's voice was a hoarse scream in her ear.

'I know every sound my machine should make. It is wrong. All of it is wrong. What did you do?' Mandragora threw Eleanora down and slapped her across the cheek.

'It was Edgar,' said Eleanora. 'Edgar put an end to this. He only played his music box once. The vibrating pin was unstable. That was the pin you put in your machine, Mandragora. An imperfect copy of his great work. I meant to swap them, and you did the job for me. I dropped the real pin into the gears.'

Mandragora's face was a picture of horror. She aimed her pistol at Eleanora with a quivering hand.

A black figure crashed into Mandragora and knocked her off her feet. The gun fired, but the bullet went wild. Valentin tore the gun from her hand and threw it aside. Mandragora dug her fingers into Valentin's face and pulled herself out from under him. She scrambled across the concrete, not towards the gun, but towards the airship.

'I can try again,' said Mandragora. 'We have another pin in the airship. I will fetch it. I will fix this. End them, Mr Saxon. Shoot them now.'

175

Eleanora turned to find Arek Saxon's gun aimed at her head.

'Put it down, Arek,' said Valentin. He stood on the other side of Eleanora, with Mandragora's gun in his hand.

Arek laughed, but his laughter had no humour in it.

'We could have been kings, God damn you,' he said.

'This is not the end,' said Valentin. 'Lower your weapon and you will live. If you do not, I will shoot you dead.'

Arek shook his head. 'Then shoot me, Sacha, because God knows—'

Arek's head snapped back and a jet of blood spurted from his brow. He dropped to the dirt, not with grace and poise, but like any common thug.

Valentin did not tremble. He did not weep. He slipped the smoking gun into his pocket and helped Eleanora to her feet.

Eleanora looked back at the Mandrake Machine and saw it pulling itself apart. The tremors that rattled their bodies were not an earthquake, but the vibrations of a machine in its death throes. One of the pistons tore free and wrenched a tear through the machine. A fire burst up from the grinding gears, and smoke billowed out of its guts.

'We must go,' said Valentin.

Another loud wail sounded, and Eleanora looked for its source. This time it was not the machine, but the woman who shared its name.

Mandragora stood at the top of the dry dock and watched the devastation. It was too late for her to do anything. Her dream was dead. With tear-filled eyes she looked at Eleanora, and Eleanora recognised her expression as grief. More than that, she recognised who the grief was for. He was dead to both of them now.

Mandragora ran back towards the airship. No sooner had she disappeared over the lip of the dry dock than the airship slowly ascended, piloted by Mandragora's terrified hired hands.

'Come,' said Valentin.

Eleanora had to be dragged away from the destruction. They ran towards the warehouses, and something whizzed past Eleanora's ear like a bullet. Wood chips stabbed at her stocking feet, and she stumbled. She looked back and saw shrapnel flying from the Mandrake Machine in all directions. A steel bar shot out of the heart of the machine like a javelin and struck the airship's balloon. Eleanora gasped in horror as it ignited.

Valentin grabbed Eleanora by the elbow and yanked her to her feet. He dragged her behind a wall of iron girders and pushed her to the ground. Scraps of ballistic debris flew over their heads, and an explosion sent a warm wind rushing past. A loud grinding groan followed, and a second explosion, and at last there was silence.

Once she was sure the silence was not a pause, Eleanora raised her head above the girders and looked at the machine.

Rosettes of fire blossomed from its broken body, and the blazing skeleton of the airship jutted out of its heart like a fatal dagger.

The concrete of the dock was cracked and blackened. The machine was a wreck of jagged metal. Bitter smoke stung at Eleanora's eyes. She could hear nothing but the echo of the screaming machine. She spotted a three-inch bolt on the ground and picked it up. It was warm.

The ground shook.

Another tremor? The earthquake she thought she had prevented?

Eleanora turned and found an army rushing towards her.

Valentin stood up and placed his arms behind his back. 'Do as I do,' he said.

The soldiers fanned around them and aimed their rifles, and a man stepped forward and shouted something at Eleanora in Mandarin. Eleanora was too shocked and confused to know what to do, so she shouted back.

'I am a British citizen, and I insist you take me at once to the British consulate,' she said.

'There won't be any need for that,' said a familiar voice. Dorian Bloom pushed his way through the crowd of soldiers and whispered something to their leader. The man seemed to want to argue the point, but Dorian was very firm, and the soldier stepped back.

'Well, this is a mess,' said Dorian.

'What happened?' asked Eleanora. 'How is Shanghai? Is the city still standing?'

'Shaken, but standing,' said Dorian. 'You did it, Eleanora.

You averted disaster.'

Eleanora felt like she was about to cry. She threw her arms around Dorian and gripped him tight.

'I think I need a drink, Dorian,' she whispered.

'We'll get you one on the plane,' said Dorian. 'They can't prove you saved the city, but they can prove you assaulted a police officer, so I plan to get you out of here just as soon as we possibly can.'

'That suits me just fine,' said Eleanora. 'I've had quite enough of Shanghai.'

Eleanora looked up over Dorian's shoulder and saw Valentin standing alone, his head bowed, his expression grim. He must have realised that she was watching him, because he looked up and gave her a smile.

The smile did not reach his eyes.

∽

Singapore. Two days later. In the smoke-filled rooms of the Mercia Club, two gentlemen enjoyed post-supper cigars in hushed, replete bliss. Unfortunately for the elder gentleman, the younger did not seem to understand the importance of quiet contemplation after a five-course meal.

'Did you hear about Shanghai, Francis?' asked the young man.

Sir Francis let out a wearied sigh and opened his eyes. He glowered at his frog-faced companion. Despite himself, he was curious to know what the man had heard.

'What about Shanghai, Ogie?' he asked.

Ogie's eyes bulged. 'I heard some beastly savages tried to sink it,' he said.

Sir Francis shook his head. 'Nonsense. There's nothing of the sort in the news.' He put his head down and closed his eyes.

'I've heard it from some excellent sources,' said Ogie. 'Terrible business. Wonderful place, Shanghai. City of the future.'

Sir Francis shot his companion a deathly glare. 'It is no such thing, Ogie, and if this story of yours were true, don't you think that I would have heard about it? Do please settle down, there's a good chap.'

Sir Francis picked up a newspaper, not because he wanted to read it, but because it would place a wall between him and his bothersome companion. He took a further draw from his cigar and tried to relax into the smoke.

There was a disturbance in the corridor. Voices were raised. A shrill man loudly insisted, 'Madam, we have not allowed women through the doors of the Mercia Club in over 200 years. You absolutely cannot enter this—'

His protests were suddenly and inexplicably curtailed.

The oak double doors parted. Heads craned around the wings of armchairs, and waiters attempted to appear insouciant as they stared.

A woman in a black silk dress and a veiled hat marched

across the plush red carpet. She made a beeline for Sir Francis.

Sir Francis set down his newspaper, rested his cigar in the ashtray, and steepled his fingers. He did not need to see past the veil to know who this was.

'Good evening, Ellie,' he said.

'Don't get up, Sir Francis. I shan't be long,' said Eleanora. She reached into her purse. She pulled out a lump of metal and tossed it onto the newspaper on Sir Francis's lap.

It was a steel bolt.

'I wanted to bring you a souvenir,' said Eleanora. Even through the veil, Sir Francis imagined he could see the glimmer in her eye, like the glint of a knife.

'You need to understand that, whatever you build, I will dismantle,' said Eleanora. 'Even if I must do it piece by piece.'

Sir Francis let out a hiss of disdain.

'You are a foolish little girl,' he said.

Eleanora's lips curled into a narrow smile. 'Please, *do* underestimate me, Sir Francis,' she said. 'You will suffer a brutal awakening. We may be the weak, the savage, and the strange, but we are going to tear the carpet out from under you.'

Sir Francis could see through her bravado. She was a slight and feeble woman with no power to speak of. Her will would evaporate once this confrontation was over, and she would scurry back to the comforts of her English home. He said nothing. He merely smiled.

He was unnerved to see that she kept smiling back.

'I will see you soon, Sir Francis,' she said. 'No doubt you won't expect me.'

She walked out through the tall oak doors.

Sir Francis reached for the onyx ring on his finger and twisted it. He stopped when he realised what he was doing.

'What a queer filly,' said Ogie. 'Whatever was she talking about, Francis?'

'Nothing, Ogie,' said Sir Francis. 'The grief-stricken ramblings of an anguished widow. Nothing for anyone to be concerned about.'

❦

Eleanora stepped out into the evening air with a broad smile on her face. The doorman, glad to see her leave, doffed his cap respectfully. She slipped him a generous tip.

Valentin stood by the door of a black Bentley, dressed in a smart charcoal uniform.

'Everything is well, ma'am?' he asked.

'Everything is very well, Valentin,' said Eleanora. She climbed in, and Valentin walked around and took the driver's seat.

They proceeded in silence, but Eleanora could see Valentin's eyes darting back to check on her every few seconds. She knew there was something he wanted to say.

'Is something wrong, Valentin?' she asked.

'No, Lady Rosewood,' said Valentin. 'It is just... Sir Francis is a very powerful man, yes?'

Eleanora smiled. 'I understand your concern,' she said, 'but please don't worry. I will do my best to protect you.'

Sacha Valentin grinned.

'I believe that you will, Lady Rosewood,' he said.

'Quite right. Drive on, Valentin.'

THE FLOWERS OF MRS MOORE

Under the fat, wet leaves of the palms, where the evening breeze tickles the ferns, on the rock-edge of the ink-dark sea, in the curl of the orange-oil-scented night, there sat a dark little bar with no name: a worn-down shanty shack with chipped lime stucco walls and a smoke-blackened interior.

This was a place for vagabonds, sailors and rogues. A place for vulgar, working, drinking men, and for a few tired girls from the dockside, to spend their hard-earned coin.

On this evening, there was one woman at the bar who was not in business, though for her own safety's sake she kept the other girls company. This woman had wrapped herself in a high-collared black coat with fur trim, and tidied her hair in a beret. It was suitable dress for hiding in shadows, but a markedly modest outfit for an establishment like this.

'You don't work around here, señora?' asked one of the local girls, a long-faced woman named Luisa with a sardonic droop to her eyes. She dealt the cards around the table.

'She don't work at all,' said her friend, Marya, a girl with a wide smirking mouth. 'Look at that coat. Expensive. Landed a rich husband, this one. We're still playing the game; she already won.'

Eleanora picked up her cards and glanced at them.

'For what it's worth, Marya, I lost,' she replied. 'My husband died.'

'Too bad,' said Luisa.

Marya laughed scornfully. 'Too bad? Why is that too bad? You don't even have to live with the man! You don't win better than that!'

Luisa hissed at her friend like a cat, but Marya hooted at her own joke. Eleanora chose not to give her the satisfaction of a response.

The last player at the table was a sharp-featured girl named Rosara, with sun-streaked brown hair and a particularly impressive bosom. She did not speak much, but she kept an eye on Eleanora, to Eleanora's annoyance.

For her part, Eleanora glanced across the bar every few seconds towards two men at a far-off table. Luisa caught Rosara's smile, and followed both women's eyes across the room. Marya was the last to catch on.

'Are we playing cards or aren't we?' asked Eleanora, irritated that the girls were all imitating her gaze.

'She likes them big, huh?' said Marya, catching sight of the heavy-browed, broad-shouldered giant at the other table.

Marya licked her lips salaciously. 'Or were you looking at the other one?' She jabbed a finger in the direction of the man's drinking companion: a skinny fellow with short brown hair, dressed in a faded red shirt and grey dungarees.

'She's not looking,' said Rosara. 'She's watching. You working a scam, huh? That how you make your money?'

Eleanora's mouth fell open. 'I am doing no such thing!' she said.

'Sure, you are,' said Rosara. 'Don't worry. I don't want a cut. I'll win my share.' She picked up a couple of matches and threw them into the middle of the table. 'Your bet, señora.'

∾

Across the room at the other table, Sacha Valentin downed another shot and slammed the glass on the tin tray on the table. He belched, and his skinny new friend snickered.

'Having a little trouble keeping that one down, are you?' asked Aiden. 'Just because you're big, doesn't mean you can put it away, does it now?'

'You talk, my friend, when you should drink,' said Sacha. He passed a shot glass across the table and dropped it in front of Aiden. 'Drink, and I will buy us more, and we will drink more!'

'Feeling flush, then?' asked Aiden. 'Where's all your money coming from, a merchant seaman like yourself? I might be in the wrong line of work.'

'I do not have much, but what I have goes on drink,' said Sacha. He winked and Aiden laughed. 'But yes, join the navy. It is man's work. Not like this... flowers. This thing you do.'

Aiden knocked back the shot and gasped as the alcohol hit.

'Sweating out on the land all day is man's work enough for me, I'll tell you,' the Irishman scowled. 'And I'll tell you this, as well; it's a paradise of a place to work.' He beckoned for Sacha to come closer, and the Russian obligingly leaned in.

'I work at the finishing school,' said Aiden.

Sacha screwed up his face in incomprehension.

'For ladies,' Aiden explained. 'Where young women go to get turned into... wives.' He drawled the words, loaded them with private meaning. 'Full of American girls, it is. Rich old bastards ship their sweet young daughters out to Havana, so when they go home they're worth a bit extra in the old marital negotiations. Lands them a decent son-in-law to trust the business to, that sort of malarkey.'

'They are pretty, these girls?' asked Sacha, hoping he was following the conversation properly.

'Oh, but you get some stunners,' said Aiden. 'Prime of life, they are, too. Fifteen, sixteen. Perfect little blossoming beauties. But that's not the best of it. You should meet the lady of the house. The headmistress, Mrs Moore. I don't think any Mr Moore has been in the picture for a while. The lady has to find her satisfaction other places, if you follow my meaning.' Aiden jabbed his thumb against his chest, just in case Sacha didn't.

'You have been... involved with your mistress?' asked Sacha. 'She has taken you to her bed?'

'Oh, I've been with the lady of the house, aye,' said Aiden proudly. 'But it wasn't in the boudoir, I'll tell you that. Let me paint a picture for you, lad. A spring morning, not long after dawn, there's me out tending to the roses. The rose garden is right out by her bedroom; she likes to look out on them. Special to her, they are.

'Anyways, I look up, and there she is standing out on the balcony with a sort of look in her eye. She's a beautiful woman, let me tell you. Long legs, perfect curves; lightly bronzed skin that's as flawless as fine china, and this gorgeous long black hair. And she has bright, dangerous eyes like you're lucky she even looks at you at all. And there she is on the balcony, smiling at me, wearing this see-through little robe and a red silk nightdress that clings to her like sin.

'So, I ask her if there's anything the matter, but she says nothing. She comes down the little staircase from her room and brushes between the lemon trees, and she's stood there in front of me with the morning dew dimpling the pale skin of her breasts. She reaches down and plucks a rose and pricks her finger on the thorns, and she takes this red little spot of blood, and she presses it to my lips. And then she kisses me. And let me tell you something, my Russian friend; I gave her a right good seeing to on the rose beds that morning, and that's no lie.'

Aiden sat back in his chair, beaming proudly. He slammed his empty shot glass on the tray.

'How's that for a man, Sacha? Think about that the next time you're out on the ocean with nothing but men in any direction for a thousand miles.'

Sacha blushed. 'It sounds... interesting,' he said. He busied himself by setting all the empty shot glasses on the tray. 'I will get us more drink, yes?' He picked up the tray and headed for the bar.

As he weaved across the room, Lady Rosewood excused herself from the ladies' table and went to the bar to meet him. They stood next to each other, both facing the barman. Sacha gestured for Lady Rosewood to order first, and she asked for a glass of water and three glasses of rum and lime. Sacha ordered another tray of shots.

'Is he drunk?' asked Lady Rosewood in a sideways whisper.

'He is lecherous,' said Sacha.

'We need him drunk, Sacha. You look like you're drinking as much as he is!'

'I am Russian,' Sacha boasted.

'Yes, and he's Irish. You're weaned on vodka, he's weaned on whiskey, and you're both drinking rum,' said Lady Rosewood. 'Just be careful, please. It's barely nine o'clock and you're both in your cups. It's no good getting him drunk if you're not sober enough to carry him out of here.'

'I will be fine,' insisted Sacha. 'It is you I am worried for.

You should not be in a place like this, talking to women like that. I told you I could do this alone.'

'Yes, well, someone must stay sober enough to get the man to the boat, and I don't know what sort of drunk you are,' said Lady Rosewood.

'I am Russian,' repeated Sacha loudly. He threw his arms out wide and smacked the beer bottle out of the hand of the man next to him.

'Oh, heavens,' said Lady Rosewood.

The offended man was a fleshy, moustachioed fisherman with arms like ham hocks. His vest was now sodden with beer. He looked down at the beer bottle spinning on the floor, and up at Sacha's slightly surprised expression, and he punched him in the face.

Sacha wheeled backwards into a table and knocked another four drinks to the floor. One of the patrons at the table tried to grab Sacha by the neck of his shirt. Sacha rammed the ball of his hand into his face.

Another patron turned his displeasure on the man with the moustache, running at him with an upturned bottle. The man with the moustache was not drinking alone. He ducked the swing of the bottle, and his friends rose from their table to give his attacker a pasting. Someone picked up a chair and threw it across the room, but he missed his target and hit a watching Creole man.

A stray punch here, an incautious blow there, and soon all

the local feuds were remembered, and all the petty resentments of the evening were unleashed. Half the bar brawled, while the other half watched and shouted and waited for an excuse to pile on.

In the middle of it all, Sacha ducked one swing and delivered the next. He was happy to throw his fists at any man who came near him. It had been a long time since he had seen a good honest bar fight, but all the old moves came back to him, and his instincts were intact.

Except there was one thing he had forgotten; he had not come here alone. He heard someone call his name, and looked around to see Lady Rosewood cornered against the wall by a strawberry-nosed drunk with a tangled muddy beard and a hungry eye. She snapped warnings at the man with starchy indignation, but he leaned in closer and squeezed her arm, and his other hand searched for the buttons of her coat.

Sacha pushed into the crowd towards her, only to be met by a chair leg to the face that probably was not meant for him. As he tried to shake off the blow, the churning tide of the fight pushed him backwards. Lady Rosewood smacked the old man with the back of her hand, but he was not easily discouraged.

One of the local girls appeared behind the old man and brought a bottle of rum down on his head. The old man staggered, swayed and fell. Sacha breathed a sigh of relief.

The relief was short lived. The girl drew a knife and held it to Lady Rosewood's throat. She looked around for Sacha, offered him a horrible wide-mouthed smile, and pushed Lady Rosewood out of the bar and into the night.

A man dropped in front of Sacha. Another tried to push himself up onto his hands and knees. Sacha stepped on the back of one, then the other, and up onto the bar. He raced along the length of it, skipped over a beer bottle as it swung at his legs, and threw himself through the air. He smashed through the doors of the bar and rolled onto the street.

There was no sign of Lady Rosewood. Sacha looked at the slums that lined the street on one side, and down over the craggy rocks that led to the sea on the other. He stopped. He listened. He heard a voice in the alleys and ran to follow it.

'You give me your purse, I let you live,' hissed the girl.

Lady Rosewood stood paralysed with fear as the girl rifled through the pockets of her coat, one hand still holding the knife to her throat. 'Someone like you, in a bar like that? You're lucky it is me who robs you and not one of these fishermen.'

Sacha stepped up behind her and blocked out the moonlight. The girl looked up with an expression of sudden terror.

'Come any closer and I cut her,' she said.

Sacha said nothing. He cracked the knuckles of his right hand in the palm of his left.

The girl lost her nerve. She dropped the knife and slipped through a narrow crevice between the buildings. Sacha stepped after her, but the gap was too small for him to follow through.

Lady Rosewood fell against the wall and caught her breath. 'Let her go,' she said. 'She did not take anything.'

'Are you hurt?' asked Sacha.

Lady Rosewood shook her head. 'I'm sorry,' she said. 'I think I made a very silly mistake going in there.'

'I think we both made mistakes,' said Sacha glumly. 'I too am sorry. I did not get the Irishman drunk. The ship leaves within the half hour and we will not have him on it. We must think of something else.'

They stepped back into the street. A figure flailed out of the bar and landed at Sacha's feet. He picked himself up and brushed himself down.

'Hell of a fight, eh there, fella?' said Aiden, his eyes mad with panic.

Sacha punched him in the face and caught him before he fell. He slung him up over his shoulder and started walking.

'It is exactly as we planned,' said Sacha.

❧

One hour later, Eleanora stepped through the arched doors of the San Cristobal Hotel; a world away from the rough nameless bar on the water's edge, and a place where the lady thought she ought to feel at home. Yet, as she entered, she experienced an unmistakeable shiver of dread.

Havana was a fresh battlefield in her personal war with

her late husband's legacy, and as dangerous as the bar had been, it was here in the grandeur of polite society that she thought she might discover the most unpleasant truths, and that thought made her more afraid than any consideration of her personal safety.

Eleanora handed her high-collared coat to the girl at the cloakroom and wrapped a crocheted shawl tight around her shoulders, as if it might ward off evil. She took a steadying breath and stepped through the grand lobby to the ballroom.

The hour was late, but the party was still alive and lively. The big band was swinging, the champagne was pouring, and the chatter was high enough to raise the roof. This was Havana, after all, and the city had built its reputation as America's backyard party town ever since the US chased out the Spaniards. Havana did not keep civilised hours.

The occasion this night was the 50th birthday of American industrialist Renfield Vandevere, but that was not why Eleanora was here. She had come to Havana to uncover the secrets of the Moore School for Young Women, to which she had become a patron at her husband's urging. Since learning of her late husband's involvement in a dastardly cabal named Dominion, she now viewed all his activities in a new light.

Edgar had encountered the Moore School almost two years ago, while courting investors for the air speed record attempt that so recently claimed his life. He had returned from Havana full of praise for the Moore School and its methods, and had shared with Eleanora a letter from the headmistress.

Eleanora was so impressed by Mrs Moore's talk of empowering young women to take control of their choices that she agreed to sponsor a few less fortunate girls to take advantage of its opportunities. Mrs Moore held it as an article of faith that any woman could thrive, if given a chance in life.

Those promising words now rang false to Eleanora. During her mission to destroy her husband's earthquake machine in Shanghai, she had uncovered a letter on Moore School stationery sent by her husband to the wicked woman who oversaw the machine's construction. The letter had read, "My dear M; What an age. I am shocked to the core by the things we teach our girls these days." The implication seemed sordid, and quite unlike the words Eleanora had read in the school's prospectus.

Eleanora could not be sure that the school was part of Dominion's plans. If it was, she could not imagine what role it might play, yet because she had paid for girls to attend, she felt responsible for any wrongs that might be done there. For that reason, an investigation of the Moore School was her top priority after the incident in Shanghai. Yet it was a mystery she was terrified to unravel.

Eleanora stood at the edge of the ballroom under a naked golden statue that held two illuminated fan lights, and she looked for a familiar face.

To learn anything, Eleanora would need to venture into

the school itself. The easiest way to do that was to meet with Mrs Moore, and the least suspicious way to do so seemed to be to be a chance meeting at a social function.

This was not a course without dangers. Eleanora had placed herself in open opposition to Dominion, and Mrs Moore might be an agent. Would Sir Francis Hardie, one of Dominion's leading lights, have warned Mrs Moore of the threat that Eleanora posed – if he saw her as a threat at all?

Eleanora had to hope that Mrs Moore was not part of Dominion, or if she was, that she had not been briefed. She would not know the facts without a personal investigation, and that began with a social introduction. If that approach was a failure, she had a contingency plan in place.

The concierge at Eleanora's hotel had assured her that the headmistress would be at the Vandevere party. Eleanora was an old friend of Mrs Vandevere, so she secured a last-minute invitation.

Now, fresh from a bar brawl and an attempted mugging, Eleanora had to be at her gracious and convivial best.

'Eleanora! My God, you really are here!'

Temperance Vandevere swept across the room with her arms stretched in front of her. She snared Eleanora in a hug.

'It is so lovely that you're here. I'm so heartbroken about Edgar.' Mrs Vandevere's soft round face creased with sympathy.

'Thank you, Temperance,' said Eleanora. 'How are the twins? Are they here in Havana?'

'You will have to meet them tomorrow. We will take breakfast together. They are monsters, both of them, but angels, too.' Temperance grabbed Eleanora's hand. 'Are you all right to meet a few people?'

'Of course,' said Eleanora. "Do your worst.'

Temperance chuckled. 'Come on, then.'

Temperance Vandevere was a good woman to know at a party. Though she was as sober as her name suggested, she had a great skill for ingratiating her way into any group of people on the power of presumption alone.

Temperance was a proud American from Philadelphia – she liked to say that the Liberty Bell had been melted down to make her – and she came from railway money, while her husband claimed his fortune from oil.

Eleanora and Temperance had met in 1916, when they both served as nurse administrators at Base Hospital 21, an American-run field hospital on a racetrack in Rouen, just miles from the front line.

They had not been friends from the first. Temperance had seniority, and placed strict emphasis on efficiency. War, she said, was not a place for soft hearts. But they both had men at the front – Eleanora's husband and Temperance's brother – and the fear that this brought them had bound them together.

'Have you met Senator Hapley?' asked Temperance. She deposited Eleanora in front of a robust red-faced man with white hair and a moustache to match. 'Harlan, this is Eleanora Rosewood, the Lady Rosewood. Eleanora, this is Harlan Hapley.'

'Pleasure to make your acquaintance, Lady Rosewood,' said Senator Hapley. He spoke with a slow Southern drawl and had a lively gleam in his eye. 'You must call me Happy. Everyone does.' He took her hand and kissed it.

Temperance gestured to the man next to the senator, a serious young fellow in a pale brown suit. He had dark brown hair and sharply handsome features.

'And this, I believe, is Mr Brand Blackwell, the magazine writer. Am I correct, sir?'

The young man nodded, but did not smile. 'You are, indeed,' he said.

'My mother-in-law is a great admirer,' said Temperance.

'Is that so?' said Blackwell. His expression revealed his scepticism. 'Then you must send her my kind regards,' he said, without much kindness. 'It is a pleasure to meet you both. Lady Rosewood, Mrs Vandevere.' He gave them each a firm handshake.

'What is it that brings you out here to Cuba, Lady Rosewood?' the senator asked.

'What brings anyone to Cuba, Senator Hapley?' said Eleanora. 'Rest and relaxation, sir.' She smiled, and he laughed.

'We have to watch ourselves in front of Mrs Vandevere,' said the senator. 'She thinks this place is Sodom and Gomorrah entwined.'

'I am never so draconian,' protested Temperance. She seemed amused rather than offended by his caricature. 'Renfield's business partners like to come here, and you know I would never stand in his way.'

'I know you stand at his back and drive him on,' said the senator. He whispered to Eleanora conspiratorially: 'Rumours say that Mrs Vandevere intends to run for public office in Illinois – through the person of her husband, naturally.'

'Scurrilous talk,' said Temperance with an easy smile.

'So, Mr Vandevere is not going to throw his hat in the ring?' asked Blackwell sceptically.

'I leave it to Renfield to make his own decisions,' said Temperance. 'You shan't get anything more from me than that, Mr Blackwell.'

'If it's all the same, I think I'd prefer he didn't run,' suggested the senator. 'You husband has a lot of money, and I don't think he'd bring it to my side of the aisle.' The senator laughed at his own joke, and shook his head and looked at Eleanora. 'I do apologise, Lady Rosewood. I'm sure our American politics can't be of much interest to you.'

'Think nothing of it, Senator,' said Eleanora. 'I've found of late that I'm increasingly intrigued by the subject of power.'

'Are you, indeed?' said Brand Blackwell. 'Why ever would that be?'

He spoke with a knowing dryness that Eleanora did not like. She wondered if all journalists spoke that way. Before she could think of a sensible response, Temperance took her by the arm.

'You can interrogate my friend another time, Mr Blackwell. I'm duty bound to make sure her ladyship gets a chance to circulate,' said Temperance. 'We shall dance later, Harlan.'

'I look forward to it, my dear,' said the senator. 'Good night, Lady Rosewood.'

'Good night, Senator Hapley. Mr Blackwell.'

Blackwell nodded, but his expression was fixed and dour. He seemed a miserable creature, and Eleanora was glad to turn her back on him as Temperance swept her off through the crowd.

'What did you think?' asked Temperance confidentially.

'Well, the senator seemed lovely,' offered Eleanora with diplomatic finesse.

Temperance leaned in close. 'It's not my nature to gossip, as you know, but I'll say this about the senator; he has a wife and some loudly declared principles back home, and he leaves them both behind when he comes to Cuba. They say he enjoys the local… colour.'

'Temperance, you're being scandalous,' said Eleanora. In spite of herself she added, 'What do you know of Mr Blackwell?'

'Oh, it's terrible,' said Temperance. 'He was at the Somme. He took a piece of shrapnel in a place we cannot mention, and they say he's never been the same since. I can quite forgive his demeanour in the circumstances, but I must say I'm not endeared. Now, who else can I introduce you to?'

'I would very much like to meet Mrs Moore from the finishing school, if she is here,' said Eleanora. 'I've sponsored some of her girls, and I would welcome the chance to see that my money is in good hands.'

'Well, of course you would,' agreed Temperance. 'I have a feeling we'll find her in the garden courtyard.'

❦

Courtyards, parks and public squares: Havana was a city rich with shared spaces. Beyond the walls of the San Cristobal was a square that buzzed with life on this sultry, starry evening. The youth of the city convened at cafés and bars and on the benches beneath the golden fig trees.

Sacha Valentin sat alone on the steps of the hotel and watched the world. The adrenaline of the fight had flushed the alcohol from his system, and his body now bristled with boundless voltage.

A group of young women in extravagant dresses gathered in front of a dance hall, where they hooted and catcalled to the fresh-faced American marines who dallied in their dress uniforms at the café across the square. The boys had presumably come from a more formal dance, and were now in the mood for something less regimental.

'No puedes sentarte aquí.'

The concierge tapped Sacha on the shoulder.

'You understand me? You cannot sit here. You must leave.'

Sacha brushed him off. He stepped down into the square and looked for a bench to occupy. They were all taken, mostly by kissing couples. The proprietor of the café called over to Sacha and gestured to an empty table.

'Come! Sit! Drink!' he said.

Sacha shook his head.

He was not happy here, surrounded by all this movement and noise. He was used to the ocean, and solitude. Whenever he came ashore he preferred to be alone – to eat and drink alone, to sit alone and think alone. Working for Lady Rosewood took him away from the safety of loneliness, and dropped him back in the swarm, where he would have to suffer the imposition of others and all the questions that he had pulled away from.

Sacha circled the square without purpose, without paying attention to the nuisances around him. Some of the girls caught sight of him, and one of them whistled and another laughed. Sacha turned on his heel to avoid them, and collided with one of the marines. The marine dropped his beer bottle and it smashed on the stone cobbles. This was becoming a pattern for the evening.

Sacha stepped back and glared angrily at the American. The energy that itched at his knuckles needed to go somewhere, and this might be as good a target as any.

The marine was a tan and square-headed youth with wide brown eyes and a down-turned mouth. His uniform was fresh-pressed and immaculate, but for a spurt of foam where the beer had splashed him. He rested his hand on the hilt of his ceremonial sword, and his lips curled into a smile.

'You looking for trouble there, buddy? You don't want to go pick a fight with a United States Marine.'

Sacha closed his fists and rolled his shoulders. Past the marine, he could see the boy's friends watching. Two of them rose to their feet. It would be a challenge to take them all on, but he thought he could do it.

Then he remembered that he needed to stay out of trouble. He needed to be here when her ladyship returned. He could not be caught brawling in the street. He could not be locked up in a local jail.

'I am sorry,' said Sacha. He squeezed the words out through gritted teeth. 'I will stay out of your way.'

'You owe me a drink, friend.'

A woman stepped up behind the marine and slipped her hand over his. She laced their fingers together and slid her hand over the sword hilt.

'Don't be that way, Mark,' she whispered to the marine. 'Look at this wretched soul. Show him some charity.'

The girl was nearly as tall as the boy, and as pale as snow – a rare sight on this dusky island. She wore a pink flower in her crimped blonde hair, and a fluted blue dress with a dark blue collar that brought out the chill in her eyes. Those eyes tore into Sacha like a diamond whip.

'Look at you,' she said. 'How sad you are. You have a thousand unhappy days hanging over you.'

'Let's get out of here, Sunna,' said the marine. 'This guy is a waste of time.'

The girl pulled away and pressed her hand to Sacha's cheek. He flinched.

'I know a mooncalf when I see one,' said Sunna. 'What a misery you are. I should sap the sadness out of you.' She stepped back and slipped her arm around the marine's shoulder. Her other hand rested on his thigh.

'Mark won a medal tonight,' she said. 'A reward from the people of Cuba for slaughtering pirates off the bay of Santa Clara. There's a little bar I know in Vedado, where they'll give us rum and glasses and a small room where we can celebrate in private. We should go there together. The three of us. We can get liberated together.'

Sacha and the marine locked eyes. Sacha expected the marine to look away. He was disconcerted when he did not.

'You can buy me that drink,' the marine said. There was a kind of courage and curiosity in his eyes.

Sacha was dry-mouthed. He looked from the couple to the hotel and back. 'I cannot,' he said. 'I am waiting for a friend. I cannot.'

'Bring your friend,' said the girl.

Sacha shook his head. 'I cannot,' he said again. He turned and fled back to the hotel. He reached the foot of the steps and saw the concierge watching through the glass doors with a sour eye. Sacha glanced back over his shoulder and saw the girl and her marine walk away.

This world of men was too much for Sacha. It would destroy him.

⁓

A hundred feet away, and a stratosphere removed, Eleanora and Temperance stepped through two tall glass-panelled doors into a covered courtyard full of lushly verdant life. Eleanora caught her breath at the panoply of palms and ferns. Emerald leaves of ancient nature divided the space with elegant geometry. The courtyard was a small and perfect Eden in the Cuban heat.

Through the curtain of this curated jungle, Eleanora spotted a matronly middle-aged woman on a white wicker bench, and beside her a grey tweedy man in pince-nez spectacles. The woman had the look of a headmistress, and the man had to be her husband.

'Hello,' said Eleanora. 'Are you Mrs Moore?'

'Oh, me? Oh, no,' said the woman. She seemed embarrassed by the confusion. She pointed to Eleanora's right, and Eleanora turned and discovered the real headmistress.

208

Mrs Moore was a strikingly beautiful woman in her mid-30s, with olive skin that glowed with health, bright topaz eyes, and jet black hair. She sat enthroned on a high-backed bamboo seat, haloed by a burst of bright red flowers, and wreathed in grey smoke. She wore a pale peach shirt under an open-necked dark-emerald dress embroidered with golden flowers. There was a coiled potency in the way she held herself. She was a regal and commanding presence.

Mrs Moore lifted a cigar to her unpainted lips and took a pull. The smoke curled from her mouth in languid tendrils and transformed her eyes into breathing embers. She held her eyes on Eleanora's as she stubbed out the cigar in an ashtray. Every movement was as precise as a dancer's.

'Can I help you?' she asked. Her accent was American, but much softer than Temperance's.

Eleanora gave no answer. This woman was not like any teacher she had ever encountered. She was not demure or strident or restless; instead, she seemed wholly possessed of herself. If this courtyard was Eden, this woman was an Eve who ate gladly of the tree of wisdom. She was confident and corporeal, and that made Eleanora all the more concerned about what she might teach young women.

'Mrs Moore, this is Lady Rosewood,' said Temperance. 'Lady Rosewood, this is Phaedra Moore. I thought you two should get acquainted.'

Mrs Moore seemed to make some invisible calculation

in her head. The result was a narrow smile.

'Well, of course,' said Mrs Moore.

She stood and offered Eleanora her hand. Her grip was firm, but not oppressive.

'What an honour to meet you at last. You have been such a generous benefactor to our school. I was so very, very sorry to hear about your husband.'

'That is kind of you to say,' said Eleanora.

'I hope we didn't interrupt,' said Temperance.

Mrs Moore shook her head.

'Not at all. The Baskins and I were just enjoying a moment's respite from the band. Mrs Vandevere, Lady Rosewood, this is Dean and Deborah Baskin. Their daughter Cora started at the school this week.'

Dean Baskin stood to greet them. 'It's a privilege,' said Dean Baskin. 'You are a patron of the school, Lady Rosewood? You must speak well of it.'

'My husband spoke well of it,' said Eleanora. 'To my shame, I have never visited.'

'That is a situation we must rectify,' said Mrs Moore. 'You and your husband have given so many young women such wonderful opportunities. You are always welcome at our school. Where are you staying, Lady Rosewood? We would be glad to have you as our guest.'

Eleanora allowed herself a smile. That invitation was exactly what she needed.

'I would like very much to stay at the school,' said Eleanora.

'Then it is agreed,' said Mrs Moore. 'We shall expect you tomorrow afternoon.'

A tall and handsome man came prowling through the ferns. He had long and prematurely grey hair, and he wore a grey suit that seemed to match. He touched Mrs Moore's arm and leaned in to her ear. Mrs Moore nodded.

'Thank you, Mr Kaiser. It appears that our car is ready and we must away. Oh, but Mr Kaiser, first I must introduce you to Lady Rosewood. Lady Rosewood, this is my aide de camp, our school's resident music master, Aldrich Kaiser.'

The man took Eleanora's hand and bowed to kiss it, just as the senator had done. What had seemed charming from the older man seemed disconcerting here. There was something lupine about Mr Kaiser, and most especially about the way he looked at Eleanora. She recognised him immediately as an intelligent and dangerous predator.

'Enchanted to make your acquaintance, milady,' he said.

Eleanora drew back her hand as quickly as propriety would allow. The existence of Aldrich Kaiser put a different complexion on her plans. He was surely ex-military, as most men of his generation were, and if the school belonged to Dominion, he might be one of that group's deadly agents. He might be a plausible threat even if he were truly just the music master.

'We must take our leave, as well, Lady Rosewood,' said Dean Baskin. 'We depart Havana in the early morning.

If you see our daughter at the school, please remind her that she is forever in our prayers.'

'Of course, Mr Baskin, Mrs Baskin. It was lovely to meet you both.'

The Baskins exchanged good nights with Mrs Moore. As they left, a pretty young waitress stepped in to the courtyard with a tray of empty glasses on her arm. Mrs Moore stooped to gather her shawl from her seat, and Eleanora caught the music master admiring the waitress as she collected empty glasses. There was a sudden look of confusion on Kaiser's face, followed by a look of alarm.

'Dominique?' he said.

The waitress dropped her tray of glasses and revealed a pistol in her hand. There was a mad, wild and angry cast to her eyes.

'You recognise me, Mr Kaiser?' she said. 'Am I still myself, after all?'

'Dominique, what is the meaning of this?' said Mrs Moore. 'What are you doing?'

'You know very well,' said Dominique. 'This is your reckoning, Mrs Moore. This is a reckoning for all of you!' She pointed the gun at Eleanora. 'I know your part in this. You'll pay with the rest of them. You'll pay for what you did to me!'

They were laughing. They were merry. The chirrup of flirtatious exchanges filled the air.

Sacha tried to bury himself in the shadow of an alley and push all sense of the whirling world away, but even here he heard them whispering.

He knew it was the voice of the dangerous girl with the light blue eyes, and with it the voice of the bronzed and handsome marine. He heard the boy groan. He heard the girl tell him, 'shush, shush'. He realised with embarrassment that he was straining to listen, and that this was not what he wanted at all.

Sacha turned his back to their sounds and reapplied his attention to the lights and sounds from the square.

And he heard a gunshot.

⚜

Eleanora lay on her back in the wreckage of broken ferns, her ears ringing from the gunshot, her shoulder burning with pain. Her sleeve was damp, and a spill of red wetness pooled on the stone tiles around her.

It had happened so quickly. The waitress drew a gun. She threatened them, blamed them for some unnamed crime. She fired, and someone pushed Eleanora to the floor.

Before Eleanora could recover her senses, she heard a scream and another gunshot. Glass rained into the courtyard, and Eleanora covered her face and tried to retreat beneath the ferns.

The girl now struggled for control of the gun with a man whose face Eleanora could not see. It was not Kaiser, as he was across the courtyard, hugging his left leg with blood-covered hands. Temperance Vandevere tried to hide behind the bamboo chair, and there was no sign of Mrs Moore.

'Stay where you are.'

Eleanora looked over her shoulder and found Mrs Moore crouched behind her. She realised Mrs Moore was the one who had thrown her to the ground. The woman Eleanora assumed was her enemy had perhaps just saved her life.

'Don't move,' said Mrs Moore. 'The girl is my responsibility.'

She stood and stepped out among the green of the garden and the glimmer of broken glass. She approached the girl with outstretched arms.

'Dominique, listen to me.'

Dominique shivered. She tried to wrench her wrist free from the grip of the man behind her. There was a panic in her eyes, and hot tears ran down her red cheeks. A whimper escaped her throat. 'Stay away from me. Stay away.'

'Dominique, remember paternoster,' said Mrs Moore. 'Cease this foolishness.'

The fight went out of the girl all at once, like a candle extinguished. Her body slackened, and the man wrested the gun from her grip. It was the journalist, Brand Blackwell. With a deft gesture, he spun out the chamber and shook the bullets onto the ground.

Mrs Moore put a hand to Dominique's cheek. 'Remember paternoster, Dominique. Be a good girl.'

The girl gasped and fainted into Blackwell's arms. He caught her weight and lowered her gently to the floor.

Mrs Moore turned away, trembling. She sat back down on the bamboo throne.

Eleanora breathed out. She tried to shake off the shock of the moment, and felt her arm for a wound. She was only bruised. The pool on the floor was only wine.

Temperance Vandevere stepped out of her cover and knelt to take the girl's pulse.

'Overcome with hysteria, poor thing,' she said. 'Was anyone hurt? Ellie, how are you?'

'I'm all right.'

'Then see to Mr Kaiser, would you please?'

Eleanora nodded. She felt transported back to Rouen, back to the war, where there had been few opportunities for self-indulgent worry, and she and Temperance had faced many worse scenes than this. Temperance always slipped so easily into that mode of stern efficiency, perhaps because for all her geniality she was only ever half a step out of it. Eleanora found it more difficult to set her fears aside.

The music master waved off Eleanora's approach. 'A little blood, it is not serious,' he said. 'The bullet struck a planter. I'm fine.' He tried to drag himself onto a bench, and Eleanora put his arm across her shoulders to help him. As soon as he was seated, she tore the seam of his trouser leg to inspect the injury. The bullet had torn a gash in his calf, but it was not too deep. She wrapped the torn cloth over the wound.

Kaiser smiled down at her. 'You make a pretty nurse.'

'You will need to have that cleaned and bandaged, Mr Kaiser, and keep your weight off this leg. Get yourself a sturdy stick.' After a moment's thought, she added. 'I may do the same.'

With Dominique and Kaiser seen to, that left Mrs Moore. She sat very still on her high-backed chair and stared into the middle distance.

'Are you well, Mrs Moore?'

She nodded.

'Can you tell me what happened? Is this girl one of your students?'

Mrs Moore replied with a hushed voice: 'No. Not anymore. She was a troubled girl. So many demons.' Mrs Moore remembered herself and looked up at Eleanora. 'We used to pray together, you see. We would say the rosary. The Lord's Prayer. The paternoster. I always thought the words hadn't reached her, but in some small way it seems they did.'

The courtyard filled with curious strangers and hotel staff. Senator Hapley pushed through the crowd with two United States Marines and one Havana police officer in his wake. A familiar Russian voice bellowed angrily from somewhere in the hotel, and Eleanora realised that if

Valentin came in here it would endanger their plans. She needed to intercept him.

'The hotel must have a doctor,' said Eleanora. 'I shall see to it.' She forced her way through the crowd and caught sight of Valentin through the glass of the lobby doors, arguing with a small phalanx of poor unfortunate porters who nervously held the line against him.

Eleanora knocked on the glass. Valentin's attention snapped to her as if he meant to shout at her next, but recognition softened his expression. Eleanora signalled that she would like to come out, and one of the porters produced a key and unlocked the door.

'Valentin, bring the car around.' She put a hand on the porter's arm. 'You, fetch the doctor, tell him to bring bandages, antiseptic and smelling salts.'

'My lady. You are unharmed? I heard gunshots.'

'I'm fine, Valentin. Shaken. One of Mrs Moore's former students attempted an assassination, which means we were right to come here.'

Valentin nodded and narrowed his eyes. 'The school, it will be dangerous?'

'We must assume so. Mrs Moore is a curiosity, and her music master puts me ill at ease.'

Someone called Eleanora's name from the ballroom, and Eleanora glanced through the window and saw Temperance waving to her from afar.

'We will discuss this at the hotel. The car, please, Valentin.'

Eleanora turned to the porter, who had already re-locked the door. She stared him down until he unlocked it.

'The doctor is on his way,' Eleanora called to Temperance. 'Is there anything else I can do?'

Temperance crossed the floor and grabbed Eleanora's hand. 'Not tonight, I'm sure,' she said. 'Go and rest, Ellie. You look positively ashen. It's been a while since either one of us went to war.'

'The war is always with us,' said Eleanora. 'I shall take a brandy and go directly to bed.'

Temperance tutted at the brandy. She leaned in close to whisper.

'You mustn't go anywhere near that school tomorrow. There's something not right about the place. This whole island is a danger. Let me call for an escort to take you back to your hotel.'

'No, thank you,' said Eleanora. 'I have just the man for the job.'

✺

Sacha Valentin was not the right man for the job.

It was the following morning, and the Moore School for Young Women stood before him: an elegant Colonial Spanish building with pink walls and white colonnades, fringed with terracotta-tiled balconies and accompanied by its own small chapel with a handsome bell tower. Stretching off behind the house was a sloping plantation of emerald green tobacco bushes poised in regimental lines. In front of the house were Mrs Moore's sculpted gardens, with a broken mosaic path leading across a cultivated lawn to a sunken patio and a simple stone fountain. Rich palms and ferns divided the perfectly appointed flower gardens, the most beautiful of which was the rose garden.

The gardener, unfortunately for Mrs Moore, had been stashed away on a cruise ship headed for Panama with a hastily purchased ticket stuffed in his pocket. Aiden had probably freed himself of the ropes by now, but there was no likelihood that the ship might turn around, and he certainly could not swim back.

That left the Moore School – and the very particular Mrs Moore – short by one gardener. Fortunately for her, there was a young man in town who happened to have an excellent letter of recommendation from an English lord. The letter was a fake, but it would be days before Mrs Moore could verify that. She would learn much sooner that Sacha Valentin was not the least bit equipped to tend a garden.

Sacha arrived at the school in the early hours. A man in a grey linen suit limped out onto the porch to meet him. He was tall and long-limbed, with a mane of thick grey hair, and he walked with a black cane.

He had to be Aldrich Kaiser, the same man that Lady Rosewood identified as a possible threat.

'This is private property,' shouted Kaiser. 'You cannot be here. If you are looking for work, the plantation is along the road.'

'I have message for lady of house,' said Sacha, choosing his words with stilted inelegance.

Kaiser looked Sacha over with revolted contempt. He held out his hand.

'Give it to me.'

Sacha shook his head.

'It is for lady of house,' he said.

Kaiser rolled his eyes.

'I see,' he said. 'Wait there, please.' He pointed to a bench by the porch, and went inside.

Sacha took off his cap and sat and wiped his brow. It was already too warm. Today promised to be as sweltering as yesterday, and there was barely a cloud in the sky to offer relief. Sacha looked again at the garden, and wondered how many flowers would die under his care.

After a couple of minutes, there was a knock at the window behind him. Sacha turned, and a manicured hand beckoned him inside. The front door opened and Sacha stepped in.

The lady of the house stood in the centre of the reception hall, a mosaic of knotted white roses spilling out on the tiles at her feet.

Mrs Moore wore a sheer green silk nightgown. Her hair was pinned up in a braid and tucked under a sleeping mask. She showed no embarrassment at presenting herself this way. She stood in the hall like an empress in her finery.

'You have a message?' she said.

Sacha nodded. 'My name is Nicolae. I am Romanian—'

'I do not care what you are. What is your message?'

'Ma'am. I sorry, I speak bad English. Your gardener, Aiden, he is gone to Mexico.'

Mrs Moore raised an eyebrow.

'We play at cards in evening,' said Sacha. 'He win much money and go adventure.'

Mrs Moore showed her displeasure at this turn of events with the merest curl of her lips.

'I see,' said Mrs Moore. She clicked her fingers. Aldrich Kaiser stepped out of the shadow of an arch and handed her a black purse. She pulled out an American quarter and tossed it to him. It landed at his feet.

'You may go.'

'Ma'am,' said Sacha. 'I am gardener. Aiden say you will need help.'

Mrs Moore dismissed him with a wave and turned and walked up the stairs.

'I do not hire hobos on a whim,' she said. 'Leave. At once.'

Aldrich Kaiser stepped in front of Sacha to reinforce the point. 'Take your money and be grateful,' he said.

Sacha picked up the quarter. It was a sad token of his fail-ure. He had not got his foot in the door at the Moore School, which meant he would not be able to spy, and he would not be able to protect Lady Rosewood during her visit.

His mind raced for a last-minute solution, even as his feet carried him out through the front door. Strategy was not his forte. Fists were his forte. He debated the merits of starting a fight with Aldrich Kaiser, if only to remove one danger from the board, but before he could settle on a decision he heard the door click shut behind him.

'Hello, mooncalf.'

The tall pale blonde girl from the previous night now stood on the gravel driveway. She wore a white dress with a thick blue ribbon around her waist. She held her hands behind her back, and one foot pointed like a dancer's. She was a picture of innocence and sweetness, but for the smile on her face, and the predatory glint of her pale blue eyes.

'What a thing, to find you here on my doorstep,' she said. 'Did you come all this way for me?'

'This isn't you at all,' said Temperance Vandevere.

The ladies met for breakfast under a flower-strewn gaze-bo on the water's edge at Temperance's hotel. While they took tea and toast with quince marmalade, a young nanny sat a distance away at a smaller table with sleeping twin babies, a boy and a girl. They were Temperance's children: Charles Arthur David and Miriam Mary Elizabeth.

'I'm not sure what you mean,' said Eleanora. 'I am a benefactor of this school, and I have always taken an active interest in charity.'

'As you should, my dear, but there is no need to be incautious. We were held at gunpoint, Ellie! The headmistress admitted that the girl was her student! Leave this whole business to the police. You have no obligation to that school.'

'I have an obligation to its girls,' said Eleanora. 'I have an obligation to Cora Baskin.'

'Cora Baskin's parents barely missed being held at gunpoint themselves. I'm sure they have heard about what happened and are capable of making their own decisions.'

'And what of the other girls? You say this is not like me, but what sort of person would I be to invest in such a venture and wash my hands of the consequences?'

'It's a bad investment, that's all,' said Temperance. 'I'm as pious as they come, but I don't go looking for trouble.'

'You saw that girl's madness. Have you no curiosity about what could have caused it? Do you not wonder what could make her want to shoot her former teacher?'

One of the babies stirred. The nanny was quick to her feet, but Temperance was quicker. She scooped the child up before it could finish its first scream, and it seemed to calm almost instantly against the warmth of its mother's bosom.

'Hush hush hush, Charles,' said Temperance. 'I quite understand your anguish. Your Aunt Eleanora is utterly unreasonable.'

'I am holding myself responsible.'

'For something you did not cause. Madness comes from many places, Eleanora. From love, from injustice, from demon drink. All too often it comes from grief.'

Eleanora narrowed her eyes and pursed her lips. Her anger was contained by her wish not to further disturb the baby.

'Do you think I came to Havana for want of anything better to do with my widowhood?' she asked.

'I'll tell you what I know,' said Temperance. 'People love scandal, and a widow racing around the globe within weeks of her husband's passing is the sort of peculiarity that attracts it. If you will not think of your safety, think of your reputation.'

'Damn my reputation.'

Temperance covered her son's ears. 'Eleanora!'

Eleanora shook her head and looked out over the placid waters of the Florida Straits. The concierge had warned her to expect inclement weather, but the sky and the sea offered only serenity and splendour, and Eleanora wished there was some way she could draw that calm into herself.

'I apologise for my language,' said Eleanora. 'There is simply more at stake here than you can understand.'

Temperance set her son back in his basket and tucked his

blanket around him. 'If you need to talk, you know I will listen,' she said.

'Of course,' said Eleanora. 'As always, I appreciate your friendship.'

Yet Eleanora could not bring herself to tell the sordid story of her husband's betrayal to another trusted friend. It was too embarrassing to admit what sort of man Edgar had been. It was too embarrassing to admit how greatly she had been deceived.

If Eleanora needed Temperance's help, she would tell her the whole story then. She would tell her about the papers in Edgar's study, the foul words that condemned much of the world as no better than mongrels, and the blueprints for machines that would keep those dogs at heel. She would tell her about the Mandrake Machine in Shanghai, and the late Madam Mandragora, and Dominion and Sir Francis. She would tell her about Edgar's letters, which had condemned the Moore School long before the incident with the girl and the gun. She would tell her friend everything, just as soon as she had to.

Until that time, she would hold on to her shame as a secret. For in truth, her reputation mattered very much, and she was in no hurry to tell her friend how great a fool she had been.

Sacha Valentin played dumb. The girl with the dangerous eyes approached with a sprightly step and spoke in a singsong tone.

'Why have you come here, Caliban? Did you follow me home last night? Did you watch me through the window? Will you tell me what you saw?'

She leaned in close, her hands still folded behind her back. She was tall enough on tiptoe to bring her face within inches of his, and she seemed able to balance that way without a tremble.

'Speak,' she said. 'Your tongue has many uses. I know that speaking is one of them.'

Sasha was dry-mouthed and humiliated. He had never felt so threatened in his life.

'My English, very bad,' he said.

The girl grinned from ear to ear. 'Then you shan't have to write me poetry. My name is Sunna. Sunna Kristjansdottir.' She took a step back and offered her hand. Nervously, he shook it.

'I am Nicolae,' said Sasha. 'I am Romanian.' He was relieved to have remembered those lies. If Lady Rosewood was known to travel with a Russian named Sacha Valentin, he could not use that name or nationality.

'Well, that's something new,' said Sunna. 'I was born in Iceland, but I'm a mutt, I've travelled everywhere, and who belongs to anywhere anymore? What are you doing here,

Nicolae? I'm sure you can't really have followed me home. I'm sure I would have noticed a rhinoceros on my shoulder.'

'Your gardener, Aiden, he is gone to Mexico,' said Sacha, repeating word for word the lies he had told Mrs Moore. 'We play at cards in evening. He win much money and go adventure.' Lady Rosewood had drilled these lines into him, knowing that Sacha had little facility for guile. The hope was that he could pretend his English was even worse than it was, both so that he could avoid difficult questions, and so that he could eavesdrop without arousing suspicion.

Sunna evidently found the explanation unsatisfying. She cocked her head to one side and waited for more.

'I am gardener,' said Sacha. 'Aiden say you will need help.'

'Did he indeed?' said Sunna. 'Yet here you are, walking away with a quarter in your hand and the look of a lost wretch. Mrs Moore must not have been so taken with you. She has a great deal on her mind this morning.'

Sacha stared at her. He had no idea how to interact with a creature like this, and he was grateful that he could hide behind poor English, but that did not seem to discourage her from speaking to him.

'But of course, I'll help you,' said Sunna. 'Come on, you monster.' She grabbed him by the hand and led him back to the house. She knocked on the door.

The lady of the house answered. She stared unhappily at Sunna, and did not acknowledge Sasha at all.

227

'I am not in the mood for this, Sunna,' said Mrs Moore.

'Rose blight,' said Sunna.

'I beg your pardon?'

'On the other side of the island. There's a terrible rose blight, and it's coming this way. Your precious rose garden will be ruined if you don't have someone to take care of it.'

Mrs Moore looked Sacha up and down, her frown unmoving.

'Where did you work before?' she asked.

Sacha handed her his letter of recommendation. She scanned it and passed it to Sunna.

'Send a telegram to Lord Stanhope for verification,' Mrs Moore instructed. She pointed a finger at Sacha. 'What is your name?'

'I am Nicolae. I am Romanian.'

'You will save my roses, Nicolae, or your meat will feed my garden. Is that understood?'

Sasha nodded.

'Sunna, show him to his quarters.'

Sasha tried to smile, but he could not manage it. His failure had become a success, but he was terrified to think what Sunna might ask in exchange for her assistance. He felt he had wandered into a strange captivity as the young woman's pet, and he could only pray that Lady Rosewood might rescue him before he was forced to do anything he would regret.

On the other side of the city, Eleanora Rosewood stepped into a more conventional prison. She had decided to stop by the police station in the hope that she might speak to the girl from the previous night.

The desk sergeant listened to her plea without interest, and accepted a bribe without giving any confirmation that the girl was here, or that Eleanora could speak to her. He merely pocketed the money and stepped away from the desk, and Eleanora took a seat on a polished wooden bench and watched the shadows of the slatted fans spin slowly on the white walls.

Eleanora waited for more than an hour. The desk sergeant did not return to his post, and his replacement stepped away every time Eleanora looked his way. She was ready to give up and leave, when at last the door to the cells opened and a familiar face stepped through, his suit crumpled, his tie askew, his expression exhausted.

Brand Blackwell.

The journalist spotted Eleanora and chose to pretend he had not. Eleanora rushed to her feet to intercept him.

'Mr Blackwell. I did not have the chance to thank you for your heroic actions last night.' She thrust out her hand and he took it.

'I wrestled a girl, Lady Rosewood. There was nothing heroic about it. If you will excuse me.' He tried to push past her, but she would not allow it.

'Have you spoken to the girl? How is she? Do you have any idea why she behaved as she did?'

Blackwell looked at her as if she were the very Hun who had so heinously wounded him on the battlefield.

'It is not your concern,' he said. 'Go home, Lady Rosewood.'

'Surely it is as much my concern as it is yours,' said Eleanora. 'I have every right to inquire after the girl's condition.'

'You can ask all you like, but you're entitled to nothing.'

'What exactly is your role here, Mr Blackwell?'

'I am of the world and for it, Lady Rosewood. Now, please step aside. The girl will not see any other visitors. I've made sure of that.'

Eleanora would not give ground, but Blackwell was done with civility. He forced her aside and strode out of the police station without a backwards glance. Eleanora looked back to the desk sergeant and reached for her purse. He shook his head and pointed to the door.

Eleanora knew she was defeated. She could not reach this girl. She might yet hope to save the others.

There were eight girls in residence at the Moore School, by Sacha Valentin's reckoning, most of them aged around 16 or 17. They all wore modest and unpretentious smock dresses in pale pastel colours, tied at the waist with thick ribbon. They also wore white socks and flat black shoes, and they had long hair that some of them kept back off their faces with a second ribbon.

Throughout his morning at the school, Sacha had very little contact with the girls. His first glimpse was during their morning poetry recital. While he trimmed the sloping lawn, the girls stood at the top of it and tried to project their voices to Mr Kaiser without raising them, all while speaking in verse of urns and daffodils. Seven girls took their turn. Sunna Kristjansdottir was not among them. She would make eight in total.

Sacha next saw the girls in pairs as they progressed from the main building to the chapel. The chapel was Kaiser's domain, a music studio dominated by a grand piano. Here the girls would practise their party pieces – dance, music or song. Sacha decided to take a closer look at Kaiser by pretending to tidy the floral borders, but when he peered inside he saw nothing out of the ordinary. One girl practised her piano octaves, while another sat bored with a book that she had no interest in. She spotted Sacha, and he ducked down out of view.

Sacha piled his cuttings in a wheelbarrow and tried to think where he could go next. The only other person he had seen at the school was a young Afro-Cuban girl who performed all the domestic chores. He thought she was the most likely person to know the school's secrets, but she never seemed to have a moment to talk.

The kitchen was the one place where the two of them might have privacy, so Sacha decided to stop by there. He picked up the wheelbarrow and almost collided with Kaiser coming out of the chapel. The barrow tipped and spilled on the lawn.

'Watch where you go, you idiot ape,' said Kaiser. He smacked the barrow with his cane. 'Clean that up at once.'

Sasha swallowed his anger. He nodded and touched his forelock. Kaiser strode towards the house, and Sacha got down on his knees to throw the clippings back in the barrow.

The piano music stopped abruptly. A moment later two dainty black shoes appeared at Sacha's side. He looked up and found the girl who didn't like to read looking down on him, while the girl who played scales watched from the doorway.

'Hey,' said the first girl. 'What happened to the Irish guy?'

The girl was strawberry blonde and freckled. She looked older than the other girls, eighteen at least, and impressively long-legged and full-hipped even in her unflattering dress.

'My English bad,' said Sacha.

'You're German?' asked the girl.

'I am Romanian. I am Nicolae.'

The girl grinned and took a seat on the chapel steps. 'My patron is German. He's a baron of someplace *und* someplace.

He's going to send me to Paris to study ballet, but he wants me to be able to present myself like a lady first. Honestly, I can't tell one Slavic accent from another. They all sound so masculine and heavy. I much prefer Romance languages, don't you? I'm sorry, I talk too much. It's nice to meet you, Nicolae. I'm Adeline. This is Cora. She's new.'

The other girl smiled from the shade of the doorway. She was dark haired and moon faced, with a stubby nose and burning red cheeks. She crossed her arms and squeezed herself tight.

Sacha nodded dumbly and threw the last few cuttings in the barrow. He felt conflicted about talking to these girls. On the one hand, it was against the rules of the house, and anyway he wasn't meant to be talking. On the other, this was the best chance he'd had to get any information. He needed to make the most of this opportunity.

'Is good school, yes?' said Sacha. He picked out a trowel from the barrow and dug at the roots of something in the flower bed that he hoped was a weed.

'I guess so,' said Adeline. She kicked the air. 'It's a funny place, you know? Most of the girls come from money, like Cora here. She's mad because her brother got to go to Egypt and dig up old bones, and she had to come here and learn royal orders of precedence and which spoon is for soup. And a few of the girls don't have money, but they have good names, and that's worth something, too, if the girls can be made respectable. Some of us don't have either one, but we get ourselves a patron and we're treated just the same. Speak nice, be polite, stand up straight and watch your elbows.'

Sacha nodded, but he did not look up from the flower bed.

'Cora thinks you're handsome,' said Adeline.

Cora ran out from her cover and slapped Adeline on the arm. 'Shut up, Adeline.' She retreated just as quickly. Sacha smiled and nodded at the girls. His incomprehension was not entirely an act.

'You worry too much,' said Adeline. 'He barely understands a word we're saying.'

'We're not meant to talk to the help, and I don't want to get into trouble! What if the Kaiser comes back?'

'We'll say we're reciting Keats,' said Adeline.

None of this was helping Sasha, so he tried to steer the conversation back to the school.

'Your teachers, they are good?'

'Not Kaiser,' said Adeline. 'He's an S.O.B.' Cora gasped, but Adeline ignored her. 'I guess Mrs Moore is all right. She's plainspoken, and she looks amazing. I wish I had her skin. But she plays favourites, and I'm not one of them.'

'What is this, this "favourites"?'

'Oh, you know, there are girls who get chosen for private instruction. They usually graduate out of here in a hurry. I think they're the girls Mrs Moore found a suitor for. This place is basically a high class…' Adeline let the thought go unfinished, and looked self-consciously over her shoulder at Cora.

'I mean, that's just the world we live in,' said Adeline. 'We're daughters, and then we're wives, and then I guess we're widows. This is where they turn us into wives, and… I don't know where they turn us into widows.'

Sacha reached into the earth and tore a plant out by its roots. 'I do,' he said quietly.

'What was that?'

Sacha looked up at the girls and forced a smile, and pretended he had not said anything at all. Adeline looked at him expectantly, so he offered a question.

'There is Mr Moore?'

'There is not,' said Adeline. 'He's dead. I think he was much older than her. She never talks about him, though. I think he was a bit of a—'

'Girls! You girls!'

Kaiser limped across the lawn as fast as his leg would allow. Cora disappeared into the chapel, and Adeline jumped to her feet and ran after her.

Sacha stood with a dead weed in one hand and the trowel in the other, and wrestled with the urge to throw down both and ready his fists. This man meant to make trouble for him, but Sacha knew that the wise course was to shy from it, for Lady Rosewood's sake and for the sake of these girls. It was not a course he had ever taken before.

'You do not talk to them, do you hear?' said Kaiser. He stabbed the end of his stick against Sacha's chest. 'You are here to work, not to fraternise.'

Sacha gritted his teeth and flexed his arms. Kaiser recognised a fighting stance when he saw it, and he was not impressed. He cracked the stick against Sacha's arm.

'Do not talk to them. Do not look at me. Know your place, you dog.'

Sacha took the blow with a wince and lowered his head. This was too much. No self-respecting man should be expected to suffer such treatment. Whatever Kaiser's training, Sacha felt confident he could take him down. And if Kaiser was out of the way, wouldn't that make the school much safer? Wouldn't that be for the best?

A horn sounded. Sacha looked over his shoulder and saw a taxicab approaching up the drive. He recognised Lady Rosewood's veiled hat through the back window.

Sacha's body sagged in defeat.

'Sir,' he said. 'Very sorry, sir.'

'Get back to work,' said Kaiser.

Sacha nodded and picked up the handles of the wheelbarrow. He caught sight of Adeline peering through the chapel window. She mouthed a 'sorry' and ducked back down.

Eleanora was immediately impressed by the school, with its handsome pink-stained stucco walls under rows of buckled red terracotta tiles. She was met at the door by a beautiful dark-skinned girl in a powder-blue pinafore dress, who invited her into a round hallway that flourished with white flower mosaics and ornate woodwork in the Spanish baroque style.

Having grown up in a church, Eleanora knew when a place had God in its walls, but as an Anglican her soul thumped in rebellion at the presence of Catholicism in these stones. This finishing school for young women had once been a convent. She was sure of it.

The maid led Eleanora to a private study, where a dry earthy perfume hung in the air. It was a generous space, and the beams in the walls and ceiling suggested it had once been three separate rooms. Now it was a place for Mrs Moore to work at her snakeskin-top French mahogany desk, to study for her lessons from the tall white wood bookcases that stretched the long wall opposite the arch windows, or to meet with parents in lushly padded black velvet armchairs set around a low oval glass table.

Eleanora took a seat with a view of the beautiful gardens and the manicured lawn that sloped towards the ocean, and the maid went to fetch the lady of the house. The door was barely closed when Eleanora jumped out of her seat and crossed to the desk to look for incriminating evidence.

She found it more quickly than she expected to. An

applewood cigar box sat on top of the desk. On top of the box was a ring.

Black onyx, engraved with an angel brandishing a thunderbolt.

Edgar had owned a ring like this, and had kept it hidden. Sir Francis had worn one the last time Eleanora saw him, and Shanghai agent Arek Saxon had worn one when he died.

This ring was a mark of membership that confirmed Eleanora's fears. Mrs Moore was part of Dominion, and this school was surely part of their dastardly plans.

'What do you have there, Lady Rosewood?'

Eleanora jumped and spun around. The headmistress had entered the room without a sound.

'Oh dear,' said Mrs Moore. 'Are you getting into mischief?'

Sacha wondered how long it might take for Lady Rosewood to make trouble for herself. Now that she was on the premises, his primary role in this subterfuge switched from spy to guardian, and he would need to be alert and on hand to come to her aid if she called.

But for the moment, she was most likely taking tea, and that meant he had a chance to cool down from his encounter with Kaiser.

Sacha wheeled his barrow back to the old tobacco-drying shed that served as his personal quarters, tucked away at the far end of the grounds in a copse of trees at the foot of the plantation hills. The shed was also storage for a strange collection of glass flasks and iron clamps; scientific apparatuses that apparently had no place at a school for girls.

Sacha tipped his cuttings into the mulch pile and sat on an upturned oil can to collect his breath and wipe his brow.

With Lady Rosewood here, he decided he would need to carry his gun on his person. The weapon was a last memento of Shanghai, a woman's pistol engraved along the barrel with two sinewy dragons. Lady Rosewood had taken it from Madam Mandragora, and Sacha had used it to kill that woman's lieutenant. That was not a memory that Sacha cherished, but the weapon's size made it useful. He could hide it in a pocket of the kit bag that contained Aiden's tools.

Sacha stepped in to the shed to retrieve the gun, and found he was not alone.

Sunna Kristjansdottir waited in the shadows of the tobacco shed. She held the dragon pistol in her hand.

She gripped the pistol comfortably, as if she had held such a weapon many times before, her finger light on the trigger guard, and she turned the barrel to admire the engraved dragons.

'And what does a gardener do with this, Nicolae?' she asked. 'Is this how you chase the greenfly off the roses?'

Sacha searched his thoughts for a convincing lie.

'Rabbits,' he offered. He was proud of himself for that, but it was clear from Sunna's expression that it had not worked.

'Rabbits, indeed. Well, you can't have this here,' she said. 'It's not safe for the girls. And anyway, you won't need it. What could possibly happen to a man like you at a school for girls?'

'It is… sentimental,' said Sacha.

'Is it?' said Sunna. 'That's a long word. But it does explain why you would have a woman's gun. Mother, was it? Lover? I shall hide it somewhere safe, and you can have it back when you leave us. Don't worry, I won't tell the headmistress.'

Sunna slid the gun into the pocket of her dress and picked up two glass bottles from an orange-box table.

'Anyway, I didn't come to cause trouble,' said Sunna. 'I thought you might be thirsty. You've been working awfully hard.'

Sacha took one of the bottles. It was ice cold and oddly curved, and the liquid inside was brown and sparkling.

'Coca-Cola,' said Sunna. 'Do you like sweet things?'

'You should not be here,' said Sacha. 'I must not talk to girls.'

'Your English is not so bad as you pretend, is it?' said Sunna. 'Don't worry, you're allowed to talk to me.'

Sacha was frustrated that he had said too much. He twisted the cap off the bottle and took a swig to stop himself saying anything more. The drink was fizzy and syrupy, but cold enough to refresh on such a hot day. Sunna sat on the edge of the cot and opened her bottle and drank. Sacha stayed standing.

'The other girls are students,' said Sunna. 'I'm the chaperone.

I make sure everyone is on their best behaviour. So, you see, you and I, we're allowed to fraternise.'

Sacha nodded slowly.

He thought back to last night, and his first meeting with this girl. She had offered to take him drinking with the handsome marine; a strange temptation to a too-human world that Sacha found terrifying.

She had not seemed like a girl who knew how to behave. She had not seemed like anyone's chaperone. She seemed predatory then, and she seemed predatory now, and Sacha was not used to being anyone's prey. He did not want to fraternise with this girl. He did not want to be anywhere near her. He wanted to be a thousand miles away at sea, where none of the intimacies of the land could reach him.

'Excuse, please,' said Sacha. 'I must work.'

'Of course you must,' said Sunna. 'And I must, as well.' She stood up quickly and kissed him on the cheek. Sacha jumped back in alarm.

'You must let me know when you have time to play,' she said.

Sacha watched her run back to the house, taking his pistol with her. Sacha felt no wiser about the dangers of the Moore School, but he was confident of the dangers of Miss Sunna.

Eleanora Rosewood had a better understanding of the dangers of the Moore School. She held the evidence in the palm of her hand: the black onyx ring of a Dominion agent.

'How naughty you are, Lady Rosewood,' said Mrs Moore. She held out her empty hand, palm up.

Eleanora had never been the sort of student to get in trouble with teachers. She had never been called to the headmaster's study, and she had never been caught with something she wasn't meant to have. If she had been naughtier in school, she might have a better idea how to get out of a situation like this. She put the ring in Mrs Moore's hand.

'How embarrassing,' said Eleanora. 'I meant only to admire the craftsmanship of this fine desk, but I thought the ring so interesting that I took a closer look.'

'The secret to bad behaviour is to avoid getting caught,' said Mrs Moore. 'That's not something I teach my girls, of course, but it's something they try to teach me. You've lost your colour, Lady Rosewood. Please don't be upset. I'm only having a little fun. I quite understand your curiosity. The ring belonged to my late husband. It is the only jewellery he ever wore, so I keep it where I see it every day.'

'Your husband?'

Mrs Moore slipped the ring onto her finger; it was much too large. 'I've thought about having it refitted so I might wear it, but it's rather a gauche design.'

This admission put a different complexion on everything.

If it was Mr Moore who was a member of Dominion, it was possible that his widow was in a similar situation to Eleanora herself. She might not be an adversary at all.

'I've seen a ring of its type before,' said Eleanora. 'My husband had one in his study.'

'Oh, but of course he did,' said Mrs Moore. 'Our husbands belonged to the same fraternity. I believe that's how they met. Would you like some tea, or should we start with a tour?'

Eleanora was never normally one to turn down a cup of tea, but she was keen to leave the confines of the headmistress's study and see more of the school.

'Thank you, I think I'd like the tour,' said Eleanora.

'Very well. Follow me.'

Mrs Moore led Eleanora through to the classroom, which shared the study's view of the lawns, and across the corridor to a refectory that looked uphill towards the tobacco fields. A spiral staircase took the women up to the girls' dormitories, and another led them down to an antechamber and out across the lawns to the chapel.

Eleanora listened with one ear as Mrs Moore talked about the building's history; it had indeed once been a convent, and briefly a sanatorium. Yet as interested as Eleanora was in the school's pre-history, her thoughts always returned to the Dominion ring. Mrs Moore might be as innocent – as ignorant – as Eleanora herself had been, but that was by no means guaranteed, and the school itself remained suspect. She could not lower her guard.

'We shall end our tour in the library,' said Mrs Moore. 'The girls are excited to meet you.'

'Mrs Moore, before we go in, might I ask an indelicate question?' asked Eleanora.

Mrs Moore gripped the handle of the library door.

'You wish to talk about last night, of course,' said Mrs Moore.

'That girl. Dominique. She spoke of a reckoning. She spoke of making you pay. What did she mean?'

Mrs Moore eased her grip on the handle. She bowed her head.

'I apologise. That was a terrible scene. Dominique was a wayward girl, prone to fits of anger. She had to be removed, and the experience clearly haunts her. I can only imagine she has come to blame us for her condition, but she was always quite unwell. I will see that she gets the care and attention she deserves.'

'She has no family that can see to her?' asked Eleanora.

'She is one of the unfortunates that we took in under patronage,' said Mrs Moore. 'She is my one failure, and my great regret, and I'm sorry that she gave you such a poor first impression of our school. I'm grateful that you've allowed us the chance to correct any misconceptions. Shall we go in?'

Eleanora nodded, and Mrs Moore opened the library door.

❦

Several rooms away in the kitchen was the one girl at the Moore School more unfortunate than all the rest. Her name was Zodie Seacole, and she was the only Havana-born girl among them. While the students practised French verbs, she French-polished the cabinets.

Zodie was not at the school for her social advancement. She was there as cook and maid. She had already achieved her social plateau, and that was understood. There had only ever been one dark-skinned student at the school, before Zodie's time, but that was an Indian girl, and Zodie did not know the particulars of her unique case.

Zodie was Yoruban, a descendant of people brought to the island in chains, and there was no value on the marriage market for an African girl. The best an illiterate dark-skinned orphan could hope for was a good job and a roof above her head, and the school gave her both these things. That was why she had to stay here, no matter how it tested her.

So Zodie asked for strength every day from the statues in the store room.

All the saints and virgins from the convent were crammed together in one small space just off the kitchen, and there was room enough for Zodie to kneel and say her prayers to

Yemaya, the holy mother, who stood with her palms open, her blue robes filled with white stars, her strangely pale face raised to the sky.

Zodie clasped her hands together and whispered a petition.

'Yemaya, I am your servant and I do not ask for much. Mrs Moore works me very hard, from before the sun rises until after it sets, and I endure, because it is good to have work, and I am grateful. I see strange things that I should not see, but it is not my place to speak of them, so I keep my tongue and I am obedient.

'Even so, I must ask for your help, because I am afraid for these girls. I am afraid for myself. I see the way Mr Kaiser looks at us. It is not good. He is not kind. I ask that you keep us safe, or give me the strength to send him away. Help me, holy mother. Help these girls. Send us protection from evil men.'

Zodie crossed herself, as she had seen others do, and pushed a plate of sugar cane in front of the statue.

She put on her apron, opened the store room door, and returned to the kitchen.

She saw the knife first, and then the man holding it.

❧

Eleanora spread butter on a scone while Mrs Moore poured the tea. They were back in the headmistress's study after the tour, and Eleanora found herself perplexed by all she had seen, because all of it had seemed so normal.

The school was a finishing school after all. It taught all the classes that a finishing school was expected to teach and, based on available evidence, it produced girls with grace, intelligence and charm. The seven students were faultlessly polite and proper.

What, then, was the secret of the Moore School? What had Edgar meant in his letter when he suggested that what they taught these girls was shocking? Was Dominique truly no more than a troubled child? Was Mrs Moore only another Dominion widow? Was Mr Kaiser just a music master after all?

'You are caught up in your thoughts, Lady Rosewood,' said Mrs Moore. 'Will you tell me what you think of our girls?'

'I think them delightful,' said Eleanora. 'You have done a fine job. Yet I find myself wondering, Mrs Moore, how you came to be here in Cuba running this school. Was it something you started with your husband? Was he a teacher, as well?'

Mrs Moore smiled and shook her head.

'He was, but not of young ladies. He taught science in New York. He was a biological chemist, and I was his assistant.'

'How fascinating. Has he been gone long from this world?'

'Two years. A lifetime. The school is a project to keep me occupied, as I suppose we widows must be. Have you found an occupation of your own, Lady Rosewood?'

Mrs Moore's dark eyes fixed expectantly on Eleanora. It was not an insubstantial question. Eleanora's occupation was the downfall of Dominion, but to what extent was Mrs Moore wise to that reality?

'What do you mean, Mrs Moore?'

'To have an occupation is one of the few virtues of widowhood, Lady Rosewood,' said Mrs Moore. 'Uniquely among women, widows have both liberty and status. We have a man's name without a man's agenda. We are empowered to reinvent ourselves.'

Eleanora did not know how to respond to this. It seemed a coldly calculated view of bereavement, and too blunt for such a fresh wound.

'Have I shocked you?' asked Mrs Moore.

'I think perhaps you have,' said Eleanora. 'You make widowhood sound like a trophy.'

'You misunderstand me. I was devoted to my husband, and I would give anything to have him back. I mean only that we should make what we can of our lot. Given my husband's obsession with taxonomy, I think he would be amused to hear two women addressing each other by the names of absent men. And yet that is the world we live in: a world made for men. A woman's only hope is a man's name.

'That is what I offer my girls; the opportunity for a good name. Once they have secured it, I teach them to make something more of themselves. If we cannot be independent, we can at least be strong.'

'Is this the modern thinking?'

'It is my thinking. In the event of widowhood, should I tell these girls to abandon what they have built and shrink into the shadows? I don't think that's what you would teach them, Lady Rosewood. If you believed that widows should be retiring and quiet, you would not be here.'

There was too much code in this language, and Eleanora wished to untangle it.

'Might I ask, Mrs Moore, why it is you think I am here?'

'To do good, of course. And how glad I am to have you.'

The door opened and a girl stepped in. Eleanora had not seen her before. She was pale and Nordic, as tall as a Valkyrie and with eyes like glaciers, and she smiled like she knew all the secret jokes of the world.

'Mrs Moore, the girls are with Mr Kaiser,' she said. 'I thought perhaps I might join you for tea?'

Mrs Moore tensed her shoulders and pursed her lips. She glanced across at Eleanora and saw her watching, and she answered in a forced tone.

'Of course, Sunna. You would be most welcome. Lady Rosewood, this is our girls' chaperone, Miss Kristjansdottir.'

'Please don't let me interrupt,' said Sunna. She sat and poured herself a cup. 'What were we discussing?'

Mrs Moore looked again at Eleanora and this time maintained eye contact.

'The weather,' said Mrs Moore. 'We were saying how humid it is.'

'Is that so?'

Sunna looked pointedly at Eleanora. Eleanora chose to take her cue from her host.

'Quite so,' said Eleanora. 'I hear we are expecting quite a storm this evening.'

'Ah, *le déluge*,' said Sunna. 'Should I be worried, headmistress? Is the school quite secure?'

'Very secure, Miss Kristjansdottir. No cause for concern.'

Sunna Kristjansdottir smiled at Eleanora. Whatever joke she was smiling at now, Eleanora was quite sure it was not funny.

∽

She was hysterical. Her scream filled the air, and Sacha panicked and dropped the knife.

'No,' he said. 'I'm sorry! No, I was not... I did not...' He took a step towards the young maid and she screamed again, so he took a step backwards. 'Please, I did not mean to scare you. I was only looking...'

He could not finish the sentence. He was looking for a weapon to replace his stolen pistol, and that sentiment was not likely to ease the girl's mind. Sacha put his hands in the air and backed against the wall.

'I do not mean you any harm. Please. I am the gardener.'

The girl grabbed a copper saucepan and heaved for breath. Recognition flickered in her eyes.

'My name is Sach... my name is Nicolae,' said Sacha. 'You have seen me on the grounds, yes?'

The girl nodded.

'I was looking for you, that is all. I need your help.'

The girl narrowed her eyes. She swooped on the knife and retreated, the saucepan still gripped in her other hand.

'You do not come in here,' she said. 'This is mine. This place is mine.'

'I'm sorry. I did not mean to frighten you. I will leave, if that is what you want.'

She nodded again.

Sacha edged towards the door. Without turning his back on her, he found the handle and turned it. The girl kept both the knife and the saucepan raised, but her shoulders relaxed a little when she saw that he really meant to leave.

'Wait,' she said.

Sacha froze.

'Why did you want my help?'

'For the girls,' said Sacha. 'I was sent here for the girls.'

'Sent? Sent by who?' asked the maid.

Sacha could not give that answer.

'By... a lady,' he said.

The maid lowered her weapons.

In the late afternoon, the girls performed their party pieces for Lady Rosewood. She was at once interested to see what they had learned, and desperate to get away.

The last girl to perform was an American named Adeline Laligne, who was a very fine dancer with masterful self-control. Yet Eleanora had no time for an encore. As soon as Adeline was finished, Eleanora applauded politely and excused herself, saying that she would like to see the flowers in the gardens while the light was still favourable. Mr Kaiser offered to accompany her on her walk. She firmly declined.

Eleanora explored the gardens quite casually while still in full view of the school, and wended her way towards a secluded grotto that offered a view of the sea. She took a seat, opened her copy of Kate Chopin's *The Awakening*, and proceeded to gaze out over the silver-blue waters. It was a beautiful, tranquil spot that offered a moment of peace that she wanted to cherish.

The peace was disturbed by a squeaking sound. Eleanora looked around to see Valentin pushing a wheelbarrow full of cut grass.

'Beautiful, isn't it?' said Eleanora.

'The sea can deceive,' said Valentin. He didn't look at her.

Neither made any gesture to show that they were talking, in case they were being watched.

'Beauty has no agenda, Valentin,' said Eleanora. 'Near as I can tell, the same is true of this place. It's all poetry and piano recitals. Have you been able to discover anything untoward?'

'I do not know,' said Valentin. 'I have spoken with the maid. She says there are secrets here. Maids have been sent away because of Mr Kaiser, so she does the work of three. Miss Sunna slips away in the night on private errands, and I am sure this is true, because I have seen her with American boys. Also, there is a room that the maid cannot enter even to clean. It is the room where girls take private instruction.'

Eleanora let her excitement get the better of her and turned to look at Valentin. 'A secret room? Do you know where it is?'

Valentin looked away. 'It is in the private house, at the eastern end of the building. It is part of Mrs Moore's personal quarters.'

'Well, that wasn't on the tour. We must hope it is close to the guest room where they have me tonight.'

'My lady, you cannot stay here tonight. I have no gun, and I do not like these people. I do not know if I can protect you.'

'This is our best chance, Valentin. We shall find some ruse to lure Mrs Moore from her room, and I shall investigate. See if you can find a mouse, or a grass snake; we shall release it in the girl's dormitory.'

'It is not safe, Lady Rosewood.'

'If you don't know which snakes are poisonous...'

'That is not my meaning. It is not safe for you.'

'I'll be fine. You keep an eye on Mr Kaiser and I shall do the rest.'

'It is not Mr Kaiser that concerns me,' said Valentin. 'It is Miss Sunna.'

'A strange and striking creature, but surely not a worry?'

'She is bold.'

'She is modern, Valentin, we don't hold that against her. What else have you noticed?'

'The girls,' said Valentin. 'They whisper and speak in code. They giggle and watch me too closely. I do not like it.'

Eleanora laughed and covered her mouth. If she did not contain her laughter she would bring the whole school over.

'You should maintain a safe distance at all times,' said Eleanora. 'Young women can be relentless and terrifying, especially in packs.' She knew it was cruel to tease, but the temptation was irresistible.

'Lady Rosewood!'

Aldrich Kaiser approached across the lawns.

'Lady Rosewood, you are wasting your time with this one! Nicolae does not speak English, I'm afraid. Uneducated peasant stock. I'm not sure what you could possibly want to ask him about. Perhaps there is something I might help you with?'

'I am a keen gardener, Mr Kaiser,' Eleanora called back. 'I

want to know what grows best in this warm climate. Is that your area of expertise?'

'Not mine, but you could ask Mrs Moore. She is a gifted botanist. Away with you, Nicolae, you wretch. You are not to speak to guests. You'll be disciplined for this.'

Valentin touched his forelock and pushed his squeaking wheelbarrow off towards the tree line.

'You mustn't be harsh with him, Mr Kaiser. I addressed him, not the other way around.'

'Then perhaps you should be disciplined, Lady Rosewood?' He grinned from ear-to-ear.

Eleanora did not dignify the remark. She stood up and walked towards the school.

Mr Kaiser grabbed her by the arm. He leaned in close.

'Do not walk away, Lady Rosewood,' he whispered. 'I thought we might have a private word.' His eyes raked over her like claws, and Eleanora choked on the scent of his musk. 'This garden was designed to arouse the spirits. The perfumes, the colours, the shapes and textures: it is a feast for the senses. One finds one can get lost in it.'

'Then I wish, Mr Kaiser, that you would,' said Eleanora. She pulled herself free.

Mr Kaiser was not so easily shaken off. He followed her across the lawn and placed his hand on her shoulder. She turned around ready to slap him, but she hesitated when she saw Valentin behind him with his spade raised.

Eleanora shook her head.

Kaiser realised she was looking past him. He turned and flinched in alarm.

'Mr Kaiser, I have question,' said Valentin gravely. 'Tell me, please, where I put this?'

Kaiser paled. Eleanora hurried back to the house.

❧

Eleanora changed for dinner and stepped out into the warm evening air to find a table laid on the veranda. Her companions for the evening were Mrs Moore and Mr Kaiser, while Miss Kristjansdottir was occupied seeing the girls to bed.

Dinner comprised clam broth, sausage-stuffed beef tenderloin, and tense conversation about trivial affairs. The trio spoke of art and popular music, of Paris and New York, and of flowers.

It emerged that Mrs Moore truly was an experienced botanist. She had made her own perfumes, and she and her husband had travelled twice to the African interior on a search for rare wild flowers. On this subject Eleanora was fascinated, as it at last brought the conversation back to the late Mr Moore.

'You said that our husbands were of the same fraternity,' said Eleanora. 'I'm afraid I don't know much about it.'

'I'm afraid there is nothing much to say,' said Mrs Moore. 'Boys and their secret clubs. I'm sure whatever they got up to, we were better left in the dark.'

The maid set down a tray of rum, cheese and quince jam. She moved the plates into the centre of the table. Mrs Moore uncorked the rum and poured two glasses. She passed one to Eleanora, and kept the other for herself.

'Mr Kaiser, would you be so kind as to see if Miss Kristjansdottir is finished for the evening? She may wish to join us.'

Kaiser hesitated.

'Our guest would love to hear more from her about how the girls are faring. Miss Kristjansdottir offers a unique perspective.'

Kaiser was clearly reluctant, but it would be rude to refuse. 'I will send her directly,' he said. He stood and left.

Mrs Moore stared at Eleanora, her expression inscrutable. Eleanora took a sip of rum. Mrs Moore knocked hers back in one shot.

'I'm afraid we've run out of time for delicacy, Lady Rosewood. You must tell me what are you doing here.'

'I am here for the children, of course.'

Mrs Moore leaned closer. 'Do you understand my question?'

Eleanora was taken aback by the intensity of her tone.

'I think I do,' she said. 'My answer remains; I am here for the children. I am here for the girls.'

Mrs Moore nodded.

'I want to be sure that I understand your position, and I want you to understand mine. When my husband passed, I saw an open window that I might have fled through. Instead, I tried to master my domain, and the walls closed around me. I was foolish, and I would not see you repeat my mistakes.'

'These are riddles, Mrs Moore. If you mean to be blunt, be blunt.'

'Very well.' Mrs Moore poured another glass of rum. 'I am not the master here, and I believe that a widow should be master. Yet if one tries to fight the world, one will find it has little patience for one's efforts. You wish me to be blunt, Lady Rosewood? You should never have come here. You cannot help. I will call a car and you will leave tonight. I absolve you of your obligation to this school.'

'Are you also rescinding my invitation?'

'That is not in my power. Do you understand? Go home and make the most of your freedom, and hope it does not bring you to a precipice. I thought you and I might find some common purpose, but the lords and masters have watched us too closely, and they will not allow it.'

Mrs Moore heard the door open behind her, and she sat back and said no more.

Sunna Kristjansdottir stepped out onto the veranda. She took a long deep breath.

'Oh my, the air is electric,' she said. 'Is it the weather, or has the conversation turned to politics?'

Mrs Moore looked away, and Eleanora could not read her. If she had understood Mrs Moore's warning correctly, the headmistress was not in charge of her school. She was a prisoner here. Did that mean that Kaiser and Kristjans-dottir were her jailors, or was there another player's hand at work here? Who were the lords and masters?

'We were talking about flowers,' said Eleanora.

'Oh, flowers,' said Sunna. She took Mr Kaiser's seat at the table. 'What precious treasures. Is there anything more beautiful than wild flowers clipped and trimmed and pre-sented in the parlour?'

'I think there is,' said Mrs Moore. 'Wild flowers are more beautiful in the wild.'

'You are right, of course,' said Sunna. 'Yet we do keep our gardens just so, don't we? Everything in order, kept at its best. On which subject, Mrs Moore, I worry that our new garden-er is too much of a brute. He's admirably strong, but not at all deft. A rose would never survive his care.'

Eleanora shivered and bit her lip. Was it Sunna Krist-jansdottir that made the temperature drop, or was it the sudden wind?

'You think my roses are in danger?' asked Mrs Moore.

'I think your roses are doomed.'

At once the heavens opened. A thunderous rumble; a dramatic downpour of rain. All three women jumped to their feet.

'That puts an end to it,' said Mrs Moore. 'Lady Rose-wood, I will call for your car.'

'Nonsense, she must stay here tonight,' said Miss Krist-jansdottir. 'I insist on it. I have already lit the incense in the guest room to keep the mosquitoes at bay.'

Miss Kristjansdottir held the doors open and the women hurried inside.

Eleanora shook the rain from her shawl. She looked out at the wall of rain and wondered if she was wise to ignore Mrs Moore's warning and remain. Valentin was right; she was in very real danger here, and Sunna Kristjansdottir was not to trifled with. Yet what could Eleanora accomplish if she fled?

'I mean to stay, if that is acceptable to you, Mrs Moore,' said Eleanora.

Mrs Moore pulled the bolts across the door.

'But of course,' said Mrs Moore. 'I will see that you are well taken care of.'

She pulled the curtains closed.

∞

The rain poured, the wind roared, and the storm raged against the house. Sacha huddled in the draughty cover of his shack and looked up at the silhouette of the house and the roiling clouds in the purple velvet sky.

Almost the whole house was sleeping. The only lights

came from the kitchen. That suited Sacha's purposes. The rain would chase all mice and snakes into hiding, but Sacha had his own strategy to cause a diversion. He planned to smash the dormitory windows with a stone. The storm could take the blame for it, and Mrs Moore would surely rouse from her bed so that Eleanora could uncover the secret room.

Sacha pulled on his gloves and waded into the night. He slipped between the trees and knelt to find a suitable rock to throw.

A glimmer caught his eye. The kitchen lights were not the only lights after all. A low glow pulsed through the narrow windows of the chapel.

Sacha crept up to the window and peered inside.

Long white candles in iron stands were arranged haphazardly across the floor of the chapel. Standing among them was a slender figure with a blue cloth wrapped around their head like a bandana, covering their hair and eyes. The figure wore a constrictively fastened fencing jacket, and socks and breeches, and brandished a Mameluke, a US marine dress sword. Perhaps it was the young man that Sunna had entrapped the previous evening?

The figure was absolutely still. Breathing. The candlelight flickered against their face, painting their skin with night and flame.

Suddenly, the figure moved. He spun on one foot, slipped between the candles, sliced his blade through a candle wick and put out the fire. He turned and turned in an elegant dance, snuffing one candle and the next with the flick of his blade, without ever disturbing the candles, without once even brushing against them.

Sacha watched in rapt amazement. He had never seen such grace, such confidence.

The stranger was completely blinded by the bandana; at most, he might feel the whisper of the flames. Yet he moved without hesitation, until there was only one candle left. With a pivot and a sweep, he struck that flame, as well, and the room fell into darkness.

A flash of lightning illuminated the sky, and Sacha ducked behind the wall. Had he been spotted? No, of course not; the man was blindfolded. But perhaps Sacha had been sensed? The man moved like a cat. He might feel the world the way a cat does. He might notice every tremor, every breath, just as he felt the flicker of a flame.

Sacha slipped away from the window, afraid of discovery. He hastened past the tall dark windows of the house and around the corner into the recess of the kitchen door. Who was this man who moved with such elegance? Was it really the marine? Could it be Kaiser, the only other man in residence at the school? Or some secret lover of one of the girls, or some lover of Mrs Moore herself?

Sacha heard a scream.

The sound came from behind him; not from the main house,

and not from the chapel. The scream came from the kitchen.

Sacha tried the door. It was locked. He threw his weight against it, and it did not move. There was the sound of a scuffle, a muffled shriek. Sacha took a step back and threw his weight again. This time he put a crack around the lock. With a third hard shove, he forced the door open.

The kitchen was empty.

There were unbaked croissants on baking trays, and the oven door was open and raging heat. A dusting of flour covered the worktop and trailed across the tiled floor.

It ended at the closet door, the same one that the maid had stepped out of earlier in the day.

Sacha leaned against the closed door and heard a voice inside whisper, 'Shh shh shh. Don't struggle, there's a good girl.'

Sacha pulled open the door.

Aldrich Kaiser knelt on the floor, surrounded by all the angels and saints. The maid sat on the floor in front of him, an arm across her chest and a kitchen knife pressed to her throat. Tears ran down her cheeks.

'Turn around now, Nicolae,' said Kaiser. 'Forget you saw anything here.'

Sacha flexed his fingers in his gardening gloves.

In a house full of hidden dangers, Eleanora did not think it possible that she might fall asleep. It certainly wasn't her plan. She intended to remain vigilant through the night, ready for whatever might come her way, ready to investigate the mysteries of the school at the first opportunity. She would not let them surprise her. Not Kaiser, not Kristjansdottir, not any one of them.

Yet the bed was so soft. The house was just cool enough in the rain. The sweet, warm fragrance of the incense worked its way into her thoughts and eased her tensions, chasing away even the anxiety and fear that she cherished to keep her alive. Against all will, against all want, Eleanora sank into a deep and restful sleep.

She heard a voice as she dreamed. She heard someone whisper in her ear. It did not disturb her. It seemed familiar and right.

And then, suddenly, she was wide awake.

'Remember amaryllis, Lady Rosewood. Stay perfectly still.'

Eleanora felt warm breath on her cheek, and the pressure of two fingers against the back of her neck. Her eyes slowly adjusted to the darkness, and she saw a silhouette looming over her. The figure pulled back, and Eleanora recognised Mrs Moore, dressed in a lace camisole with her long hair loose over her shoulders.

'We could have been such friends,' said Mrs Moore.

Eleanora tried to speak, to ask what was happening, but

her lips, her tongue would not move. She remembered the steak knife she had secreted under the pillow and tried to reach for it, but her arms would not move either. No part of her body would respond. She could breathe, she could blink, but her body did nothing she willed it to do. She was a prisoner bound by invisible chains.

Mrs Moore looked Eleanora over. She ran a hand along Eleanora's body, from shoulder to breast to hip.

'You are a better woman than me,' she said.

Eleanora felt a tear welling in her eye. She had that, at least. She could still weep.

'You stayed for the girls,' said Mrs Moore. 'You will die for these girls. How I admire you for that. I have weighed my soul against theirs so many times, and always found in my favour. There was only one way out for me, you see. Or you'll see soon enough, I suppose.'

Mrs Moore stood and went to the window. She drew back the curtains, and a rattle of lightning etched white lines against her tall, strong body. She opened the windows and let the wind roar in. It carried with it a whirling flurry of rain. Eleanora felt the water dapple her arms and soak the bedsheets.

'You have to understand, I did not want you dead,' said Mrs Moore. 'Quite the opposite. I prayed for you.'

She turned back to Eleanora, her skin jewelled with rain drops; her hair wild from the wind.

'I never pray any more. Perhaps I am being punished for my insolence? But you see, I thought it was wonderful, what you did in Shanghai. I hate to see a woman scorned, but I love to see how scorn transforms her.

'My prayer was that you would come here next. Burn this place to the ground. Wouldn't that be something? You would break me out of my prison, and I would give you what you need to take them all down, once and for all.'

Mrs Moore sat on the bed and leaned forward. She put her hand to Eleanora's cheek, and the rain water dripped onto Eleanora's face.

'But they watch me, you see. They always watch. If you had come some other time, we might have made it work. But not when one of the five is here. That is what cursed us both. I am cursed to live, and you are cursed to die.'

The rain fell so fast, so heavy. Eleanora was soaked to the skin, and she could not even shiver. Mrs Moore wiped the wet hair back from her face.

'Think what we could have achieved, you and I.'

She slid back and sat upright, and took Eleanora's hand. She pressed an object into it and closed her fingers around it. She held Eleanora's hand up so that she might see.

It was a straight razor.

'Remember amaryllis, Lady Rosewood,' said Mrs Moore. 'When I say those words again, you will take this razor and go to the mirror. You will cut open your wrists along the vein, and watch as the life floods out of you. Speak, if you understand me.'

Eleanora could manage only two words.

'Do not—'

Mrs Moore put a finger to her lips. 'That is enough.' She stood and went to the door. 'I will find you in the morning. The papers will say you despaired at the loss of your husband; that you could not stand to live in such a beautiful world without him. There is poetry in it. Everyone will understand.'

She opened the door and stepped into the dark corridor.

'Remember amaryllis, Lady Rosewood.'

Mrs Moore was gone.

Eleanora tried to will herself to stay, to remain in bed, to go back to sleep and make a nightmare of this memory. Yet where before she could not will herself to move, now she could not will herself to stay.

Eleanora rose from the bed, her hand tight around the handle of the razor, and walked to the mirror. She stood alone with her treacherous reflection, raised her bare arm, and held the straight razor against her skin.

She wanted to scream at herself to stop, as if the person doing this terrible thing was someone else entirely, but she lacked even the self-control to speak.

She was a puppet, robbed of all volition. Any resolve she could muster was not enough to steer her through the maze of her mind and back to herself.

The square tip of the blade pricked her arm and a perfect droplet of blood formed on her skin.

She could not even scream at this.

⁓

Kaiser pressed the knife to the maid's throat, and Zodie closed her eyes and whispered a prayer. Not one of the worthy saints that cluttered the small store room would intercede on the girl's behalf. Only Sacha could help her.

'Turn around, you dull-witted oaf,' said Kaiser. 'I will cut her. I will ruin her pretty face if you do not leave and forget what you saw.'

'Cut her, and I will kill you,' said Sacha. He flexed his fingers in his thick leather gardening gloves. 'Hurt her, and I will kill you. Release her now, and perhaps I will not kill you. Do we understand each other?'

Kaiser snarled out a laugh.

'How old are you, Romanian? Were you old enough to serve? Were you at Focsani when your people surrendered? Turn on your heel, you dog. It is what your people do.'

'I was not at Focsani,' said Sacha. 'I was at Lutsk, under General Brusilov, where we slaughtered your men and broke your advance.'

Kaiser narrowed his eyes and gritted his teeth. He tightened his grip on the girl and pointed the tip of his knife at

Sacha. 'You lie. The Romanians played no part at Lutsk.'

'No,' said Sacha. 'They did not.'

Zodie bit down on Kaiser's wrist and he screamed. He closed his other hand over her throat and tried to choke her. Sacha lunged and grabbed for the knife, and Kaiser flicked the blade at him. Sacha closed his fingers over the blade and slammed his other fist into Kaiser's face. He felt the edge of the blade press through the leather of his glove. He punched again. He felt blood trickle along his palm. He punched, and he punched again.

At last, Kaiser let go of the knife and slumped against a statue of the Virgin Mary. Three more statues shook from their shelves and toppled on top of him.

Kaiser did not move again. Sacha grabbed the maid's hand, pulled her free of his clutches, and dragged her out of the room.

'You are bleeding,' said Zodie.

Sacha slapped the knife down on the butcher's block in the kitchen. Blood ran thick down his wrist. Sacha peeled off the glove and inspected the injury. There was a deep cut along his index finger and shallower cuts across his other fingers.

'It is nothing,' said Sacha. 'I will be fine.' He grabbed a white kitchen towel from an open drawer and wrapped it around his hand. 'You must fetch Mrs Moore. Tell her what has happened. I will take Kaiser outside and tie him up.'

Zodie wiped tears from her eyes.

'Do you think it matters what I tell Mrs Moore?' she said. 'She will send me away, that is all. You should not have come. I should not have prayed for you.'

Sacha did not understand her.

'He would have hurt you.'

Zodie nodded. 'Yes. And I would have kept my job.'

The girl's dress was torn, so Sacha pulled off his dirty gardening shirt and handed it to her.

'The lady will know what to do,' said Sacha. 'The lady will—'

Kaiser surged out of the store room with a furious cry and struck Sacha in the temple with his walking cane. The blow took Sacha by surprise and hit him hard; he spun around and bounced off the worktable and onto the floor.

Sacha put a hand to his head and tried to force his senses back together. His skull was ringing, and three Aldrich Kaisers loomed over him, each of them raising their cane like a club. Sacha rolled onto his left side and under the worktable. He heard the crack of the cane on the tiles.

Sacha closed his eyes for just a second. He thought he was going to pass out. Zodie screamed and he lifted his head in time to see her thud against the wall and crumple as the knife clattered from her hand to the floor.

Sacha emerged from under the table and went for the knife, only to receive a kick to the chin. He landed on his back again.

There were only two Aldrich Kaiser's hovering over him now, but they both had the knife.

'You are not as dumb as you play, are you, Nicolae?' said Kaiser.

Sacha searched the tiles around him for a weapon, something to defend himself with. His hand landed on a croissant. He slid along the tiles on his elbows until he found himself backed against the wall.

Kaiser smiled at him. Both Kaisers.

'First I will cut out your heart,' said Kaiser. 'Then I will cut your lying tongue from your head.'

Kaiser lunged with the knife. Sacha swung a baking tray over his chest and gripped it there with both hands. The knife cut through just far enough for the point to prick his skin, but could drive no further. Kaiser pushed down. Sacha pushed back.

'Was it worth it?' asked Kaiser. He knelt on Sacha's legs and put both hands on the blade. Sacha's arms shook as he tried to stop the knife slipping further. 'Was it worth your life, the virtue of this ignorant little—'

A gush of blood exploded over Sacha. He looked up into Kaiser's wide-eyed, open-mouthed face as blood flooded down his chest. There was a cleaver buried in his neck.

The knife slipped further, and Sacha used all the strength he could muster to roll Kaiser's dead weight off. He spat out the other man's blood and tried to catch his breath.

There was only one Kaiser now, dead beside him in a rapidly spreading pool.

Zodie stood over them both, shaking and crying. She wiped her tears from her face and spread the dead man's blood over her cheek.

❦

How amazing, thought Eleanora, that even pain was not enough to stir her from her trance. Mrs Moore's words had snaked deep into her brain and taken root. Eleanora would kill herself because she had been willed to do so. Pain would not stop her. Blood would not stop her. Nothing would.

A flash of light flooded the sky.

Eleanora shrieked, but the sound of her cry was drowned by the sky-shaking echo of the thunder. The air tasted like metal. A plume of flame shot up from the garden.

It took Eleanora a moment to realise that she had stopped. The straight razor was still against her arm, and the pain seemed greater now, but she was no longer cutting herself.

With a fearful breath, Eleanora willed herself to draw the blade away.

Her body responded, and she sobbed with relief. She threw the razor to the floor and sat, sank, fell onto the bed and tried all at once to stem the flow of blood and cover her mouth and wipe her tears.

She was alive.

Through the window, on the edge of the garden, she saw a lonely tree blazing with fire no more than a hundred feet away. A lightning strike. Somehow that had snapped her out of the spell.

Eleanora grabbed the towelling cloth that hung on the back of the bedroom door and used the belt to wrap her wound. She slung the robe over her nightdress, slipped on her shoes, and grabbed the knife from under her pillow.

Faced with the choice of walking out into a storm or spending another moment in this house, Eleanora chose the storm.

~~~

The fire consumed the thick-bellied banyan tree. The bright flames seemed untroubled by the rain, empowered by the wind. The tree had been a stately figure against the horizon; now it died a stately death, a beautiful bonfire in the storm.

Sacha watched in awe as the wind rushed his bones and the rain pummelled his face. The sky crackled and threatened, and the devils danced on the black twisted trunk of the ancient tree. The spectacle revived Sacha's senses.

'Nicolae! The fire! Do something! Put out the fire!'

Mrs Moore stood on her balcony, soaked to the skin in her camisole and a thin robe, shivering, lit up by the glow of the light from her room. Sacha scanned the house to see if any other lights were on, but it was only hers. Lady Rosewood's room was dark.

Sacha turned back to the fire. He could not let Mrs Moore see the glossy blood stains that soaked the front of his undershirt.

'We can do nothing,' said Sacha.

'We must save it!' Mrs Moore's anguish was extreme, as if she could not believe that nature might reclaim her garden with such savagery and cruelty. This one loss seemed to devastate her.

Sacha shook his head. 'It is dead,' he said.

'Oh, this ugly world,' said Mrs Moore. 'This cursed, ugly world.'

He heard her slam shut her balcony doors.

The fire was too far from the house and from the other trees to be any danger. It would burn itself out in the rain. Sacha hugged himself for warmth and returned to the kitchen.

Zodie jumped at his return, but breathed again when she saw it was him. She knelt in the middle of the floor with a bucket and a cloth. There was still blood everywhere.

'There is a place where I can bury him,' said Sacha. 'I will do it tonight, when the storm is passed. It will be a muddy grave, but it will serve.'

'We should give him to the sea,' said Zodie.

'The waters would bring him back. Give me everything that will burn, and I will make a fire in the morning.' Sacha scooped up blood-splattered dough from the table. 'What will you feed the girls for breakfast?'

Zodie laughed. It was a bitter sound.

'I have killed a man,' she said.

'To save us both.'

'And now I must think what to feed the girls for breakfast.'

'Everything must be as normal when the sun rises. I will speak to my lady and she will take you somewhere safe. You understand, Zodie?'

Zodie nodded.

'There is dough for bread. I will make fresh rolls. You must see to your hand, Nicolae.'

Sacha saw she had laid out cotton bandages and a bottle of spirit alcohol. He washed his cuts over the sink and wrapped bandages around his fingers. With this done, he joined Zodie on the floor and pulled a cloth from the bucket.

They scrubbed together in silence for more than half an hour, until the floors and walls and surfaces were as clean as they could be, and every trace of Kaiser was gone. When Sacha was sure he had done all he could to help, he went out to see if the storm had passed.

It was still raining, but the winds had eased. The banyan tree smoked and its guts crackled, but the worst of the fire was over.

There was no life in the night. The house was quiet. The chapel was dark. Mrs Moore was not at her balcony.

Sacha picked up a spade from in front of the tobacco shed. He hesitated for a moment, thinking he heard a noise. Nothing. Perhaps a bird.

There was a patch of turned earth by the grotto, out of sight of the house and the road. This would be Aldrich Kaiser's grave.

Sacha dug for three hours in the darkness, fighting against mud, wind and rain to make a hole deep enough to hide the man.

He returned to the kitchen and found it exactly as it should be, with two trays of unbaked rolls laid out under cloths. Zodie was gone, and Sacha hoped she had salvaged some hours of sleep.

A potato sack by the door contained Zodie's blood-stained clothes and the shirt that Sacha had given her, as well as all the rags they had used to clean. Sacha realised that his own clothes were still bloody, but now caked with mud, as well. He would need to find something of Aiden's to change into, but not until he was finished with his work.

Sacha opened the store room. A long, bundled shape lay out among the saints in a blanket that blossomed with a streak of brownish-red.

Sacha hauled the body onto his shoulder and carried it out to the grave. He lay Kaiser down and recited the Magnificat in French.

The sky was calm and tinted with the purple of the dawn by the time he finished. He thought the ground looked as it had the day before. It would have to be enough.

Sacha returned to the kitchen to retrieve the potato sack. The room now smelled of fresh bread. Sacha hauled the sack behind the tobacco shed, to an ashen patch of ground where a hundred bonfires had been lit in the past. He knew it would be wise to start the fire before the house stirred, so he needed to go back to the shed to change.

The shed smelled of tar. Sacha wiped his eyes and stared sadly at the bed that he would not get to sleep in this night.

There was someone in it.

Lady Rosewood lay curled up under the blankets, fast asleep, her knife resting inches from her hand. The last embers of a fire crackled in the small brazier in the middle of the room

Sacha grabbed a work shirt and a pair of dungarees from the trunk beside the bed and left the lady to her rest.

∽

Every morning, Zodie brought Mrs Moore her coffee on a tray. Every morning, she cut a fresh flower and set it in a tiny crystal vase beside a steaming French press pot, a bowl of Demerara sugar, and a gilded demitasse cup.

This morning, the tray rattled with each step, and it was a rattle that revealed Zodie's fear. It was a rattle that revealed her guilt. It was a rattle that said she was a murderer, and that rattle would be her confession, and she would lose her place at the school and end her days in jail. All because she dared to pray. All because she did not accept her lot.

Zodie set the tray down on the small table in front of Mrs Moore's door and knocked. Only then did she notice that the door to the guest bedroom was open.

She heard laughter.

Zodie looked into the guest bedroom.

Mrs Moore sat on the bed among damp tangled bed-sheets with a straight razor in her hand. There were tears in her eyes, but she was smiling. She was laughing.

'Mrs Moore? Ma'am?'

Mrs Moore looked up, surprised.

'Zodie. Oh. Good morning.' The headmistress did not look her normal self. She looked wild.

'Ma'am, is everything all right?'

Mrs Moore folded the straight razor shut and set it down on the crumpled bed sheets. She wiped tears from her eyes and swept her hair back from her face.

'Everything is just as it must be, my dear,' she said. 'We are all in the hands of the gods, don't you find?'

Zodie swallowed her nerves and replied very quietly, 'Yes, ma'am.'

'Go fetch Miss Kristjansdottir, would you please?' said Mrs Moore. 'Tell her our guest has departed. No, let us be clearer than that. Tell her our guest has disappeared.'

'The... the lady?' asked Zodie.

'That's right,' said Mrs Moore. 'The miraculous lady.'

Zodie nodded. The lady was gone. The lady who would take Zodie somewhere safe.

There was no salvation for sinners, and Zodie Seacole would end her days in jail.

❧

Eleanora woke in a sweat. Her fingers closed over the handle of her blade and she sat up.

A wooden shed. Draughty, dirty, an empire of spider-webs. Garden tools. Crates. Dusty glass beakers. The air tinged with smoke.

She remembered where she was. She remembered why. She covered her mouth with her hand and tried to steady her heart.

The memories made Eleanora shudder.

To have her will turned against her, to have her sense of self so violated, was devastating. To think that Mrs Moore held that power was terrifying.

Eleanora inspected the self-inflicted cut on her arm and thought it looked like nothing now. It would heal without a scar. The wound to her soul was deeper. She now understood Dominique's madness; she understood how an experience like this could break a person's mind.

Paternoster. Amaryllis. These were words that Mrs

Moore used to control her victims. Eleanora was now an alumna of that unhappy company.

A pristine white dress hung from a nail on a rafter. Eleanora pulled off the blankets, removed her coat, and put on the dress. It was loose and shapeless. She put on her boots and her coat, slipped the knife into her sleeve, and peered out through a crack in the door.

It was a fresh, warm day, and the air was clear. The sun was low on the horizon; the world not fully awake. Eleanora dared to venture a little way out.

Valentin stood on the ridge of the lawn, staring at the bare twisted tree stump of the old banyan tree. The strike of lightning that had killed it had also given Eleanora her life.

Eleanora whistled something she hoped sounded like birdsong. Valentin looked up. He saw Eleanora and very gently, very slowly, shook his head. Eleanora retreated inside the shed.

Valentin joined her a moment later. He wiped sweat from his brow and smeared his face with charcoal. His eyes were bright red against the grey of the ash.

'Lady Rosewood.'

'Valentin. I am sorry for stealing your bed. I meant to wait for you here, but I could not keep my eyes open. I hope you were able to find a place to sleep.'

'I have not had need, milady. There was an incident. Mr Kaiser is dead.'

'Oh, good heavens. Did you…?'

'The maid, ma'am. Zodie Seacole. He meant to violate her and to kill me. She did what was necessary, and I have buried him in the garden. Mrs Moore does not know. I told the maid you would help her to escape.'

Eleanora took a breath and tried to think this through. The loss of Mr Kaiser did not seem a tragedy, but it would cause consternation, as would her own disappearance. The maid deserved protection just as much as the other girls.

'Of course. We will help her, of course. Tell Miss Seacole we will do everything in our power. Oh dear, but this puts a pallor on things. My own night was... also eventful. Mrs Moore hypnotised me as I slept, and she meant for me to take my own life. The storm stirred me from the trance and I retreated here.'

'Hypnotised? I do not understand.'

'She seized control of my mind, Valentin. Like Franz Mesmer. I suspect she uses some sort of narcotic, and I am sure she uses the same power on her students. To what end I cannot imagine. Have you seen Mrs Moore this morning?'

Valentin shook his head. 'I have heard her arguing with Miss Kristjansdottir. I am sure they must be looking for you.'

'Then we must leave at once. We will fetch reinforcements and come back for Miss Seacole and the girls. I feel we now know enough about the school to close it down.'

'Ma'am. I promised Miss Seacole that I would—'

'Nicolae!'

The voice was Sunna Kristjansdottir's. Valentin put a finger to his lips. He stepped out of the shed and closed the door.

Eleanora pressed against the wall and stood very still. Through a crack between the boards she saw Sunna approach with her hands folded behind her back, her face drawn into a stern frown.

'Nicolae. Good morning.'

Valentin bowed his head. 'Miss Kristjansdottir.'

'How was your night?'

'Very poor, miss. The storm.'

Sunna allowed a smile at that. 'Were you afraid?' she asked.

'What is you want, miss?'

Sunna stretched out her long slender arms and breathed a sigh. The morning sun glowed against her pale skin.

'I slept beautifully,' she said. 'But it seems I missed the fun. We have lost our guest, Lady Rosewood, and our music master, as well. Have you seen either one of them this morning?'

Eleanora realised, a little too late, that there was an easy lie to tell here. She wished she could transmit the thought somehow from her mind to Valentin's.

Valentin shook his head. 'I have not seen,' he said.

'You did not hear strange noises in the night? I suppose not, if you were cowering from the storm. Well, if you do... oh, Nicolae, what have you done to yourself?'

Sunna reached for Valentin's bandaged hand and grabbed it before he could pull it away.

'Did you cut yourself?'

Valentin nodded. 'Glass,' he said.

'Oh, Nicolae. You must be careful.' She held his hand between hers and smiled up at his face. 'What a beast,' she said. 'But that reminds me. Mrs Moore says you are to pull up the tree stump. She says it is a blight and an insult and she will not tolerate the sight of it.'

Sunna let Valentin go, and turned back for the house.

'Of course, I think it's rather beautiful,' said Sunna with a backward glance. 'We can't all be flowers, can we Nicolae?'

She skipped away.

Eleanora took a breath as Valentin came back inside.

'You must go,' said Valentin. 'Follow the woods to the plantation. Go to the city for help.'

'Valentin, they know that I oppose them. They may know about you, as well.'

'They think I am Nicolae.'

'Or they think they can use you to find me. Fetch the maid; the three of us shall leave together.'

Valentin frowned. 'And the girls?'

Eleanora's heart sank. She could not leave the girls unprotected. She hoped that her own impossible disappearance might be attributed to Kaiser, but if Valentin and the maid also disappeared, Mrs Moore would know her school was under siege. What might she do then to these girls? How might her control of them manifest itself? Eleanora was so determined to get away from this place that she had not thought clearly of the consequences to others.

'All right,' said Eleanora. 'You stay and keep watch. I will find Temperance and her husband and... oh, the senator! I will seek out Harlan Hapley. I will bring back an army if I must, as soon as I am able. If I am not back within a couple of hours—'

'You will be back,' said Valentin. 'But you must be careful. We do not know how many agents Dominion has here. I saw a man last night, in the chapel. He had a sword.'

Eleanora shivered. 'There are too many devils,' she said. 'We must both be careful.'

Valentin stepped out and checked the way was clear. He held the door open, and Eleanora slipped around the back of the shed towards the trees.

She stopped and looked back at the terrible school. Valentin stood alone by the bonfire. The flames flickered behind him.

'I am abandoning you,' said Eleanora.

Valentin did not acknowledge the remark.

'I am, Valentin, and this is not your fight. You need not be here.'

Valentin shrugged.

'It is good to have something to fight for,' he said.

Eleanora nodded. She turned and fled into the trees. When she looked back again, Valentin was gone.

These walls were soaked with murder and sin. These walls were smeared by the filth of innocence extinguished. These walls were lost to god and all her mercies.

Within these walls, Zodie Seacole performed her duties just as she always did. She polished away every hand print from the bannister, wiped every scuff from the skirting board, erased every mark from the cabinet glass.

Yet all the chores would end today. Zodie was sure of it. She would either escape, as the gardener had promised, or she would be caught for her crime. Zodie had prayed for protection, and her prayer had been answered in blood. There was always a price for these things. Zodie hoped for rescue, but she did not believe it would come.

At mid-morning, a telegram arrived for Mrs Moore. It weighed heavy in Zodie's hand as she stared at words she could not read. A telegram on a morning such as this could only be a bad omen.

Zodie brought the telegram to the classroom, where the girls took letter-writing classes. She stayed silent at the back of the room while Mrs Moore stood in front of her desk and delivered her lecture.

'You must imagine you are writing to a gentleman,' said Mrs Moore. 'You must be oblique and tantalising. Write about yourself, but mention yourself only sparingly.'

Mrs Moore signalled for Zodie to cross the room.

One of the girls put up her hand.

'Mrs Moore, I don't think I understand.'

Mrs Moore took the telegram but did not read it. 'Which part, Cora?' she asked.

'Any of it, ma'am,' said Cora. 'What am I writing to him for?'

'To fascinate him, Cora. To place the best thought of yourself in his head.'

Mrs Moore read the telegram. She pursed her lips and creased her brow. Zodie bobbed a curtsy, a reminder that she was still there, and Mrs Moore held up a finger to assure her that she had not been forgotten.

Cora's hand was back in the air.

'Mrs Moore, I don't know how.'

Mrs Moore did not look up from the telegram. The printed words absorbed her.

'Write about what you know,' said Mrs Moore. 'Write about what he does not.'

'But I don't know what I know,' said Cora. 'And he isn't real, so I don't know what he doesn't.'

Mrs Moore looked up and out of the window. Zodie thought she was looking at the gardener, who was stripped to the waist, sweating, hacking away at the banyan tree with an axe. But Mrs Moore's attention was on the vase of flowers in the window. Some sort of sweet pea, with a lemon-shaped bud jutting out from between butterfly wings. She walked over and pulled out a stem.

'You are a garden, Cora,' said Mrs Moore. 'All men are ignorant in the same way. What they do not know is women. You are a garden of mysteries. You must not surrender them easily.' She inhaled the flower's perfume.

'Reveal yourself in inches. Tease him and draw him in. Touch lightly in delicate places and stimulate his interest with the merest breath. Do not be obvious or brash. Do not give yourself away.'

Mrs Moore put the flower in Cora's hand.

'That is how you write to a gentleman. Tell him about your garden, and tell him he will only discover its secrets if he is kind.'

Zodie felt a flush come to her cheeks.

All of the girls had stopped writing. Almost every one of them looked as confused as Cora. One of them, the baron's girl, kept her head bowed so as not to show the redness of her cheeks.

Cora stared at the flower. She looked as though she had another question, but it had not quite formed.

Mrs Moore gave the telegram back to Zodie.

'Take this to Miss Kristjansdottir,' she told Zodie. 'You are both to meet me in my personal quarters at the turn of the hour.'

Zodie curtsied. As she left the room, her stomach tightened. She felt certain now that this telegram revealed her fate.

❦

Sacha hacked at the banyan tree and forced all thought and fear from his mind. He could not worry about Lady Rosewood. He could not worry about Aldrich Kaiser. He could not worry about the agent with the sword, or the girls, or Zodie Seacole. There was nothing he could do about any of them. He could do this, and only this, and be vigilant and invisible, until Lady Rosewood returned.

He had chopped away as much of the trunk as he could, and he needed next to dig a trench so he could cut through the roots. He needed his spade.

Sacha returned to the tobacco shed and saw that the spade was not there. The nail it usually hung on was bare.

He remembered in a flash where he had used it last. He remembered where he had left it.

Sacha bolted from the shed, across the lawn and between the flower beds.

Sunna stood by the grotto with the spade in her hands. She used it to draw lines in the earth of Kaiser's grave.

Sunna looked up at Sacha with a smile.

'What have you buried here, Nicolae?'

Sacha snatched the spade from her. 'I am turning earth,' he said.

'Is that so?' Sunna kicked the ground with her black shoe. Sacha saw that she had drawn a heart on the grave. 'Aiden planted a fresh bed of seedlings here. They seem to all be gone now.'

Sacha scowled at his own stupidity. Of course this plot was here for a reason.

'I did not know,' he said.

'You'll have to plant something new,' said Sunna. She brushed dirt off her fingertips. 'Plant a black cypress to replace the old banyan.' She drew closer to Sacha and looked him in the eyes. 'I thought you might have buried Aiden here.'

Sacha's skin burned

'Aiden is gone to Mexico.'

'You said. But I have a sordid mind. I always think only of two things.' She ran a finger along the shaft of the spade. 'One of them is death.'

'Miss Kristjansdottir, I must work.'

'Shhh. No-one can see us back here.'

Sunna gripped the spade and rose on tip-toe. She kissed Sacha on the lips.

Sacha pulled away.

'Miss Kristjansdottir!'

'Will you stop me, Caliban?'

'I do not want to use force,' said Sacha.

Sunna chewed on her lip and tipped the corner of her mouth.

'I think you do,' she said. 'You have a dark light around you. You are all sadness and rage. I see these things, you know, but I see them clearest when a thing is dying, and there is life left in you. You should live it.' She slipped her arm over his shoulder and kissed him again. Her other hand grabbed the hem of his rolled-down dungarees.

Sacha pushed the spade against her and knocked her off her feet. She landed on the bare earth.

Sunna laughed and wiped her mouth.

'I think you do not care for me, Nicolae, and I suspect that I understand why. Do you know that I have a twin brother? He is my very image. Perhaps if you imagine I am him…?' She stretched out and squeezed the earth between her fingers. 'Have you ever made love on a grave, Nicolae? But of course, your first time—'

'It is not—' Sacha protested.

'Oh, hush. We have company.'

Sacha looked around and saw Zodie approach with a telegram in her hand.

Sunna held out her hand to Sacha. Sacha did not want to touch her again, but she refused to pick herself up, so he took her hand and pulled her off the ground. She fell against him and whispered in his ear.

'The whole world is a charnel house. We always make love on corpses.'

She kissed him on the cheek and slipped off to meet Zodie.

Sacha shivered and looked out to sea. How he missed the frozen comforts of the waves. It kept him safe from the warm horrors of the body.

❧

Eleanora Rosewood stared out at the same still ocean from the poolside café at the San Cristobal hotel while her tea turned cold in front of her. According to the reception desk, Temperance Vandevere was spending the day touring churches in Camagüey, and could not be reached. Neither the American nor British ambassadors could make an appointment for Eleanora until after lunch, and the local police were unresponsive to her inquiries. She considered Brand Blackwell, but after their encounter the previous day, she felt certain he was not an ally.

That left Senator Harlan Hapley as her best hope for aid. He was also a guest at this hotel, but he was on his way back from the naval base at Guantanamo. The hotel promised to page her as soon as he was back. Eleanora was unsure what else she might do, and she was anxious to only return to the school with a cavalry at her back.

So, she waited in the shade of a parasol, and watched the sea and the strangers on the promenade, and her fingers idled against the bandage on her wrist. Every few minutes she would thoughtlessly press against the wound, as if the experience of that faded pain was all that kept her in herself.

Hypnosis. That was within Mrs Moore's power. Or something worse than hypnosis; something worse than the stage magic she had read about in magazines and cheap novels. Mrs Moore had a way to make people betray themselves. To kill themselves.

Yet what use was that power over a group of schoolgirls? Young women driven to suicide were a danger only to themselves. There had to be more to it than that. She had to understand. She had to speak to...

Dominique.

It was her. She walked up the steps from the promenade, her hair hidden under a scarf, her pace quick and her movements nervous. How was she out of prison, and what was she doing here, at the scene of her crime?

Eleanora rose to her feet and hurried around the pool to intercept her. She hesitated. The girl had meant to kill her two nights ago. What if she was armed again?

Dominique caught sight of Eleanora and froze.

'Dominique. We must talk.'

The girl regarded Eleanora with undisguised terror.

'You! Did you lure me here? Did you trick me?'

'Dominique, please, I want to help you!'

'Help me?' The terror turned to rage, a red fire rising in her eyes. 'You did this to me! You and your husband put me in that school! You turned me into this!'

The girl charged at Eleanora, and Eleanora was so surprised that she did not know how to respond. All at once Dominque had her hands at Eleanora's throat, and the two women tumbled backwards and landed with a splash in the pool.

Eleanora gasped too late for air and swallowed a mouthful of water. Bubbles streamed from Dominique's mouth and nose. Eleanora tried to prise her off, but it was no use. The girl was powered by her fury. Eleanora remembered her code word, paternoster, the word that Mrs Moore had used to calm the girl, but she could not speak it now.

Eleanora kicked and struggled, but the girl was determined. She held her down and choked the last air from her body, and the darkness crept in.

We pay a price for answered prayers.

Zodie Seacole stared at her reflection, mirrored back at her into infinity, and wondered what form that price would take.

In amongst all the images of herself, she saw the shadow of Mrs Moore and the phantom of Miss Kristjansdottir to her left and right.

The room was a perfect octagon, each of its eight walls a full-length mirror. Four iron stands placed around the room held bowls of burning incense, and the smoke was earthy and sweet. In the middle of the room was a padded black velvet chair.

This was Mrs Moore's private study. This was the room that Zodie was never allowed to enter. She wished she was not here now.

'Sit down, Zodie,' said Mrs Moore.

Zodie hesitated. She forced herself to resist the instruction.

'It will make me happy if you sit,' said Mrs Moore. 'You want to make me happy, don't you?'

Zodie nodded, because it was true. Mrs Moore's voice was soft and pleasant. It seemed like the voice of a friend. The longer Zodie stood in this room and breathed this smoke, the calmer and happier she felt, and the more she wanted to please Mrs Moore.

'Sit down,' said Mrs Moore again.

Zodie nodded. She sat down.

Sunna Kristjansdottir slipped behind the chair, and Zodie watched the girl's reflection. She opened a hidden panel in one of the walls and picked out a tall bottle of green glass. It was shaped like a teardrop, with a stopper that looked like a white orchid.

'What is that?' asked Zodie.

Sunna handed the decanter to Mrs Moore. She tipped the bottle on its side, and the thick dark liquid slid around. Mrs Moore handed the bottle back to Sunna, but kept the stopper. She held it over the first incense burner and let a drop of liquid fall.

'It is a distillation of a rare flower that my husband and I found in Africa,' said Mrs Moore. 'We call it Mother of Lies.'

Sunna frowned at Zodie with obvious scepticism.

'Are you sure about her?' she asked. 'She has had no conditioning. The other girls—'

'The other girls may spend years in peaceful bliss before we call on them,' said Mrs Moore. She continued around the room, placing a drop of dark liquid in each of the burners.

'We are rushing this. We have a girl for Senator Hapley. Cora Baxter is his goddaughter. She can get to him at any—'

'You saw the telegram, Kristjansdottir. If Lady Rosewood gets to the senator, we are finished. We must do this now, and the maid is the only girl who suits the senator's... particular tastes.'

Zodie heard the words, and she did not fully understand their meaning, but she knew that she should be afraid. She thought that she should leave, but that thought did not reach her limbs.

'What can you accomplish in one session?' asked Sunna.

'If you understood my methods, Kristjansdottir, would your masters have need of me?' asked Mrs Moore. 'I cannot make a masterpiece, but I can do as much as is asked for.' She handed the stopper back to Sunna.

Mrs Moore crouched down beside the chair, and Zodie felt breath on her cheek.

'Your command word is blackjack,' whispered Mrs Moore.

Sunna scoffed.

'Blackjack? Why give her a command word at all, if the girl is disposable?'

Zodie caught Mrs Moore's reflection as she glared at Sunna.

'Because that is the way it is done,' she said.

Sunna sighed and crossed her arms.

Mrs Moore returned to Zodie's ear.

'Remember blackjack,' she said again. 'When you hear that word, you will fall into a trance. When you hear that word, you will do as you are told. Do you understand?'

Zodie nodded.

'Very good. I have a very special job for you, Zodie. There is an enemy of Dominion on this island who must be disposed of. A voice of progress who must be silenced. Do you hear my words, Zodie Seacole?'

Zodie wished she did not, because the weight of them was apparent to her now. Mrs Moore was about to ask her to do something terrible, and she had no power to refuse. This was her punishment for taking a life: the worst punishment imaginable. She would have to take another.

'Blackjack,' said Mrs Moore. Her voice seemed closer now – not at Zodie's ear, but inside her, in her head and in her soul.

'Today, Zodie Seacole, you will go to the San Cristobal Hotel, and you will assassinate a United States senator.'

Mary, queen of heaven, looked out through an open door at a room where a man had died a terrible death, and she was not moved to mourn. With her head slightly raised, her arms outstretched, she seemed not sad, but hopeful. Exalted. Raised out of sin.

Sacha took a battered cigarette tin from his pocket. He opened it and removed his silver cross. He offered three prayers.

The first was for his mother, who had taught him and raised him on her own until taken by typhus when he was 14. His mamulya had given him strength and heart. She also gave him the cross, and she was always first in his prayers. He prayed in the French his mother taught him.

The second prayer was for Lady Rosewood. She had left this place afraid, with a promise to soon return. Hours had passed, and the afternoon slipped away without word or sign. Sacha remained at the school to protect the girls, but that left Lady Rosewood unprotected, and he feared what might have happened to her on an island full of enemies.

The third prayer was for Zodie Seacole. There was no sign of her in the kitchen, no sign that she had prepared any lunch for the school. Sacha's rumbling stomach had sent him looking for her, and only now did he realise she was gone. His third prayer was for God to give his protection to Zodie, because Sacha's own protection may have failed her.

Sacha took a bread roll from the waste, wiped it down,

and went outside. He could not enter the main house, but he hoped he might discover Zodie through one of its windows.

Through the library window he saw the girls gathered, reading books. One of them looked up at him and he ducked down.

The girl opened the window and leaned out. It was Adeline, the same girl who had been so forward the previous day.

'Nicolae!'

Sacha put up his hands and shook his head. 'I cannot speak with you.'

Adeline tutted. She opened the window wider, climbed onto the sill and jumped down. She crushed a bay of lilies in the process. One of the other the girls cried Adeline's name in protest.

'Nicolae, what's going on?' asked Adeline. 'Kaiser's disappeared, we've only had cheese and apples for lunch, and Mrs Moore won't let us leave the library. Why is everyone acting so queer?'

Sacha wondered what to tell her. Didn't she deserve to know? Didn't all the girls deserve the truth?

'It is not safe,' said Sacha. 'Tell me, where is the maid?'

Adeline threw up her hands. 'That's what I mean! The maid went off in a taxi about an hour ago. I swear, she was wearing one of Mrs Moore's dresses. She looked like a scandal waiting to happen.'

That confirmed it. Zodie was gone, and Lady Rosewood

might not be coming back. All he could do now was protect the girls.

'Adeline, if I told you to leave this place, where would you go?'

Adeline wrinkled her nose. 'Your English is awful good all of a sudden, Nicolae.'

Sacha shook his head. 'My name is Sacha Valentin. I am not a gardener, I am... I am here to help.'

Adeline laughed nervously. 'What does that... I don't know what that means.'

'You are in danger. You are all in danger, and I do not know if anyone else can help you, so you must help yourself.'

The girl paled.

'You're scaring me,' she said.

'Very good,' said Sacha. 'Talk to the girls. Tell them to leave. Take them through the trees to the city, and find the American embassy. I will follow you if I am able. Stay away from the roads. Yes?'

Adeline's lips quivered and her eyes watered.

'If you're trying to be funny—'

'Look at me, Adeline.'

Adeline swallowed a sob and wiped at her eyes. She nodded.

'All right,' she said. 'I'll talk to them.'

Adeline reached for the windowsill. Sacha boosted her up and she climbed inside. She looked back down at Sacha as she pulled the window shut.

'Mr Valentin?'

'Yes, Adeline?'

'Thank you,' she said. 'No-one ever tells us the truth.'

'Yes,' said Sacha. 'This is a very bad school.'

❧

Eleanora Rosewood strained against the tangled briar of Mrs Moore's garden, screaming without sound as the vines wrapped around her limbs and tore at her skin.

Mrs Moore looked down on her from her throne of flowers and mocked her misery. Sweet, dark smoke filled the air, and it snaked into Eleanora's nose and mouth. It filled her up and snared her bones, and as Mrs Moore twitched her fingers, the smoke shook Eleanora's limbs.

Eleanora woke with a start.

She found herself cocooned in blankets in a strange bed ringed by green curtains. She threw off the blankets and discovered she was wearing a hospital robe and nothing else. Her clothes hung on a hook on the door, wrinkled but dry. She dressed quickly.

She was just straightening her sleeves when the door opened and a young Cuban doctor stepped through.

'Lady Rosewood, back with us at last. How are you feeling?'

Eleanora searched under the bed for her boots. She found only a pair of slippers.

'What time is it, doctor? What happened?'

'You shouldn't be getting dressed. You almost drowned, ma'am. A young lady pushed you into the pool. You were only under a few seconds before the lifeguard got to you, but you've been out for a few hours. We were quite worried about you.'

Eleanora remembered her dream. 'An induced delirium. Nothing more,' she said. 'I am quite well. Where are my boots?'

'Ruined, I'm afraid. You cannot leave, Lady Rosewood. You may yet have water in your lungs. We will get you to the hospital as soon as we're able.'

Eleanora looked around at the room.

'This isn't the hospital?'

'You are at the Hotel San Cristobal. I am the doctor in residence, Dr Prado.'

'I'm still at the hotel? Has Senator Hapley returned from Guantanamo? Can you place a call to his room? Tell him I need to see him at once.'

Dr Prado chuckled. 'The senator has returned. I saw him just now in the lobby, receiving a gift of cigars from a very beautiful young woman.'

'What about the girl who attacked me? Where is she?'

'I have just now taken her to the lobby so that she can be handed to the police.'

Eleanora leapt from the bed and pushed past the doctor.

'Now, wait a moment, Lady Rosewood, you can't... Now, listen here...'

'I'm sorry, doctor. I simply don't have time to be feeble.'

She rushed out of the doctor's rooms and ran down the corridor in stolen slippers.

❧

Four storeys up, Zodie Seacole waited like a marionette while Senator Harlan Hapley struggled with the keys to his hotel room door. His giddiness got the better of him, and he dropped the keys on the carpeted floor.

'Now tell me again where it is they sent you from, my darling?'

Zodie wanted to tell him that she came from a poisonous place, a school of sin; that she came carrying death. She wanted to scream or cry; to run.

That was not in her power. She could only do those things that served her mission. She could only smile politely and say what she had been told to say.

'I am from Cigar Nacional,' said Zodie. 'I am here to show the gratitude of the people of Cuba.'

There was no charm in her voice, only a dull monotone, but Hapley looked at her bosom and her legs in that bright red dress and seemed not to care at all for charm.

'Well, isn't that just delightful,' said Senator Hapley. He finally got the door unlocked. 'Come on inside then, my dear, and let's celebrate our two great nations together.'

A black bull terrier ran across the room, barking loudly.

Zodie did not like dogs, and always flinched at their approach. The poison that gripped her mind would not allow it, and she stood her ground and appeared perfectly calm as the dog circled her legs. On the inside, she screamed.

'Hey now, that's enough,' said the senator. 'You've had your feed and your water, right, sport? You're pleased to see me, is that it?'

An aide stepped through from an adjoining room, a young spectacled man in a smart suit. 'I'm sorry, senator, he got away from me.'

'That's OK, Bob, I'll take him from here. You go on down and get yourself a drink.'

Bob looked at Zodie and smiled in a way that Zodie did not like. She wanted to send him a signal, a message. *Help me. Get me away from here.*

The message was not received. Bob left the room and closed the door behind him.

Senator Hapley sat on the couch and scruffed his dog behind the ears.

'Well, why don't we light up one of those fine cigars,' said Senator Hapley. 'That'll shake some of the tension out of the day.'

Zodie nodded. She set the cigar box down on the side table and lifted the lid. There were the cigars in a tidy row, and beside them, a clipper and a box of matches. Underneath all of that was a dainty lady's pistol, engraved with two dragons.

∽∾

Sacha wanted his gun back.

He hated that gun. The woman that had owned it. The man he had killed with it. The gun itself was ridiculous. Ugly and small. He did not like that gun at all, but he was happier with it than without it.

Instead of a gun, Sacha had a spade. He carried it across his shoulder as he slowly climbed the stairs to the private rooms.

He had seen no sign of Mrs Moore or Sunna or the swordsman. He hoped they were in conference down in the main study, or in the chapel. He hoped he could uncover the secrets of Mrs Moore's private rooms without discovery, and be gone from this cursed place in minutes.

Sacha pushed open the first door on the main landing and found a man's valet stand hung with a white shirt, and piano music scattered across a made-up bed. Aldrich Kaiser's room.

The second room was a simple one with no personal touches. The bed was a mess, the pillows in disarray. A straight razor lay on the bed. Sacha slipped it into his pocket.

The third room was the grandest, with thick red carpet, and wallpaper patterned like lavish jungle. The dark wood four-poster bed was made up in emerald silk. A padded love seat stood by the balcony window

304

with a book folded down on top of it.

And there were flowers. Two vases on the mantel, a bowl of giant blooms in the fireplace, flourishing cacti at the foot of the bed, a miniature tree on the windowsill, tall and handsome spears of red by the dressing table.

A private bathroom stood just off the bedroom. Sacha could not see the room where Mrs Moore took the girls for private instruction.

Sacha looked at the shape of the room, the L formed by the bathroom and the corridor, and tried to understand where another room might hide.

He saw it. A tapestry of magnolias hung on one wall. He pushed it aside and found a brass ring set in a panel. He slipped his finger into the ring and slid back the hidden door.

Sacha jumped back at the sight of three men, five men, eight men lurching towards him.

He was stupid. They were only mirrors.

The room was a small chamber panelled with mirrors, with four braziers and a chair in the middle.

This was where Mrs Moore subjected the girls to her wicked power.

Sacha noticed movement in the mirrors. Someone had appeared behind him. He spun around and swung the spade and it shattered one of the mirrors.

Mrs Moore leaned in the doorway with a cigar in her hand. 'Hello, Nicolae,' she said. 'We should talk, you and I.'

❧

Eleanora's twice-failed assassin Dominique sat with her head bowed, her hands folded together, a position of prayer or supplication. One of her hands was cuffed to the arm of a bench in the hotel lobby, and a uniformed porter sat beside her.

'Dominique!'

They both looked up in surprise at the woman rushing towards them in slippers, but only Dominique tempered her surprise with horror. She tried to rise from the bench but the handcuffs and the porter both restrained her.

'Dominique, please, I am not your enemy,' said Eleanora. 'I want to help you. Tell me what they did to you at the school, and I will see to it that you get the care you need.'

'You know what they did,' said Dominique. 'It was you. You did this.'

The porter interceded. 'Lady, keep your distance. This is a dangerous criminal.'

Eleanora shook her head. 'No, sir,' said Eleanora. 'She is a poor innocent, and I am her patron.' She got down on her knees in front of Dominique. 'I am very sorry about what happened to you. I swear, I did not know about it, and if you tell me what happened, I will see that it never happens again.'

Dominique narrowed her eyes.

'Your husband knew,' she said. 'Your husband was there when they did this to me.'

That was a knife to Eleanora's heart.

'My husband is dead,' she said. 'I have come to put right his mistakes. The people who hurt you have hurt me, as well.'

Eleanora offered her hands to Dominique.

Dominique looked into her eyes.

She took her hands.

She wept.

'How?' Dominique asked. 'How can you put this right? Every night I see her in my dreams. Every night I hear her voice. I was meant to forget. They told me I would forget. All I do is remember. Always and every day I remember.'

'I will see that you get help,' said Eleanora. 'Only tell me why they did this. Tell me what they asked you to do.'

'It is because of my uncle,' said Dominique. 'My family comes from nothing, but my uncle is now French minister of foreign affairs. He is a Radical Socialist, and they meant for me to take his life.'

Eleanora felt a chill go through her.

She had not wanted to think it possible, but she saw the truth in it at once. These girls were being sent out to kill. They were assassins who did not know what they were. Assassins who could be placed in powerful families, never suspected until called upon to act against their will.

'How?' asked Eleanora. 'How do they do it? How do they make you kill?'

'With incense,' said Dominique. 'There is a potion, a distillation from an African flower. When it burns, our targets become dull and slow, and when we smell its perfume, we remember. We remember our orders, and we kill.'

Eleanora thought of the incense in her room, the incense that Sunna had lit to keep out mosquitoes. The smell of it seemed to linger still in her thoughts.

'How is that possible?' asked Eleanora. 'If they need incense to trigger the action, how do they persuade you to burn the incense?'

'Oh, Lady Rosewood, isn't it obvious?' said Dominique. 'The targets are always powerful men. They send them cigars! The incense is in the cigars!'

Zodie clipped the cigar with trembling hands. She turned to the senator and found he had stripped to his shorts, vest, socks and suspenders. He smiled at Zodie and waved a glass of ice rum.

'Would you like a drink, my dear?' he asked.

Zodie shook her head.

She gave him the cigar. He held it under his nose.

'Divine,' he said. 'My God, I do love this town. They grow

them good in Havana.' He slapped Zodie on the backside.

The senator's dog sniffed at Zodie's feet. She tried to ignore the animal and focus on her hands, on willing them to stop as she pulled out the matchbox from on top of the pistol and struck a match. She could not stop herself. The match sparked.

The senator set down his rum, took the match and held it under the cigar. He puffed until the cigar took fire. Smoke curled out of his mouth and formed a cloud around his head.

'Smell that,' he said. 'Magnificent. Fine tobacco, fine rum and fine company. Do you know what would make this moment perfect, my little sweetheart?'

Zodie smelled the smoke. She reached for the pistol. The senator's dog barked loudly.

'Do you mind if I smoke?'

Mrs Moore showed Sacha the unlit cigar.

Sacha held the spade in front of him. 'Yes,' he said.

Mrs Moore backed away into the bedroom. 'It is just a cigar,' she said.

'No,' said Sacha. In his mind, anything that burned could be a weapon.

Mrs Moore smiled. She sat down on the bed and stabbed the cigar into the stones of the cactus pot.

'I'm not here to hurt you,' said Mrs Moore. 'You can put down the spade.'

'If you think, ma'am, that you will seduce me—'

Mrs Moore laughed. 'No, Nicolae, I don't think I will. My bed is my own, and I do not throw myself at gardeners.'

Sacha frowned. 'Aiden told me—'

'Men will say these things about women, Nicolae. I think you have quite the wrong idea.'

'I do not think so,' said Sacha. 'In this room, you hypnotise girls, yes? To what end? To steal secrets?'

'To kill,' said Mrs Moore.

Sacha nodded.

'I will stop you.'

Mrs Moore slid her fingers under her knees and slid them back under her thighs. 'In the mirrored chamber. Back panel. That is the poison we use. Go fetch it, and I will stay here and sit on my hands.'

Sacha stared at her. She did not move. He could not make sense of her. He edged towards the back of the chamber, the broken glass crunching under his boots. He could not see Mrs Moore from the back of the room, so he slid the panel open quickly and grabbed the decanter. He stepped back into the bedroom and found Mrs Moore in the same position.

She tilted her head to one side.

'You did not believe me.'

Sacha held up the decanter. 'What is this?' he asked.

'Pour it out.'

'Why?'

'It is called Mother of Lies, and I am the only one who can make it. When I am dead they will have no way—'

'When you are dead?'

'By their hand. By yours. I am finished either way, especially if my blackjack gambit pays off. They'll know I betrayed them, and you're not going to help me. I have weighed my soul and found it wanting; fallen women must die. I am far beyond hope of salvation, and I will not hurt these girls anymore.'

Sacha thought he heard a sound in the corridor. He went to the door to check, but there was nobody there.

'Pour it out, Nicolae, so they cannot rebuild when I am gone.'

Sacha examined the bottle. The liquid was thick and gelatinous. He pulled the stopper from the bottle. He tipped the bottle on its side, and the Mother of Lies trickled out slowly like syrup.

'Even now, my assassin is on the telephone to our superiors, no doubt receiving the order to terminate me and burn this place,' said Mrs Moore.

'You mean the swordsman?' asked Sacha. He looked up from the black liquid pooling on the carpet. 'I saw him in the chapel at night. He is the one who watches over you?'

Sacha sensed a presence behind him a moment too late. An arm looped around his neck and caught him in

311

a choke-hold. Sacha tried to struggle free but his assailant was strong, and had cut off the flow of blood to his brain.

'Oh, Nicolae,' said Sunna. 'There is no swordsman, you silly boy.'

The bottle dropped from Sacha's hand and he slipped into unconsciousness.

❧

Eleanora rose, floor by floor, and watched the arrow slide above the elevator doors. Fifth floor. Sixth.

Cigars. The Moore School used cigars to trigger its assassins. At this moment, Senator Hapley was in his room with a beautiful girl and a box of cigars. He might already be dead.

Ninth floor. Tenth.

Eleanora grabbed the concertina doors and slid them open before the bellhop had a chance. She hurried down the corridor towards the presidential suite, and banged on the door. There was no answer. She banged as hard as she could and called out;

'Senator Hapley! Are you in there, Senator Hapley?'

The door opened.

Senator Hapley stood in his robe with a glass of rum in his hand and a cigar hanging out of his mouth.

'Lady Rosewood?'

Eleanora snatched the cigar from his mouth and ground

312

it against the doorframe. She pushed past the senator into the room.

'Lady Rosewood, what in the world?'

Zodie Seacole was on the floor, quivering and weeping. A dog sat with its head in her lap, and she pushed her fingertips through its fur.

'Zodie?'

'Lady Rosewood, I swear, I don't know what happened to the girl,' said Senator Hapley. 'We were going to enjoy a few cigars, a little rum. Suddenly she started weeping. She just collapsed on me.'

Eleanora put her hand on Zodie's shoulder. 'Zodie, can you hear me?' The girl did not respond. 'Senator, what did you say to her? Do you remember the last thing you said?'

The senator sipped his rum and looked up at the ceiling. 'Well, I don't know, nothing of any importance. I was saying how good the cigars were. The dog was barking. She just went all peculiar all of a sudden.'

Eleanora stroked the dog's head and reached under its chin for its name tag.

'Did you say the dog's name?' asked Eleanora.

'I suppose I did,' said the senator.

Eleanora lifted Zodie's face with her hand.

'Blackjack?' said Eleanora.

Zodie nodded.

'He said, "Blackjack, stop it",' said Zodie, 'and I stopped.'

~~~

Sacha stirred into consciousness. He tried to lift himself and realised his hands were tied behind his back. His feet were also bound.

Sacha rolled onto his back and saw he was lying on Mrs Moore's bed, with Mrs Moore tied up beside him. Her eyes were closed.

The tip of a sword touched on Mrs Moore's cheek.

'She's only sleeping. It's just us monsters.'

Sacha turned his head very slowly and looked along the length of the sword to the figure holding it. Sunna Kristjansdottir. She had lost the little blue flower in her hair, and, instead of a smock dress, she wore black trousers and a white cotton shirt, with a small olive kit bag slung across her shoulders. The mischief remained in her bright, dangerous eyes.

'Hello, mooncalf. Are you surprised?' She slipped the blade to Sacha's neck and leaned forward. 'I am afraid there is no master here, Sacha Valentin. Only me.'

Sacha strained against his bindings.

'You know my real name.'

'You are such a naughty liar,' said Sunna. She brushed the hair from Sacha's brow. 'But I did enjoy your little game. I wasn't sure it was you, but I kept a close eye, don't you think? It's rather exciting, to meet the man who murdered my teacher. Did you use that silly gun? Of course you did. How foolish I was not to see it. You shot him between his eyes with it.'

Sacha was confused. She had to mean Arek Saxon, whom he had killed in just that manner in Shanghai; and yet, he and Lady Rosewood were the only people who knew how Saxon died.

'How did you—?'

He smelled smoke. Not incense, but real smoke.

'There is a fire.'

Sunna nodded.

'The Moore School is closed for business, and we will re-build without the treacherous Mrs Moore. Don't worry, I know you'll find a way out. You don't die today, my Caliban. Your lights are filled with sadness, but you do not die today.'

Sunna pressed her lips to Sacha's cheek.

'Goodbye for now, my monster,' Sunna whispered.

She picked up the decanter and fled from the room.

'This place is a mad house,' said Sacha. He raised his hips off the bed and the straight razor fell from his pocket. He opened the blade, positioned it against the rope and sawed.

'Wake up, Mrs Moore,' Sacha shouted. 'You need to wake up.'

Mrs Moore murmured. Sacha broke the frayed rope around his wrists and quickly severed the rope at his ankles. He cut Mrs Moore's ropes next, and slapped her across the cheek.

'Wake up!'

She opened her eyes a crack and rubbed her brow.

'Nicolae?'

'The liquid,' said Sacha. 'There was still a little in the decanter. If they have it, can they make more?'

'I don't know,' said Mrs Moore.

'It is possible?' said Sacha.

'Yes. It is possible, yes.'

Sacha pressed the razor into Mrs Moore's hands. 'The building is on fire.' He opened the balcony doors and leapt from the balcony to the lawn, landing with a roll.

Sunna was about a hundred feet ahead of him, walking slowly, whistling. She seemed to sense the impact of Sacha's landing, and she stopped and turned.

'Give me the decanter and I will let you live,' said Sacha.

Sunna laughed. She put down her kit bag and the decanter, and stabbed her sword into the ground.

'I told you, mooncalf, I'm not going to kill you today. But I can make you wish I had.'

Sacha roared and charged at his foe. He intended to grab her by the neck and barrel her to the ground, but the moment his fingertips merely brushed Sunna's skin, she swivelled out of his grasp. Sacha tripped on Sunna's ankle and fell face first onto the ground.

He rolled onto his back. Sunna had barely moved at all. Her hands were folded tidily behind her back.

'I and my fellows are ministers of fate,' said Sunna. 'The elements, of whom your swords are tempered, may as well wound the loud winds.'

Sacha got to his feet but kept his distance. He was wary now. He readied his fists.

'I do not understand you,' said Sacha.

Sunna rolled her shoulders and beat out a jig on pointed toes. She smiled.

'Ariel,' she said. 'I am the sweet sprite of the air, and you are the hag-born monster. We are both slaves, but one of us is merry.'

Sacha spat on the floor.

'You are mad.'

Sacha lurched at his foe, and Sunna dodged without effort. He grabbed for her arm, and Sunna snaked her arm around Sacha's, put him in a lock, and slammed the flat of her hand into Sacha's nose.

Sacha twisted and tried to land his elbow in Sunna's face. Sunna let Sacha go, and took three quick steps back.

The fighters returned to their imagined corners. Sacha wiped blood from his mouth.

'I have stepped across the roof of the world and seen its fading lights,' said Sunna. 'The world is dying. We should dance on it while we can.'

Sacha was tired of her words. He charged again. This time he did not try to grab her, but to put her down. He led with a left hook, and kept his right fist ready for a switch.

Sunna stopped him with a kick to the chest and spun on one foot to deliver a blow to his face. Sacha reeled into a backhanded left, a right to the chest, and a kick between the legs. He dropped onto his knees.

'This was fun,' said Sunna. 'But I really do have to leave.'

Sacha wheezed for breath. He noticed the sword standing just out of reach.

'Next time, we'll go a little longer,' said Sunna.

'No,' said Sacha. 'You must pay for your crimes.'

He grabbed for the sword. Sunna moved faster and snatched it away, but Sacha rolled back on himself. He grabbed the decanter and retreated out of Sunna's reach.

Sunna laughed. 'Oh, bravo,' she said. 'A feint!'

'You will pay,' said Sacha. 'But it is more important, I think, that you do not poison again.'

'It wasn't poison, my sweet, silly bull. It was liberation. Don't you see? I was those girls' best friend, and I watched them every day. I read their lights and saw their potential. They could be killers, Sacha. If women can only learn to kill, doesn't that make us the equal of any man?'

'Beasts kill,' said Sacha. He pulled the stopper from the bottle, drew back his arm, and threw the bottle as hard as he could towards the sea. It spun and spun in an extraordinary arc and landed with a splash.

Sunna watched the bottle disappear with an air of amused nonchalance.

'Well,' she said. 'That's that, I suppose. You win the day.'

She picked up her kit bag and set off across the lawn.

'Do not walk away from me,' Sacha bellowed after her. 'You think I will let you leave?'

'I think you might,' said Sunna. 'You were very wise to tell those girls to flee. Dominion has no use for them now that Lady Rosewood knows their names. Unfortunately, they didn't quite make it to the door.'

Sacha looked back towards the inferno consuming the school. Flames rose from the windows of the girls' dormitory.

'Try the library,' shouted Sunna. 'If you're not sure, it's the one with all the books.'

Sacha roared his frustration and ran for the house.

He tried the doors. They were locked. He kicked.

From down on the lawn he heard Sunna singing: 'Where the bee sucks, there lurk I. In a cowslip's bell I lie. There I couch when owls do cry. On the bat's back I... do... fly.'

If there was more to the song, Sacha did not hear it. He forced open the doors of the school with one more heavy blow and ran into the burning building.

Eleanora saw the smoke from the road.

'Faster, Senator! Drive as fast as you can!'

The senator put his foot down and sped along the last few miles and into the school driveway. The car had not even come to a full stop when Eleanora leapt and raced across the gravel towards the lawn, with Zodie Seacole directly behind. A second car drew up, and four marines sequestered by Senator Hapley came charging out.

'Senator, drive up to the plantation. Report the fire,' said Eleanora. 'Tell them we will need ambulances, and bring me towels and plenty of water. You boys, there may be girls inside. Quickly now. Quickly.'

Two girls lay out on the grass, and they were the only people Eleanora could see. They both seemed far too still for Eleanora's comfort. She knelt by one of them and checked her breathing. Zodie knelt by the other. Both were alive, and a little singed, but not badly hurt. From the glaze of their eyes it seemed they were both in a trance.

Valentin came out of the school as the marines ran in. He had a girl slung over his shoulder.

'The library,' Valentin yelled to the marines. 'Across the corridor, in front of you.'

Valentin carefully laid the third girl down beside the other two. He nodded to Lady Rosewood and returned to the building.

Two feet in dark green shoes shuffled towards the girls.

Eleanora looked up and saw Mrs Moore, red eyed and pale, a wretched ghoul with wild hair and a twisted frown. She dropped down beside the girl and whispered in her ear: 'Remember carnelian. Awake.'

The girl gasped, sat up, and coughed ferociously. Zodie put an arm around her.

'Jeroboam,' said Mrs Moore. She pointed to the girl beside Eleanora. 'Sandalwood.'

Eleanora whispered the command words to the other two girls and told them to awake, and they responded as the first girl had done. Soon all three girls were alert, but overcome with fear and horror.

The marines emerged in pairs, each pair carrying one girl between them.

'Zanzibar. Portcullis,' said Mrs Moore. She stared up at the school as the smoke rose higher. Some of the upper rooms were consumed by flame.

Valentin emerged again, soot-covered and coughing violently.

'The others,' he said. 'I cannot find—' The words died in a coughing fit.

'Cora and Adeline,' said Mrs Moore.

'They were not with the others,' said Valentin.

'They were never subjected to the process,' said Mrs Moore. 'Kristjansdottir could not control them. She must have moved them elsewhere.'

Valentin leaned forward against his knees and spat out a mouthful of black.

'I will find them,' he said. He gestured to the marines and the five of them ran in to the smoke.

Eleanora looked at the school, up at the windows, terrified she would see them there. She looked then across the lawns at the chapel.

Smoke clouded the chapel windows. A second fire had been set there.

Eleanora jumped to her feet and pulled the axe from the tree stump. There was a chain across the chapel doors, and it was padlocked shut. She swung the axe at the lock.

Her whole body shook. She swung again, and again, conjuring up every ounce of strength she had.

'Zodie, get those boys out of the school,' she shouted. 'Get them out of there now!'

Eleanora's arms ached, but she kept going. The lock cracked. Eleanora swung again and the lock shattered. She dropped the axe and staggered backwards with a sob. Mrs Moore appeared at her side and pulled the doors open. Through the black smoke, she could see two figures on the floor, bound in ropes and gagged with their own cloth belts. Mrs Moore helped one of the girls to her feet. Eleanora helped the other.

As they stepped out of the chapel, they heard a terrible creak. The roof of the school building collapsed, sending out a plume of ash and flame. The women staggered away and collapsed onto the grass. Eleanora looked up at the school as one by one the timbers gave way. She watched the door as one, two, three figures emerged. Zodie was among them. The other two were marines. The third marine appeared, and the fourth.

The building gave up another anguished groan. Eleanora screamed as part of the ground floor collapsed.

Sacha Valentin sprung from the doorway and fell to the ground. The school tumbled down, and a cloud of black smoke rolled over them.

The air was hot and poisonous. Eleanora untied the wrists of the girl she had saved, and searched for the other. 'Get to the water,' she said. 'Get away from here.'

She could not see Mrs Moore. Eleanora stood and stumbled after the girls. She looked back and saw a silhouette in the smoke, standing in the chapel doorway, ringed by an orange glow.

'Mrs Moore!'

The woman walked in to the chapel.

'Mrs Moore, what are you doing?'

Eleanora ran towards the chapel. She was intercepted by Sacha Valentin. He picked her up and slung her across his shoulder and ran across the lawn. Eleanora beat her hands on his back. 'Let me go, Valentin. We can save her.'

Valentin did not answer.

Eleanora pushed herself up against Valentin's shoulder

and through eyes stung by smoke she watched the last of the school fall against the chapel. The chapel collapsed into smouldering rubble.

It was the end of the terrible Moore School. It was the end of the tormented Mrs Moore.

~~~

A warm breeze rushed the trees and carried the ozone scent of the fresh salt sea. Eleanora Rosewood breathed deep.

Even now, three nights after her experiences at the school, Eleanora imagined she felt traces of Mrs Moore's poison in her bloodstream. She flinched at every whiff of woody perfume.

Last night she had slept terribly, too warm in the humid night. It delighted her to be restless. The agitation of feeling was much preferable to the dull numbness of mesmerised sleep.

Eleanora suppressed a yawn and looked out along the tarmacadam airstrip, the road off the island, and thanked the lord for the pains of being alive.

'Girls, come along now. It's time to board.'

The voice was Temperance Vandevere's. Eleanora watched Temperance flap and agitate the girls from their benches in a cloister of potted palms in the airport departure lounge. Today these girls would fly from Havana to Miami, and travel on to all points, to the sanctuary of their homes. Doctors had judged them physically well enough to travel. Their mental condition would be an ongoing concern.

The girls curtsied and said their thank-yous as they trooped past Eleanora towards the twin prop plane. They were admirably proper and polite.

Their graduation gift from their school was that the rest of their lives would be tainted by this scandal.

'Thank you so much for escorting them, Temperance,' said Eleanora.

'Think nothing of it, Ellie. I'm only sorry I wasn't here to help before,' said Temperance. 'My goodness, I don't know how you've coped, learning what you have about Edgar.'

Eleanora blushed. In the wake of the Moore School's destruction, she had told her friend everything of Edgar's betrayal. It brought her some relief to share the story, but also significant shame.

Temperance took Eleanora's hands tight and looked her in the eyes.

'You're not alone in this, Ellie. Tell me everything, and I will be there with you, you understand? And don't go rushing off into any more trouble on your own.'

'I appreciate your kindness. Nonetheless, it falls on me to put right my husband's—'

'All martyrs have one thing in common, Eleanora. They're all dead. We will track down the school's other students together, and we will get them the care they need. We may even find a cure. Edgar's brother is an explorer, yes? Might he not be able to find that African flower?'

'Peter hasn't been heard from in months.'

'Oh, Ellie. The Rosewoods are too touched by tragedy. Then let us focus our efforts on this secret league. I hear there's a hidden government of heretic teachers in Tibet. We should—'

'I don't think Edgar ever visited Tibet.'

'Well, we should pursue every avenue. We'll find out who these people are, and we will expose them to the world.'

'Thank you, Temperance.'

Temperance pulled Eleanora into a hug.

'Give my love to the twins,' said Eleanora.

'I will. May God in His wisdom guide you, Eleanora. Adeline, come along!'

Temperance followed the girls onto the plane.

Adeline and Cora were still in the lounge, weeping on each other's shoulders. Adeline wore a jaunty hip-length navy blue sailor shirt, with red scarf and matching skirt. Cora wore a copper-coloured sweater with sunbeam embroidery and a midcalf pleated brown skirt. They looked like smart and modern young women. More than that, they looked like themselves.

'You'll write to me,' said Cora.

'Of course I will,' said Adeline. 'And you must come visit. Tell your parents you want to see the museums.'

The girls broke apart, and Adeline headed for the plane.

She stopped to say goodbye to Eleanora.

'Thank you,' said Adeline. 'I owe you my life.'

'You don't owe me a thing, my dear,' said Eleanora. 'Just promise me you'll take good care of yourself. Paris is too full of temptations.'

'But I'm going to study ballet, Lady Rosewood! And the Baron is so mortified about sending me to that school that he's promised to take me to Maxim's!'

'Even so, you have my address if you need it, yes?'

'If I need it,' said Adeline. She hugged Eleanora and whispered to her. 'Is it wrong that I'm sad about Mrs Moore?'

Eleanora shook her head. 'Not at all, Adeline. We must remember the best and the worst of a person, and take lessons from both.'

Adeline smiled and wiped her eyes. She kissed Eleanora on the cheek and ran up the steps. She stopped at the top and turned and waved.

'We're missing one,' shouted Temperance Vandevere. She poked her head out of the door. 'We're missing one, Ellie.'

Cora put her hand to her chest. 'Not me,' she said. 'My parents are picking me up this afternoon.'

'No, not you, Cora,' said Eleanora. She stepped into the airport and explored the palms.

She found Zodie Seacole hiding in a quiet corner in a beautiful dark purple dress, her knees raised to her chest, and a black clutch purse gripped in her hands.

'Zodie, it's time to go,' said Eleanora.

Zodie shook her head.

'The plane won't leave without you.'

Zodie looked up at Eleanora with wide, wet eyes.

'Ma'am. I don't deserve to go. I am marked by sin. I am not one of these good girls.'

'You are the victim of sin, not the cause of it,' said Eleanora. 'Your aunt in Chicago is expecting you. Mrs Vandevere has agreed to find you work, I will see that you get some schooling. You're starting a new life now, Miss Seacole.'

Eleanora held out her hand. Zodie took it and stood. She followed Eleanora to the aeroplane, and stood at the bottom of the steps and crossed herself.

'You deserve that chance as much as anyone,' said Eleanora. 'More than most.'

'If you say so, ma'am,' said Zodie. She climbed the stairs.

The door closed, and a group of porters wheeled the stairs away.

Eleanora and Cora watched the plane taxi along the runway and suddenly speed and launch. It carried with it the final class of the Moore School for Young Women, who had learned truths that might serve them well for the rest of their days.

'What happens now, Lady Rosewood?' asked Cora.

'Now, we go to the hospital to visit Dominique, and see how her treatment is going,' said Eleanora. She led the way back into the terminal. 'By the time we get back to the hotel, your parents will be here to take you home.'

'And after that?' asked Cora. 'What happens next, Lady Rosewood?'

A figure stood slouched in a phone box, his hands in the pockets of his wrinkled suit. It was the journalist, Brand Blackwell. Eleanora had her suspicions about the man. She felt sure he was the one who had bribed the police to let Dominique go, but to what end she did not know. Was he for the girls, or against them?

Regardless, she was in no mood for a confrontation, especially not in Cora's presence. She held her head high and walked on

'What happens next?' said Eleanora. 'We have a bold new future to contend with, Cora. I do hope you are ready for it.'

～∞～

Sacha Valentin watched the bustle of the passing world from behind the wheel of his car as he waited outside the airport. It was not quite the sanctuary of the sea, but it kept him a safe enough distance from strangers and sentimental farewells.

Sacha leaned out of the side of the car and watched the twin-prop soar into the sky. He silently wished the girls luck, and thanked heaven that they were gone, and he would soon leave this island.

A piece of paper fluttered in from the open window on the other side of the car and landed at Sacha's feet. A woman in a green dress and a red headscarf hurried away down the street.

Sacha picked up the piece of paper. It was addressed, 'To Lady Rosewood and Company'. He unfolded it.

It was a type-written list, about thirty items long.

The first item read, 'Dominique Chevalier. Paternoster.'

The last read, 'Zodie Seacole. Blackjack.'

Underneath the list, hand-written in pen, was a note.

'A secret, from one widow to another.'

❧

THE END.

VALENTIN & THE WIDOW

WILL RETURN IN

THRONES & PRINCIPALITIES

ANDREW WHEELER is a writer, editor and journalist from Hastings, England, currently based in Toronto, Canada. His works include the subversive fantasy comic Another Castle from Oni Press, and the gay superhero series Freelance from Chapterhouse.